UNIMAGINABLE LOVER

A WARRIORS OF LEMURIA NOVEL #3

ROSALIE REDD

UNIMAGINABLE LOVER
A Warriors of Lemuria Novel #3

By

Rosalie Redd

For permissions contact: Rosalie@rosalieredd.com
Cover Design: Melody Simmons
ISBN: 9781944419110
United States of America

CHAPTER 1

DEEP IN THE CASCADE MOUNTAINS OF THE PACIFIC
NORTHWEST

PRESENT DAY

*T*he waterfall's roar drowned out Tanen's footsteps. Good.
He needed to approach his target with the utmost care.
With deliberate intent, he placed his palm against the rough bark of a
cedar tree. The fresh scent eased into his lungs, mixing with the musty
smell of damp vegetation and loam. As he glanced around the massive
tree's girth, his breath caught in his throat. He'd found his enemy
—Mauree.

Mauree was his responsibility, his burden to bear since he was
council leader, and she'd escaped on his watch. For the past week he'd
tracked her through the forests outside the underground Keep, hiding
in small caves and dense foliage during the day, away from the sun's
killing rays. He hadn't had this much exercise in years, and his jacket
and trousers hung loose from his frame. The muscles in his legs

ached, but he relished the renewed strength and energy coursing through his veins.

His goal—to capture the renegade and return her to the Keep for her execution. The marking over his chest, the one for tenacity, burned to life, fueling his resolve. *I can't fail Noeh.* The need to please the Stiyaha king ignited Tanen's fury, and he clenched his hand into a tight fist.

Mauree's naked skin glistened in the moonlight. She stood at the base of the waterfall, sluicing water away from her face and through her beautiful blonde hair. Her full breasts bobbed as she moved, her nipples peaked from the cold water. His gaze tracked to her narrow waist, over her well-rounded hips and down her perfect legs. Not long ago he'd have paid any price to see her bare flesh. Now, she was nothing but a traitor.

Her shower complete, Mauree headed for the shore. She squeezed water from her shoulder-length hair and picked up her ragged clothes. "Tanen, you can come out now. No need to hide."

Craya! His heartburn flared to life, and he swallowed the bitter taste in his mouth. Inside his coat's front pocket, he gripped the cool, rough surface of the sacred blue sunstone. The tension in his shoulders eased, if only for a moment.

For weeks he'd searched the ancient scriptures for the unusual punishment of treason. The pressure had gotten the better of him, and he'd given in to his kleptomania, stealing the magical blue sunstone from the Throne room. He'd eventually found the right text outlining the death sentence. On the way to deliver the news, he'd discovered Mauree's empty cell. He couldn't face his king on either count and had pursued the traitor on his own.

A low, bell-like laugh echoed from the water's edge. "Come now, Tanen. Did you really think I didn't know you trailed me? It's about time we talked, don't you think?"

He adjusted his collar and traced his fingers over his lapel pin. The engraved symbol stood for Lemuria or "Mu" and was his most precious adornment, signifying his status as council leader. He gritted his teeth and stepped into the open. "There's nothing to say. For assisting the Gossum, our dark enemy, *and* for attempting to kill the queen and her unborn child, I'm taking you back to the Keep to—"

"...face the death sentence? You're not as smart as I thought you were." Mauree's ragged clothes were nothing like the fine garments she used to wear as a member of the elite class.

He approached, his gaze locked onto hers. "How did you find out about your punishment?"

"That little twit of a seer, Ginnia. She seemed to think I needed to live. Maybe you should have a chat with her."

Indeed, once he got Mauree back to the Keep, he'd do just that. He took a step closer. "You will return with me and face your execution or die here."

Mauree placed her hand over her eyes and squinted, focusing her attention on the forest. "Did you bring some warriors with you? Cause there's no way I'm returning to the Keep with you."

"You're not funny, Mauree." He popped his knuckles. The idea of using force against her didn't sit well with him, but he'd do what was necessary.

An astringent smell carried along the breeze, searing his senses. *Gossum.* A bead of sweat dampened his brow. He hadn't faced the real enemy in years.

The branches of a nearby pine trembled, as if the tree feared the creature in its midst. The Gossum slid from his perch and landed on the underbrush in an eerie silence. Once human, the evil creature wore the remnants of an old sweatshirt and dirty jeans. His bald head reflected the moon, and his tongue snaked between his serrated teeth.

Tanen eased the knife from his belt. As council leader, he'd never needed his sword, and it remained in his quarters at the Keep, unused, forgotten. He held out the weapon, but couldn't stop the shake in his hand.

Mauree's shrill cry echoed off the trees.

The Gossum glanced at her. A slow hiss eased from his lips.

Tanen fought to control his voice. "Mauree, come...get behind me. I'll protect you."

Mauree's low chuckle sent goosebumps sliding along Tanen's

arms. She sauntered toward the Gossum and placed her arm around his shoulder. "Tanen, Tanen, you misunderstand. While you wasted valuable time tracking me, I made a new friend. Meet Jakar."

The urge to vomit roiled in Tanen's gut, and he spit on the ground. "Your soul is black. There's no hope for you now, Mauree."

"On the contrary. With Jakar, I have a new lease on life. One I intend to take."

His inner beast growled, eager to be set loose. Only King Noeh had recently reconnected the bond between man and beast, successfully transitioning back from his animal state. Tanen wouldn't take the risk and forced his beast into submission. "What do you intend to do?"

Mauree's smile spread across her face, and even in the dim light, her eyes shone with madness. "Get revenge against Noeh, of course. I should've been queen." Her lip quivered for a moment before her features hardened.

The muscles in Tanen's shoulders tightened. He'd do whatever it took to protect his king.

She glanced into the brightening sky, then peered at her cohort. "The sun will be up soon. We need to return to the safe house."

Jakar hissed. "My lady, what shall I do with him?"

Mauree's attention shifted to Tanen and her mouth curved into an evil grin. "Kill him, of course."

Tanen gripped the knife in his sweaty palm. He was a Stiyaha, placed here by his goddess Alora to fight for the right to claim Earth's water for the dying planet Lemuria. The last time he'd tangled with a Gossum, he'd earned the scar that ran across his chest. His desire to battle with his enemy warred with his fear. Turmoil built within and his hand shook once again.

Moonlight glinted off Jakar's serrated teeth, and a drop of saliva slid from his mouth. A loud screech burst from his chest. He launched himself into the air. Claws extended from his hands. Razor sharp, they dug through Tanen's coat and pierced his skin. The Gossum's weight knocked him to the ground.

Air whooshed from Tanen's lungs. Even after all these years of non-use, his old warrior training resurfaced. Using the Gossum's momentum, Tanen pulled Jakar with him. They rolled over the small rocks embedded in the path. The hard, sharp edges poked into Tanen's ribs.

Tanen aimed his knife for Jakar's throat, but only nicked the Gossum on the cheek. Their tumble ended when Tanen rammed into the hard trunk of a cedar tree. A sharp pang and a loud pop echoed from his chest.

The spiked tip of Jakar's long tongue hit Tanen on the elbow. Numbness spread into his muscles. His knife slipped from his fingers.

Jakar's heavy weight descended on Tanen's back, grinding his face into the ground. Bits of moss and soil raced down his windpipe. He coughed as he fought to gain leverage. Knife-like claws ripped through his coat and shirt, scraping his back, again and again.

A harsh scream tore from his throat. He squirmed, but the evil creature had him pinned.

Jakar's tongue stung him on the face, the arm, the shoulder. Each lash was a reminder of his inability to conquer his enemy. His mouth went dry. He'd be lucky to get out of this alive.

Jakar dug his claws into Tanen's arms and hauled him out of the dirt. His limbs wouldn't cooperate. The Gossum's venom worked its way into his muscles, shutting them down. His knees wobbled, and his left arm hung loose at his side. If he didn't act fast, Jakar would kill him.

Tanen's knife glinted in the path. As he reached for his only weapon, the blue sunstone tumbled from his pocket. A flash of light burst from the crystal then it went dark. Cool fingers of dread coiled around his heart.

Mauree audibly inhaled, her gaze transfixed on the sacred, legendary sunstone. She glanced at Jakar. "Get the stone."

Tanen's need to retain his treasure burned inside. His muscles remembered all he'd learned in his early warrior sessions. He'd never been a good fighter, but he'd use his intelligence and the knowledge he'd acquired over the years to defend himself.

He grabbed a handful of dirt and tossed it in Jakar's face.

Jakar screamed and covered his eyes. Tanen took advantage of his enemy's momentary distraction and punched him in the jaw. He landed a few feet away, his body motionless against the base of a tree.

Tanen's muscles gave out and he crashed to the dirt path. Pain ricocheted up his thighs and into his back. Mauree scrambled to retrieve the sunstone, but Tanen swiped the gem into his palm.

"Hey, Jim, let's go on this trail. It looks promising."

Human voices...

"Naw, look. That trail leads to the river. *This* trail takes us up the mountain to the waterfall. If we hurry we can catch the sunrise."

...drawing closer.

Tanen had never encountered a human before. His heart pounded.

To interact with humans wasn't against the rules, and the Jixies that assisted the Stiyaha in the Keep often traded with them, but if the humans discovered you weren't one of them...discovered you were something...more, then they had to become players in the game or you forfeited your life.

Mauree fled into the forest. Only the soft breeze echoed in the trees.

Jakar roused and shook his head. He followed her, disappearing without a trace.

Why had Jakar left instead of attacking the humans and turning them into Gossum? Tanen would take the bit of luck. Anything to get away from his rival. He remained still, hiding behind the thick foliage as the humans passed.

The footsteps and loud banter slowly diminished. Now that the immediate threat was over, his adrenaline surge dissipated, and the numbing effect of Jakar's venom coursed through his veins. A small twig dug into his bruised and broken ribs. He inhaled, sending another stab of agony through his body.

His attention moved past the tree's branches to the brightening sky. The first rays of the rising sun painted the scattered clouds a vibrant shade of pink. His chest tightened. Time to find shelter. He grabbed his dagger and placed it in his coat pocket.

With effort, he compelled his bruised and battered body to stand. A steady drip caught his attention. He glanced at the ground.

Droplets of blood splashed into the soft dirt, creating a small red pool.

The world spun, the trees melding together into a blur. He'd never felt so out of control in his life.

Mother Goddess, Alora, take me or show me the way.

A soft melodic twitter pierced the pre-dawn sky. Not far away, a small bird perched on a nearby branch. He'd never heard its eerily alluring song before. Infatuated, he stared at the tiny creature. Nails skittered along the bark of a tree. On the trunk of a large fir, a chipmunk stopped and tilted its head. These were morning creatures, and *he* was the odd one here.

He clenched his fist. Pushing against the fallen tree, he forced his injured leg to take the weight. His knee wobbled, but he maintained a steady balance. The putrid taste of bile filled his mouth. If it hadn't been for the humans, he'd be dead.

Humans. With a quick glance at the brightening sky, he lurched down the path. The brilliance of the day turned the world into a vibrant green. His beast growled, spurning him on, as if his alter ego knew what danger lay in that beauty.

Between the trees stood a small yellow house with a dilapidated shed. The smells of fireplace smoke and domesticated animals filled the air. *Occupied.* A sense of unease rippled under his skin. His scalp tingled.

The first rays of the sun pierced the tops of the trees. His beast screamed, and a low growl escaped his lips. He couldn't chance it, so he headed for the small structure on the edge of the property.

Despite his sense of urgency, he carefully opened the door. The last thing he needed was to call attention to his hiding place. With only a tiny squeak, the hinge gave way. The smell of dirt, grime, and oil filtered into his senses. Garden tools, an assortment of pots, and a large unfamiliar red machine with four wheels and a long handle filled the small shed. He could stay here for the day.

With a firm tug, he shut the door. Darkness enveloped him, except for the tiny ray of light that pierced through a small hole on the south side of the building. He was safe, at least for now. At the realization, his knee gave out once again, bringing him to the floor. He pushed aside a few pots, advancing as far into the corner as he could. Coated in sweat, he shivered and leaned against the structure's inner wall.

A trail of blood tracked from the entrance to his location. *Craya.* He pressed his fingers against his back. Blood oozed through his shirt and onto his hand. A sharp pain raced along his spine. Lightheaded, objects in the shadows spun in a slow circle. He blinked, fighting against the tide that threatened to take him down, and a low howl tore from his throat.

His gaze drew to the hole in the wall. Blue sky caught his attention, the color so bright, so alluring. *So beautiful...* Before he could complete the thought, the whirlpool pulled him under and darkness claimed him.

CHAPTER 2

*S*heri leaned against the counter and picked up today's list of residents at the Columbia Rehabilitation Center. Hushed voices, fingers tapping on a keyboard, and the subdued ring of a telephone formed the soothing melody of life at the nurses' station. She scanned the list and her chest constricted. "Oh, no."

Mrs. Alton, one of Sheri's favorite patients, had stood from her wheelchair unassisted, taken a tumble, and was now confined to a bed. Sheri shook her head. Helping the infirm rehabilitate back to health was a rewarding occupation, but there were just as many who ended up on the slow road to death.

Olivia, her best friend and co-worker, touched Sheri's shoulder and leaned in. "Hey, how'd your interview go?"

With a quick glance around to make sure no one else was within earshot, Sheri focused her attention on her friend. "Great, I think. Panel interviews make me nervous, but at least it was a Skype session. The job sounds wonderful. They have state of the art equipment, almost no overtime, and the people seemed so friendly, so nice—"

"Sher," Olivia squinted, "you're good at heart, but a bit naive. Are you wearing rose-colored glasses?"

Sheri exhaled. "You're right, I'm probably making it out to be better than it is, but I could really use the change, get away from here."

"Not that I want to see you go," Olivia gave her arm a gentle squeeze, "but if moving to Seattle helps you forget, then I hope it works out."

Yes, forget. That's what she needed to do. Forget all about the pain and loss she'd experienced in Portland. Her marriage to Ram had ended two years ago, and she would've left then if not for her mother. The familiar ache built in Sheri's chest. Her mom's recent death was still raw and fresh, like a scab not quite healed.

Sheri glanced at her friend. Dark circles rimmed Olivia's eyes. "Liv, how's it going with Ben?"

A brief flinch crossed Olivia's features. "He left last night. Said he tried to stay for the kids, but just couldn't—" She bit her clenched fist.

Sheri's throat tightened and she pulled Olivia into a hug. "I'm so sorry."

Olivia held on for a moment, her body trembling, but then she stepped away and wiped at her eyes. "Me and the kids, we'll be fine. At least the new puppy you gave us has provided a welcome distraction."

Sheri had a soft spot for the downtrodden, strays and orphaned animals. She'd recently nursed a litter of Labradors from the local animal shelter—five yellow, one black. The little black pup had wormed his way into Olivia's heart and she'd adopted him without a second thought.

"Max is a handful, I'm sure, but I'm glad he's given you and the kids some of his special puppy love." Her friend's troubles tightened the coil in Sheri's stomach, resurfacing painful memories. Ram's heroin addiction had turned him into a shell of his former self. At first she'd tried to help, but ultimately, she couldn't handle his problems and had fled the marriage faster than you could say "sayonara." She hadn't heard from him in over a year. He could be dead, but she didn't believe that. Ram was too mean, too tough.

Olivia sniffled and raised her chin. "I need to start my rounds. I'll catch up with you later, okay?"

"Sure thing." Sheri's chest tightened. *Maybe it wouldn't be a bad thing if I didn't get the job.*

Matt, Sheri's supervisor, strode toward her. He pushed against the bridge of his glasses, and gave her a quick smile. "Sheri, got a new arrival, came in a few minutes ago. His name's Michael Colton, car accident victim. Seems he was texting while driving...room nine." Matt nodded and pointed to Mrs. Alton's room. "I'll be in there for a few minutes. Can you handle the new guy?"

Sheri smiled. Matt had a way of cheering up the saddest residents, and right now, Mrs. Alton needed his special brand of care. "Sure, Matt, I got it covered."

She turned away from the nurses' station and headed down the hall. Her rubber-soled shoes skated across the highly polished linoleum without a sound. As she entered room nine, she got a good look at her new patient.

In his mid-thirties, the man on the bed seemed gaunt and pale. A few lacerations marred the puffy skin around his mouth. Full, dark lashes caressed his cheeks. A fiberglass cast protruded from beneath the covers, his toes visible at the end. Her breath caught in her throat. The extent of his injuries was more than she'd expected. He was lucky to have survived the car accident.

She picked up the electronic chart from the foot of his bed and scanned her new patient's history. Michael Colton—broken tibia, fractured knee, bruised kidneys, three cracked ribs, numerous lacerations, and to top it off, a broken jaw. No next of kin. *Poor guy.* After his stint in the hospital, he'd been sent here to start his rehab.

She put on her best smile and gently touched her patient's arm. "Hi Michael, my name's Sheri. Welcome to Columbia Rehab Center. I'm going to take good care of you while you're here."

He roused enough to look at her. His eyes widened, and he studied her with an intense gaze. A small, content smile formed on the good side of his lip.

Something in her stomach fluttered. Reflexively, she took a step back. He'd reacted as if he knew her, but she'd never seen him before in her life. A strange chill ran over her arms.

11

Ow! The pungent tang of blood filled her mouth. She'd bitten the inside of her cheek. Dammit, that meant she'd bite it again twice more. *At least that's what Mom always used to say.*

Her chest constricted. She missed her mother's affection, love, and support. Now that she was gone, Sheri had no one in her life. Her father had left the family when she was nine. As a child, she'd blamed herself for his departure. Even now the memory of his cutting words beat on her psyche, *I can't deal with that brat,* stirring the old guilt buried in her heart. She shook her head to clear her thoughts.

"I need to check your bandages and go over your vitals, okay?" She moved to the side of the bed.

He gave her a slow nod.

She pulled back the sheet. A large bruise bloomed from his lower rib cage, covering a good portion of his chest. A wave of compassion toward him caused her throat to tighten. After checking his blood pressure and bandages, she focused on his pelvis. His catheter bag was clear and didn't need to be emptied yet. She tugged the sheet over his chest and glanced at him.

"Ahh...mmm...mu...." Michael focused on the pitcher of water on the side table.

"Are you thirsty?" She gripped the carafe and filled the plastic glass. The straw swirled in the water. She placed the container back on the table, and her arm grazed the end of the straw. It flipped into the air, end over end, like a bizarre pixie stick and landed on the floor. "Oh, shoot. Let me see if there's another one in the drawer."

His gaze tracked her as she rounded to the other side of his bed. His muffled cries increased.

There was something intense and personal in his look. Those dark brown eyes of his, like pools of dirty oil, made her cringe, and a shiver of dread ran down her back. Why did he study her so?

She picked at the edge of her thumbnail. The skin was raw and tender to the touch. Such was her nervous habit. She hated her hands. Big as an average man's, there was nothing dainty about them, but they were just an extension of her large body. At least she was strong enough to move most of the patients when needed.

She shook her head and resumed her search for a straw. The last drawer on the right, the one closest to the window contained a small stack of straws individually wrapped in plastic.

"Ah, here we go." She gripped a green one, and pushed her hip against the drawer. The hydraulics gave a slight sigh as the drawer closed at its own pace. With a nervousness she didn't understand, she twirled the straw between her fingers, flattening the end.

She returned to his bedside. His gaze still bore into her, but a faint smile tugged at his lip. She rolled her shoulders to shake away her earlier uncertainty. He was a man in need of her assistance, and help him she would.

"Okay, Michael, you want to give the straw a whirl? Let's see if we can get this to work, shall we?" The plastic crackled as she ripped off the wrapper. She plunged the end of the straw into the water and picked up the glass.

He glanced from her eyes to the plastic cup and back again. A slight moan escaped him.

She leaned forward, one hand holding the glass, the other bending the straw. With care, she placed it against the edge of his lip. "Here you go."

His tongue snaked out of his mouth, touching the end. She pushed the small tube further between his lips.

"Go ahead, see if you can take a drink."

Pressure constricted the straw and water passed along the tube, cooling the skin on her fingers. A drop of water spilled down his chin.

"Oops. Let me get that for you." She placed the cup back on the small side table and grabbed a tissue. The sound of the thin paper easing from the box was loud in the quiet room. She dabbed at his chin, wiping the spilled liquid.

He whimpered and his eyes dilated. Had she hurt him?

She pulled back. "I'm sorry. I didn't mean to make you uncomfortable."

He blinked, and shook his head. Garbled sounds emerged from his mouth and he fisted his blanket in his good hand.

"It's okay, Michael. You'll be well taken care of here. We'll have you chatting up the nurses in no time." She winked at him. "I have to round up some things for your room. I'll be back in a few minutes."

His brows furrowed, and the edge of his lip pulled into a thin line.

With a firm squeeze, she patted him on the arm and her fingers prickled from the contact. She turned away from him, and she swore his eyes bore into her back. Blood pounded at her temple. She didn't know this guy from Adam, yet she couldn't shake the strange sense of foreboding that crested over her.

CHAPTER 3

Sheri tossed her keys into the old plastic ashtray. The faded "Eat at Sam's" lettering caught her attention. Why today? The ashtray was left over from a time in her life she'd like to forget, a time when she'd met and fallen in love with a monster. A chill ran over her arms. *I should toss that thing.* But as much as she despised Ram's self-destructive nature, he'd had a good side, too.

Soft chimes from the cuckoo clock filled the air, and she waited for the bird to chirp. *One, two, three, four, five, six, seven.* Wow, she'd worked an extra-long shift. Michael, today's new arrival had taken longer to settle than she'd anticipated, and as much as she tried, she couldn't forget the way his gaze had bothered her.

The flap of Cooper's doggie door slapped against the frame. Her German shepherd raced from the kitchen, his bright eyes shining in the light. With his legs spread wide, he barked.

"Hi Coop. What's got you all in a frenzy? Did you see another squirrel?" She scratched behind his ears, but his insistent yelps echoed around the room. Coop was an ex-police dog, and a few months ago his human partner died in a car accident, pushing Cooper into an early retirement. Unable to resist her penchant for strays, she'd taken him in. "C'mon Coop. Settle down."

She glanced into her living room. A sock lay against the foot of her couch, nestled next to one of her running shoes. Her latest paranormal romance, *Blood, Breath, and Desire*, peeked from between her blue pajama pants draped across the cushions. The urge to grab them, put them on, and snuggle up on the comfy couch with her book, called to her. She let out a sigh and peered through the window into her backyard.

Blades of grass blew in synchronization with the wind, as if taunting her. The rain over the past few days had provided an excellent excuse, and more was in the forecast. *You should mow the lawn while you can.* Her mother's voice echoed in her mind. She slumped, her head falling in mock surrender.

Not bothering to remove her coat, she unlocked the back door and stepped onto the deck. Coop raced between her legs, tangling her feet. She gripped the railing, catching herself before she fell. "Dang it, Coop."

Her companion ran across the lawn and faced the shed. His barks became more insistent, wracking his body with each woof.

The pine trees at the edge of her property cast long shadows onto the lawn. Their tips seemed like sharp claws, and goosebumps rose along her arms. She picked at her fingernail, ripping into her cuticle.

"Ow." A drop of blood formed along the edge, following the line of her nail. She wiped her hand against her scrubs and looked into the darkening sky.

With a forced lilt in her voice, she chuckled and stepped off the deck. "I'll bet that poor squirrel hid in there to get away from you. Didn't it?"

The cool grass tickled the inside of her ankle, right above the sock line. She reached the small building and stilled. Imprinted on the door were several dark smudges, like blackened fingerprints. She hadn't left those marks. Her mouth went dry and the tender spot on the inside of her cheek ached.

Coop's persistent barks added fuel to her rapid pulse. She gave him a quick pet, as much to calm herself as to quiet him. "Shh, Coop."

He whined, his body quivering with energy.

With a tentative grasp, she opened the door. A soft squeak eased from the rusty hinge.

Darkness filled the small room except for the soft shaft of light she'd let in through the opening. Her red lawnmower stood out like a beacon. All was quiet.

A nervous chuckle bubbled from her lips. "See, Coop, no problem—"

Coop pushed past her, and a low growl eased from him. In all the time she'd had him, he'd never reacted this way before. She gripped his collar, holding him in place.

Thump.

Her heart skipped a beat before revving into overdrive. Adrenaline surged through her veins, her face tingling from the rush of blood. The urge to flee overwhelmed her, and the muscles in her legs and arms tensed.

"Ahhhh..." a distinctive male voice eased from the gloom.

Coop lunged, yanking against her grip. His barks continued.

"Quiet, Coop!" Her companion hushed, but he strained against her hold.

A dark form slumped against the far wall.

She inhaled and took a step back.

The man groaned louder.

"Who are you? What are you doing in my shed?"

The only sounds, his labored breaths and her own heartbeat.

She emboldened her tone with as much confidence as she could. "You're trespassing. I'm calling the police."

"No...don't." His words were short, strained, yet the tenor of his voice weaseled its way into the deepest recesses of her soul. The sensation warmed her insides. She held her breath.

He moaned again. His dark form moved.

Her medical training kicked in and she had the urge to rush to his side and help him, but she remained wary. "Are you injured? Should I call an ambulance?"

"Is it dark outside?" His strained speech carried across the small space.

A strange desire to hear him speak again washed over her. She fisted her hand. "What difference does it make if it's dark outside? If you're injured, you need help."

"Please, tell me...is it," a quick intake of breath, "...dark yet?"

The cultured way he spoke made her still. She'd never heard his accent before. Sweat broke out on the back of her neck, dampening her collar. He seemed in pain, but she wasn't sure. Her curiosity warred with her fear, and she wavered between barricading herself in her house with Coop and rushing to aid him. Instead, she remained fixed in place.

"It's dusk," she choked out, her throat tightening from her confusion.

He leaned his head against the wall. She couldn't see his features, but from his outline, she could tell he was a large man. "Don't...fear me. I'll leave...soon...dark." His words washed over her again, stroking her insides.

With a quick move, he stood. A stifled groan eased from his lips, and he rested his shoulder against the wall.

She took a step back. It took all of her inner strength not to run.

Coop growled.

Something wet dripped onto the wooden floor, the rhythmic splashes an eerie omen.

"*Craya.*" He tipped over, his body sliding down the wall until he landed on the floor.

"Stay, Coop." Without a second thought, she raced to his side.

This close, the dim light was enough to see his features. Rough stubble on his chiseled jaw accentuated his luscious lips and broad nose, but what caught her attention was the intensity in his eyes. His gaze swept across her features, reading her, assessing her... devouring her. Warmth spread through her and she had the sudden urge to curl up to him, find out if his lips were as delectable as they appeared. Her cheeks heated, and she shook her head to clear her thoughts.

Blood stained his jacket, or what was left of it. Tattered and torn, the ragged material clung from his wide shoulders. His narrow hips led to muscular legs. He wore an odd pair of trousers that looked handmade.

With a quick tilt of his head, he glanced at her. "Don't...touch me."

Her training kicked in and her *mother nurse* side emerged. "You're injured and need help. I'm a nurse. Let me assess you."

His gaze narrowed, intensely focusing on her.

Her heart skipped a beat, but not from fear.

He tried to stand again, but failed and gripped his chest with his free hand. "I have to...leave."

"The only way you're going anywhere is in an ambulance. Let me get my phone." She turned to go, needing to get help on the way as soon as possible.

He gripped her arm, stopping her flight.

Heat and something more sensual and powerful flowed between them.

"No!" The word was a low command.

Despite knowing nothing about this man, her body responded to his order, her nipples peaking beneath her shirt. Her mind raced. Why did she react to him this way?

She glanced from his face to his hand and back again. He released her, and fell forward, his palm slapping against the wooden floor. "I'm s...sorry. No infirmary."

Infirmary? That's an odd word. She blinked. "You need medical attention. A hospital is where you belong—"

She stilled. Blood drained from her face. *What if he's a criminal?*

Coop rubbed against her leg. His chest rumbled.

The man's nostrils flared, and his intense gaze locked onto hers. "Don't fear. I'm not a danger to you."

She took a step back, toward the exit. "Are you running from the law?"

A deprecating chuckle eased from his throat then was cut short. As he inhaled, his lungs wheezed. "Not in the way you think."

"But you are running."

"I...I need to go." He rose once again, but couldn't maintain his balance.

She caught him before he fell. Even with her big bone structure, his weight was almost more than she could bear. "You're not going anywhere in this condition. You're coming inside with me, so I can take a look at you. Then, we'll talk about an ambulance. Okay?"

His nod was all the confirmation she needed.

CHAPTER 4

*R*am woke to a blinding white light. The glare pierced his brain, stabbing him like a sharp knife. All he could discern was the radiance around him. Maybe he was on the planet Lemuria, on the character board. All dead warriors in the game went there. Then again, maybe not. Unease rippled through his senses.

"You failed me, but transporting you to the character board is far too easy a death." Zedron's low, menacing tone resonated deep into Ram's mind. His god wasn't happy, and that couldn't be good for Ram.

As Zedron's Gossum leader, it was Ram's responsibility to defeat Noeh, the Stiyaha king. Unfortunately for Ram, that didn't happen. Instead, he'd been the one to die. If he'd had a voice, he would've whimpered.

"Your aura is in the palm of my hand. I could crush you—I should crush you, ending your miserable existence for all time."

Ram's essence quivered.

"For failing me...twice, you will suffer in a unique way." Zedron's steady voice was worse than if he'd laughed. "I'm returning you to Earth to live in a broken human body. From whence you came, you shall return."

The light blinked out, and Ram descended into his new hell.

Pain exploded in his arms, legs, chest, and knee, all pounding in a misery he'd never experienced before. He'd often got a kick out of little bits of pain, *enjoying the twinges and pulls on his muscles and tendons. He'd been so wrong. Real pain, the kind that knocked you on your ass...that hurt.*

A loud buzzing noise circled his head. He focused on the sound, trying to use it to distract himself from the agony. As he homed in, his own scream beat into his psyche.

Someone's warm fingers touched his throat. He opened his eyes. A man wearing a yellow hardhat came into focus.

"Medic! Here. This man needs help."

Ram's throat was raw from his screams, but he didn't stop. He couldn't.

"You! Get the jaws of life."

Nooooo! They were going to kill him, but then, maybe the pain would stop. For a brief moment, he wished that were true.

A man appeared in Ram's line of sight. He leaned in, his gaze observant. "I'm a paramedic. I'm giving you morphine for the pain."

A small pin-prick in Ram's arm, and the initial dose of morphine burst into his bloodstream, providing a small measure of relief. He hadn't had a hit of any drug since the last time he was human. His scream transformed into a bizarre laugh. How he'd longed for this high, just not under these circum-stances. The absurdity wasn't lost on him.

As the drug took hold, his laughter ceased. He peered around. His legs were pinned underneath the car's steering wheel. The pillow of an air bag lay against his chest. Shards of broken glass were everywhere, on the dash—or what was left of it—on the empty seat next to him, and embedded in his arm. Oh, yeah, this was a doozy.

A loud screech, then the ting of metal against metal permeated the air.

"Right here, yes. He hit a tree, you'll have to pry the roof off to extract him."

Someone ran a finger over his brow. "Hey buddy, you with us?"

Ram glanced at the paramedic, the same one who'd given him the drug. In Ram's messed up mind, the man's eyes blurred together and melded with his nose.

A strange light exploded behind Ram's eyes and his vision pinpointed into a white dot until even that blinked out.

The rhythmic squeak of a cart wheel in desperate need of some oil and the quiet murmur of voices filtered into Ram's mind, waking him from his recurring nightmare. He was in his new home, the Columbia Rehabilitation Center. As he inhaled, the astringent scent of rubbing alcohol invaded his senses, reminding him of what he used to be—a Gossum. Ram held his breath. His rib cage expanded and a new bout of pain raced along his nerves. The ache was nothing new. He'd experienced much agony and torture over his beleaguered life, but nothing compared to the soul-deep misery he experienced in his new body thanks to Zedron.

The meds the humans pumped into his bloodstream tempered some of the pain, but not enough. That was okay. He deserved the torture after what he'd done, and what he'd wanted to do.

He hadn't asked to be a part of this war, but sometimes, fate found you. Back when he'd been an ignorant human, a couple of Gossum had indeed found him. He'd been bitten, scooped up like dirty kitty litter, and thrown into the back of a van. *Welcome, young Gossum, have we got a job for you.* His missions—to win the war for his god, Zedron, enslave the humans, and begin the long process of transporting water back to Lemuria. He closed his eyes. *I failed.*

During the latest episode, he'd been in a battle with a couple of Alora's warriors—Demir, the Panthera leader and his second in command, Aramie. In his arrogance, he'd thought he could control them both, only to realize his mistake a tad too late. A throwing star in the eye was so not a brave way to go.

He gripped the sheet, the fingers on his right hand squeezing until his arm shook from the force. His energy depleted rapidly and he couldn't maintain his hold. As his fingers relaxed, he sighed.

Soft footsteps approached. He opened his eyes.

"Ah, you're awake. Hello, Michael. My name is Tammy. Time to change your bag." A tall nurse stood by his side. The patch of grey at her temple was in stark contrast to her dark hair, but matched the laugh lines around her eyes, giving away her age. She wasn't Sheri, and a solemn heaviness settled onto his chest.

He tensed and closed his eyes, the humiliation of having his catheter bag emptied by this female was additional insult to injury. *Thanks, Zedron, thanks a bunch.*

Tammy drew down his sheet, and cool air wafted over his skin. He detected the scent of bacon on her breath and heard the unmistakable pounding of her heart. Seems he'd kept his supernatural Gossum senses. Not that those would help him while he withered away in this bed. He needed a distraction from his torment, and fast.

Sheri...

A sense of weightlessness cascaded over him, bringing a smile to his face. Tight from puffiness, the skin around his mouth pulled, sending a small wave of discomfort through his jaw. Even though Zedron had thrown him into this broken body, maybe the finicky god had done him a favor.

Despite it all, the one thing he'd wanted more than anything was to reunite with his ex-wife, and she was here...with him. How odd he'd ended up in the one rehab center where she worked. Odd, but fortunate. He wouldn't look a gift horse in the mouth.

Shoes squeaked against the polished linoleum floor, and he peeked at the nurse. She disappeared into his adjoining bathroom. A few moments later, the toilet's flush eased around the half-closed door. She tossed the empty urine bag into the red garbage receptacle labeled "medical waste." Her mouth lifted at the corner.

His pulse quickened. He wanted to growl his displeasure, but only a small gasp escaped his lips.

She patted him on the wrist. "Let me attach a fresh bag and then we can get you some more liquids, maybe even some gelatin."

He clenched his jaw, and his broken bone sent a lance of pain through his skull. Sweat dampened his forehead. White spots swam in his vision. The pain receded, and the cool sheet swept over his chest once again.

Tammy turned to leave, but glanced back. Her gaze traveled over his features, studying him. "Well, Michael. You're going to be here for a while. I'm not the day nurse, Sheri is, but I'll do my best to take care of you when she's not around."

Through the jumbled mess of his jaw and his swollen lips and tongue, he uttered a single word. "Shh...Sheri." Saying her name out loud lightened his mood, and a sense of weightlessness slid through him.

Earlier, when he'd first seen his ex-wife, he'd tried to speak, tell her it was him, but the words wouldn't come. Good thing, too. What would he have said to her? He couldn't tell her who he was, that would freak her out, but at least he'd get to spend time with her. His chest expanded. Somehow, someway, he'd figure out a way to prove to her he was worthy and maybe, just maybe, win back her heart.

CHAPTER 5

*B*lood trickled down the back of Tanen's arm, wet and warm. Each step through the damp grass reopened the cuts on his back, and a new wave of agony tore through him. Weak from his blood loss, his head pounded. A human female, her arm wrapped around his waist, guided him toward her home. Her linen and lime fragrance worked its way into his senses. As he breathed, he committed her scent to memory.

"This way. Three steps up." The soothing tone of her voice skated over his nerves. Unbidden, his inner beast stirred. Close to a growl, a low moan burst from his lips.

Each step was an effort in muscle control. His legs shook and white spots formed in his vision. The female pushed open a wooden door. As if in protest, a small squeak issued from the metal hinges. She leaned into him, and he couldn't help but notice the fullness of her breast against the side of his chest. Even through the pain, he responded to her closeness, his heartbeat picking up speed.

As he crossed the threshold into her home, something warm and fast scooted between his legs.

"C'mon, big guy. Let's get you into—"

A deep-throated growl echoed in the room.

The menacing sound filtered past the pounding in Tanen's head. He stiffened, forcing the female to stop in her tracks.

"Cooper! Sit!" She took a step forward, pulling him further into her home. "He won't hurt you. Coop's a good dog. Aren't you, buddy?"

Cooper chuffed, but remained tense, his gaze riveted on Tanen. This animal was the source of the barking he'd heard off and on all day. *A wolf, yet...not.* Lancing pain raced over Tanen's shoulders and down his back. His vision blurred.

With her free hand, the female pulled a wooden chair away from a table. Stacks of paper were strewn across the top and even through the fog in his brain, the disorder beat against his psyche. The tension in his shoulders tightened, and a sour taste formed in his mouth. If he were capable, he'd straighten the mess. He gripped the back of the chair as the female helped ease him onto the seat.

A bead of sweat rolled over his brow and down his cheek. He couldn't control the shiver that raced over his skin. A burning desire to gaze upon his savior coursed through his veins.

Her fine features came into focus—a pair of hazel eyes surrounded by dark lashes, a pert little nose, and lips so plump, they begged to be kissed. Long strands of blonde hair cascaded around her shoulders, enticing him with their soft appeal. Mesmerized, he couldn't look away.

She left him for a moment, and a sense of loneliness bore down on him. Even in his weakened state, he understood there was something wrong about that. He shouldn't, no—couldn't be attracted to her. She was human. He needed to leave...find Mauree...bring her back to the Keep. With great effort, he pushed against the armrests, forcing his battered body to stand.

Her warm hands pressed against his chest, holding him in place with unexpected strength. "No you don't. Stay here." In his fogged mind, her command reminded him of his time in the warrior training program, when he'd followed orders without thought. He relaxed, giving in to her demand.

A short, predatory bark came from the female's companion.

"Coop, go! Sit in your bed!" Her stern voice must've done the trick for the clicking of clawed toes echoed against the floor.

A brightness in the room burned into his sensitive eyes, and he squinted at the orb in the center of the ceiling. The light provided a minimum amount of heat, but didn't compare to the sunstones lining the Keep's walls. His headache beat against his skull. Would he ever see his home again?

The female returned to his side. She pulled a chair next to him. The concern etched in her brow burrowed into him and took up residence. A pang hit him in the chest and he stiffened, riding the wave of pain until it subsided.

"Tell me where you're injured." Her words were forceful, yet gentle.

"My back." With each breath he took, air wheezed from his lungs. His Lemurian blood would heal his wounds. All he needed was rest and a little time, but he couldn't tell her that.

"And your arm, your face. Let's get this coat off you so I can take a look." She eased his jacket from his shoulders and tossed the garment over a nearby chair. With attentive care, she removed his shirt. A quick gasp escaped her lips.

Her gaze traveled from his back to his shoulders and down his chest. She focused on the three dark teardrop shapes over his heart. His marking...one each for honesty, prudence, and tenacity. She bit her lip. The sudden urge to do the same raced through his mind.

"Were you attacked by a bear?"

No, something far worse. He couldn't tell her that. To do so would break the rules...informing a human about the Lemurians. If she found out he wasn't human, he'd have to change her, make her a part of the game. No Stiyaha in recent memory had ever tried to turn a human, and Tanen wasn't about to break that tradition. He needed to keep everything about himself a secret. The lie came easier than he thought it would.

"Y...yes, a bear." His marking for honesty pulsed, and he placed his hand over his heart. He didn't want her to see the mark fade. Let her think the symbols were a tattoo.

"I have a first aid kit, but you really should go to the hospital. You may have broken ribs and internal bleeding—"

He placed two fingers against her lips, silencing her.

Her eyes widened, but he'd achieved the desired result.

The softness of her skin tingled his fingers. He longed to do more, but instead, he pulled back. "I'll be…fine. Just need…" …*to rest.*

She stood. Her fingers traveled over her mouth and her gaze met his. The deafening silence stretched on for several seconds. Placing her hands on her hip, she focused on him. "I'll get the first aid kit."

As she left the room, Coop roused from his bed. His dark eyes focused on Tanen, but he didn't move. A soft bark, a warning, burst from his mouth.

Tanen gritted his teeth and ignored her companion. Now open to the air, the wounds on his back flared anew. Warmth radiated from the cuts, pounding in a rhythm to match his heartbeats. The heatwave rushed over his shoulders and down his back. He shivered, and a clammy sheen of sweat covered his arms.

Alone for the moment, he glanced at his surroundings. Not far away, the hallway opened into a large room. A sock, a pair of pants, and an odd assortment of clothes were strewn across a couch. Atop a nearby table, an empty food carton lay on its side. An orange sauce had dribbled onto the wood, along with some rice. Neat, she was not. The clutter beat against his need for order, and despite the pain in his chest and back, he had the sudden urge to sweep the spilled contents into the container. He fisted his hand.

On the far wall, a large shelf overflowed with books. Some lay flat, others were tilted at an angle. His mouth went dry. In his pain-induced mind, the sudden urge to touch them, caress the fine leather, and smell the familiar scent of inked paper was a call he couldn't ignore. He stood and blood raced south. His vision blurred. Wavering on unsteady legs, he gripped the chair's armrest.

Soft footsteps padded down the hall.

He sat before he fell over.

She returned with a small white box emblazoned with a red cross.

"Here we go." She perched in the chair next to him and opened the container. "From what I could tell, the cuts on your back are the worst. Can you turn so I can take a look?"

Sweat beaded on his lip. The pain had reached an all new level of torment, radiating from his back into his legs. To twist would be horrific, but he wouldn't show suffering, not to her. He nodded.

Steeling himself, he twisted in the chair and faced the far wall. His teeth clamped together so hard, his jaw popped. Bits of white light flitted across his vision. *Don't pass out, don't pass out.* He swallowed. Cooper eyed him from his bed.

She audibly inhaled. "How are you able to move at all?"

He peered at her over his shoulder. With his skin stretched taut, the pain resurfaced full force. He couldn't respond even if he'd wanted to.

She shook her head. "Th...these are bad. You *need* to go to a hospital."

He exhaled, letting out the breath he'd been holding. "No."

She pursed her lips. "I'm sorry. You don't have a choice." She pulled a small, flat box from her back pocket. A small light lit up the screen. With care, she tapped her finger against the smooth surface.

"What are you doing?" he croaked.

"Calling an ambulance to take you to the hospital."

Nooooo! He couldn't go to a human infirmary. They'd find out what he was. A surge of fear rushed energy to his muscles. With the quickness of his kind, he stood, wrapped his arms around her, and trapped her against the nearby wall.

The small box fell from her fingers and bounced on the wooden floor. A loud clatter tore through the air.

The reserve energy he'd used pumped through his veins, staving off the pain. Instead, awareness of this female's body pressed against him, molding to him, reawakened his beast.

CHAPTER 6

*S*aar twirled the toothpick between his lips. The smooth wood tickled the inside of his mouth, but the routine motion calmed his nerves, at least for the moment. He stood outside Noeh's Throne room. His feet were heavy, rooting him in place.

A low growl started in his chest. His beast wanted to shred something, preferably his enemy, but at this point even a good fight with one of his warriors would do. He hadn't been able to find Tanen or Mauree. His failure stuck in his craw.

He must admit to Noeh the two of them were still at large. A tic started in his jaw, and he clamped down on his inner beast. Time to get it over with. He raised his fist and knocked on the door.

The large double doors glided open, pulling in a draft of air. Jax looked up at Saar, his curly red hair bobbing around his ears. The lines around his eyes creased and a smile bloomed on his face.

"Ooh, Saar, welcome. Good to see you, yes, indeed." The small Jixie turned his head and peered into the room. "Your Majesty, Saar is here. He is, he is!"

The little male stepped back, allowing Saar access to the king's private chamber. Saar raised his chin and entered the room. The doors closed behind him with a soft whoosh.

Noeh sat on his throne, one hand resting on his knee, the other entwined with Melissa's, his queen. He caught Saar's gaze and his smile faded. With deliberate intent, he rose from his seat. "What news do you bring?"

"Nothing that will bring you any peace." Saar removed the tooth-pick from his mouth, approached his king and bowed low. When Noeh didn't respond, his stomach tightened.

"Saar, please rise. Your formality is appreciated, but isn't necessary." Noeh's voice held a tinge of sadness.

Saar straightened. Dark circles colored the skin under his king's eyes, and he seemed tense and fatigued. The knot in Saar's gut tightened. "Your Majesty, what—"

"Waaaahhhh."

Saar glanced at Melissa. Anlon, the new prince, struggled to get down from his mother's lap. Melissa stood and placed him on the ground. He crawled the few inches to his father, gripped Noeh's pant leg, and sucked on the material. Melissa smirked. "Why does everything have to go in his mouth?"

The babe turned at the sound of his mother's voice. An arresting smile lit up his face.

Anlon brought much hope into the Keep, and Saar couldn't help the smile that tugged at his lips. After centuries without children, the young prince served as a beacon of optimism for many.

Noeh leaned over and twirled his finger in his son's blond curls. He looked at Saar. "Old friend. Tell me what's on your mind."

A rush of nausea washed over Saar, and he placed his hand over his mouth. His other curled into a tight fist. To admit to Noeh he'd failed was harder than he'd anticipated. He couldn't speak, his words trapped behind his closed throat.

Noeh's brow scrunched. He straightened and took a step toward Saar. "Now, you've got me concerned. Tell me."

At the command, Saar's throat relaxed. Forefront in his mind was the need to respond to the king's request. He met Noeh's gaze. "I've failed you, Your Majesty."

Noeh glanced at Saar's mouth, then returned his attention to

Saar's eyes. Noeh didn't speak right away, but then raised an eyebrow. "How so?"

He doesn't hear me. I forget...he's completely deaf.

Saar shook his head. "After several days of searching, I was unable to locate either Tanen or Mauree. They should be easy to find, but..." He shrugged. What else was there to say?

"Saar, no one expects you to be perfect." Melissa's words hit him like a punch to the gut. He took pride in his tracking ability and fighting skills. That's how he'd earned his status as Noeh's Commander of Arms. Nothing less was acceptable.

Unable to hold either the king's or the queen's gaze any longer, he turned around. He shoved the toothpick into his mouth, gouging his lip. Such was what he deserved. One of the elegant paintings caught his attention. A group of Stiyaha in beast form—brown fur covering their skin, claws extended—battled against their enemy, the Gossum. How he hated the evil hairless creatures. Saar paced between the statues of warriors long gone to Noeh's ornately carved desk, flipping the toothpick from side to side in his haste. "I can't believe this is happening."

Noeh's firm grip on his shoulder halted him in his tracks. Saar turned to face his king.

"Just because you haven't found them yet, doesn't mean you won't. I have faith in you, my friend." Noeh's eyes reflected his determination and belief. "They're out there. It's only a matter of time."

Saar spoke quickly, his fear pulling the words from him. "My concern is Ostrum—the spring ceremony at Roan's Rock. I wouldn't put it past Mauree to try to attack you there. She's obsessed with revenge."

Noeh shook his head. "She wouldn't be that brave or that stupid."

"But she might be that crazy." Melissa's words were tight.

Silence.

The quiet in the room was eerie. Only Anlon's soft coos broke the stillness.

"Let her try." Noeh's tone left no room for argument.

"I shall continue to search for them, but I request additional guards at the ceremony." Saar held Noeh's gaze. He wouldn't back down, not from something as important as the king's safety.

Melissa placed her hand on Noeh's arm. "I think that's a fabulous idea. Thank you, Saar."

The king glanced at his queen. A knowing look passed between them.

Noeh pursed his lips, peered at Saar and nodded. "Be sure to alert your warriors to be on the lookout."

Melissa picked up Anlon, and the baby giggled. The soft laughter pierced its way into Saar's heart, warming him to the little guy.

"As you wish, Your Majesties." He bowed before the royal family and turned to leave.

Jax opened the double doors, and the breeze blew a few wisps of hair over Saar's cheek. He gritted his teeth as a new resolve coursed through his veins. Mauree would get her due, and Tanen, too, he'd make sure of it.

CHAPTER 7

Sheri's pulse raced as a strange mixture of shock and desire coursed through her veins. The tall, muscular stranger pinned her against the wall. One second she'd pressed 9-1—on her phone and the next, she was here, in his arms.

His biceps bulged, and she had a sudden urge to run her fingers over them, feel the steel that was below the surface, but her hands were trapped at his hips. She gripped his taut waist, and his heat bore into her, warming her fingers, tingling the sensitive nerves. Although caged in his embrace, he was gentle with her, holding back the strength that ebbed from him in waves. As he leaned in, his breath cascaded over her shoulder, warm and enticing.

"No infirmary." His gravelly, rough command came out on a whisper.

She should've feared him, this stranger in her home trapping her in his arms, but instead, her insides melted, warmed by his touch, his voice, his scent. Something about him made her long for more.

So focused on the man who held her so close, she hadn't noticed Coop. His insistent barks echoed through the house.

The man tensed, and in the process his lean body pressed tighter against hers. Her skin prickled at the contact.

With a quick glance over his shoulder, she caught sight of her pet. He growled, his lips curled over his fangs.

"No, Coop. Stop!"

His back legs bunched in preparation for his attack.

The man didn't release her, but turned to face her dog. He held out one hand, palm open. "Halt."

Coop's growl faded.

He took a tentative step forward.

His nose quivered, and a small whimper eased from his chest. Her pet, an ex-police dog trained to track and defend, placed his muzzle under the stranger's palm.

She gasped. If she hadn't seen this for herself, she wouldn't have believed it. He patted Coop on the head, and the dog's tail beat against the floor.

The man's eyes were red-rimmed, and sweat coated his forehead. "I have to leave…"

His eyes glazed over, and his grip around her waist loosened.

As her hands traveled along the space between them, her fingers trailed over the firm muscles of his abdomen and chest. The strength and power under his skin lit up her nerves. She moved a stray hair away from his brow and focused on his eyes. Bottomless pools of blue, they reflected the pain hidden behind his features.

Her chest constricted. "Please, let me help you."

His gaze fell to her mouth, and he reached up to stroke her bottom lip with his thumb, teasing her. "How? Like this?"

Before she could stop him, he slipped his hand around the base of her neck and pulled her close. His mouth hovered over hers for the briefest moment. She closed her eyes, aware that doing so was an invitation all its own. Warm and welcoming, his lips tasted of musk and pepper. With unexpected tenderness, he teased her with his tongue, caressing the crease between her lips. The sensitive nerves tingled at the contact and she inhaled, parting her mouth.

Moaning softly, he deepened the kiss, and explored her. His tongue brushed the sore spot in her mouth, but instead of pain, his smooth caress eased some of the ache. The passionate need in his kiss

36

bore into her, sending a wave of desire to her core. Beneath the thin material of her shirt, her nipples peaked, and she couldn't hide her reaction to him. A slow groan rumbled in his chest.

There was no denying her yearning for this stranger, and she mewled under his onslaught. When she didn't think she could go any longer, he broke their kiss. Trailing his lips over her throat, his warm breaths tickled her skin. As she squirmed, she rubbed against him. Between the soft cloth of his pants and her scrubs, his shaft twitched. A shiver raced over her arms.

This is wrong...I shouldn't do this... Clarity filled her mind and she tensed.

With a swiftness she could barely perceive, he released her. His brow furrowed, his eyes glazed and unfocused. "What's happening?" He shook his head and glanced at the door. "I must leave...complete... my mission..."

The muscles in his arms visibly quivered, and he lost his balance. As she placed her arm under his shoulder, her legs wobbled to support his extra weight. Her hand landed against his back. Blood seeped onto her fingers.

She peered at the couch. He was far too big for the small love seat. The only place large enough was her bed. "C'mon, big guy. This way."

Using their combined strength, she led him along the short hallway. Her bed was unmade, rumpled, and had yesterday's partial load of laundry scattered across the sheet. She couldn't worry about that right now.

He landed on the bed in a heap, face down. She swallowed and took a tentative step back. Adrenaline surged through her veins, heightening her senses. She placed her hand on his shoulder. "You still with me?"

Silence. The muscles in her legs trembled. She gripped his wrist, taking his pulse. *Normal.*

Coop chuffed. He stood in the doorway, ears straight up, his attention focused on her.

"Oh, Coop, this man is in serious trouble."

Feather light, the man's eyelashes caressed the skin over his strong cheekbone. His dark blond hair cascaded over the edge of his ear. With the side of his face plastered against the pillow, his puckered lips reminded her of their kiss.

Her face heated. She was in way over her head.

No infirmary. His words echoed in her mind.

What the hell? Was he a wacko, some nut job she'd let into her house, into her bed? How quickly she'd come under his spell. That's what it had to be, because no one in their right mind would bring a stranger into their house in his condition and not call an ambulance.

Indecision tore at her, eating away at her resolve. "Well, at the very least, I can clean your injuries while I decide what to do."

She rushed to the living room and retrieved the medical kit. When she returned, Coop lay on the floor at the side of the bed, right next to the man. A chill ran over her arms. He'd never reacted this way toward strangers. With a shake of her head, she concentrated on her task. Pulling out the bottle of rubbing alcohol and some cotton balls, she dabbed the solution onto his wounds.

A bear, huh? Although she hadn't seen any, a string of recent sightings was all over the news. She'd treated a few bear attack victims when she'd interned at the hospital, but the cuts on his back didn't look like those marks. She stilled, her hand hovering over his shoulder. A drop of rubbing alcohol dripped onto his skin and ran down his spine. She shook her head. A bear was the logical answer...it had to be.

With a loud exhale, she wiped the moisture away and finished her cleaning, bandaging the worst of the wounds. After tossing her clothes off the bed, she placed a towel on the sheet. Carefully, she pushed against him. "C'mon, tough guy, roll over."

His heavy weight was a struggle, but she rolled him onto his back.

A large scar cut across his ribs, the rugged seam in stark contrast to his smooth skin. She inhaled. What would cause such a wound? A small tattoo covered the skin over his heart—three black teardrops. She'd noticed it briefly when she'd first evaluated him. The raised surface was rough and one mark was lighter than the others. She touched the outline, her fingers tingling at the contact.

"Stop...you can't...treason..." His brow bunched together and a low moan eased from his lips. "Yes, Your Majesty..."

Her heart skipped a beat. What a strange dream. Who was he?

Despite his weakened condition, he seemed strong, powerful, and his handsome features called to her, stirring a craving in her chest she'd long forgotten. *Forget it, girl. Doesn't he have disaster written all over him? Do you want another replay of Ram, version 2.0?* Determination burned in her gut, and she fisted her hand. "No. I won't open myself up again. It would end in heartache."

Her marriage to Ram, and his endless problems, was something she'd run from. She wouldn't take on another head case, yet the memory of the stranger's passionate kiss filtered into her mind. Her lips tingled in response.

She searched for any other signs of injury. Tall, strong, and beautiful—he was not the type of man she'd imagined in her bed, but an unbidden thought formed anyway. What would it be like to be with him? Curiosity got the better of her, and she lingered for a moment at the bulge between his legs. *Wow, what a package.* A slow shiver ran over her arms.

She looked him over once more then wiped the cut on his brow. "When you wake up, sleeping beauty, you're going to tell me who you are."

CHAPTER 8

Far above the surface of Lemuria, Alora raced along the platform connecting two giant Etila trees. The scaffolding swayed in the breeze and she tightened her grip on the wooden rail. With a quick glance into the sky, she caught a glimpse of Aridis, Lemuria's largest moon. Its radiance lit up the night, overpowering the soft glow coming from the lanterns spaced evenly along the path. Although well past nightfall, warmth from the day still lingered, and sweat formed on the back of her neck as much from her exertion as her unease. She'd arrived at her destination.

Carved into the thick bark of the largest Etila tree on Lemuria, the door with its intricate engravings and embellishments was unmistakable, and the gilded lettering over the frame left no doubt as to whom was inside—Councilor Radnor. He'd summoned her to his private chamber. Even though she'd been here many times before, her stomach tightened into a hard knot.

She closed her eyes and inhaled. Even the sweet fragrance of a nearby Tralum plant couldn't calm her nerves. *I should get this over with.* She pulled on her inner strength and tugged at the Yandora vines dangling near the door's entrance. Sweet chimes announced her arrival.

"Enter." Radnor's voice eased through the tiny cracks in the door.

Alora twisted the knob and stepped over the threshold. A rush of cold air, circulated from the tree's roots and through the inner bark, wafted over her face and arms. Goosebumps rose along with the hair at her nape.

Radnor approached, twirling the ends of his mustache between two fingers. A smile crossed his face, but it didn't quite reach his eyes.

She returned a forced smile. "Radnor, good to see you again."

"Ah, Alora, welcome. Come in." Radnor enveloped her in his embrace. In addition to council leader, he was also her father-in-law.

"A-hem."

She stilled. Zedron.

Against the far wall was a large table, filled with an assortment of fine nectars and wines. Zedron held a crystal goblet between his fingers. He caught her gaze and raised his glass. "Alora."

Her pulse rose. He was her rival in this war, as well as, her ex-lover. She wanted to claim Earth as a free planet, bartering knowledge and technology in exchange for Earth's water. Zedron wanted to enslave the humans and take the water by force. In either case, the dying Lemuria and its inhabitants needed the precious resource. She fisted her hand. "What are you doing here?"

"Well, isn't that a fine greeting." Zedron advanced, his eyes twinkling.

Her insides tightened into a coil. She focused on Radnor. "What's going on?"

Tension lines formed around his eyes. "Alora, Zedron brings charges against you in the battle for Earth. He claims you've cheated in the game—again. You know the rules, guidance only, no direct interference."

Her throat constricted. Earlier in the war, she'd helped her Stiyaha warriors survive the great scourge, the one that killed over half of her best characters. In an effort to save them, she'd infiltrated the water in the Keep with the antidotal serum.

She'd been caught and sanctioned. For the remainder of the war, she would never see daylight. Her mate, Veromé knew what she'd done, and the council had sanctioned him as well, to never see the night. The few minutes at dawn and dusk were their only moments together. Unfortunately, her characters in the game received a similar fate, relegated to the night and unable to handle the sun's rays, putting them at a disadvantage in the war.

The knot in her gut twisted, but she refused to let Zedron see her squirm. She pursed her lips and glared at him. "What's your proof?"

A slow smirk played along his lips. He picked up a gilded box from the councilor's desk and inclined his head to her father-in-law. "May I?"

"Proceed." Radnor nodded and settled into his chair with a tired sigh. The worn leather creaked from his weight.

Zedron's eyes glinted with purpose. "Behold, my validation."

He unhinged the box and a flurry of tratee flies flew into the air. They circled each other in the middle of the room. One by one they united until their wings combined to form a hologram. An image appeared—two characters heading for an outcropping of rocks— Demir and Aramie, two of her Panthera warriors.

Alora's mouth went dry. She stole a glance at Zedron. He sneered. Her anger burned, hot and fevered. She fisted her hand and returned her attention to the hologram.

Her two warriors huddled near the edge of a large mountain, the sun creeping down its face, closer and closer to the trapped couple. The mountain shook and an opening appeared. Demir pushed Aramie through, then followed her, but not before sunlight hit his arm, burning his skin. The stench of burnt flesh wafted into the room.

Alora clenched her jaw and her teeth ached from the pressure. A niggle of worry toyed with her psyche. *Don't let him get to you.*

Zedron swirled his hand in the air, dissipating the tratee flies. They returned to the box, and he shut the lid. His gaze met hers. "I was looking through my *visus bacin* when I saw this happen. Good thing the scrying bowl records everything."

"How did you know—"

"Alora!" Radnor's voice silenced her. "Someone created that small opening. Was it you or Veromé?"

Alora's pulse pounded loud in her ears. She couldn't speak. To do so would admit her guilt. Silence hung thick in the room.

Radnor's pinched features softened. "Alora, you know I love you like a daughter, but I must enforce the rules. No one else would have cause to do this except you or Veromé. Was it you?"

She dropped her gaze. *What do I do?*

"Tell me, Alora, or I will assume Veromé did this and punish him accordingly."

No! Adrenaline coursed through her veins. She couldn't let that happen. "I...I opened the hole. I had to. Dem—"

Radnor held up his hand. "So, your meddling saved—what are their names?" He narrowed his eyes. "Ah, yes, Demir and Aramie. You saved your characters and altered the course of the game."

He rubbed his brow then peered at Zedron. "Please, I forget the details."

Zedron bowed low. "My pleasure, Councilor."

Alora tensed, fear slithered into her stomach, squeezing her insides.

Zedron's lip curled into a grin, and her skin crawled. She'd once found that smile so attractive.

"Your knights killed my best player—Ram. If you hadn't cheated, your characters would be dead, and I'd still have my kingpin."

"That is grounds for serious punishment." Radnor turned in his chair. "Alora, this is your second offense. A third time will result in forfeiture of the game. Do you understand?"

She met Radnor's stare. Heat flushed over her skin. *I won't lose to my rival. I can't.* With all her senses screaming inside not to, she gave a slight nod.

"Pick one of your character species to allot to Zedron." Radnor's voice boomed across the room.

She shook her head. "Wh...what?" When Zedron had challenged her for access to Earth's water, she'd selected six character species to battle in this war. Since they were scattered across the globe she'd recently met with each group, encouraging them to join forces at the

Keep. Some were still on their way to the underground caves in the Pacific Northwest.

He leaned forward and placed his elbows on his desk. "Give one of your species to Zedron. I can't be any clearer."

"Radnor, please. I know Zedron has cheated, I just don't have any proof—"

The councilor's face reddened, and he glanced at Zedron. "Who would you like to have?"

"Stiyaha."

"No!" Spittle flew from Alora's lips.

Zedron laughed. "As an alternative, I would take Ursus."

"The Ursus were almost to the Keep." Tears threatened and she blinked them away.

"Decide, Alora. Ursus or Stiyaha." Radnor's mouth turned down at the corner. He was done playing games.

A heavy weight settled onto her chest. To hand over one of her character species would give her rival an advantage. Her hand curled into a fist. She hated Zedron all the more. "Fine...Ursus."

"Ursus are not my first choice, but I will take them, if you also give me Mauree."

She flinched. "You want that traitor?"

He nodded, a wicked smile plastered on his face.

"Fine, take her. May she betray you as well." Alora took one last look at her father-in-law, lifted her chin, and headed out the door. Once on the other side, the tears flowed.

CHAPTER 9

*T*anen was hot, burning, his fevered skin making him shiver. A slow breath escaped his lips, but as much as he tried, he couldn't wake up. He lay on a bed, a soft pillow cushioning his head. The scent of linen and lime buried into his senses, stroking him, settling into his pores.

His beast growled, sensing this female, her nearness so close, yet so far. He wanted to grab her, pull her tight, show her how she tempted him. A strangled cry emerged from his throat.

His mind wandered, drifting on a sea of disconnected thoughts and images until one came into focus. He didn't want to remember, to experience the rejection yet again, but he couldn't fight the tide.

Tanen stacked the remaining books onto the table. He peered around the room and shook his head. In a fit of anger toward the gods, young King Noeh had decommissioned the Hall of Scriptures. Tanen's chest ached. He understood Noeh's pain, having lost his own parents and his older brother, Remi, during the great scourge. He ran his finger over an ancient text's gilded spine. To close the library seemed harsh, but Noeh's decree was firm. Tanen had no choice but to comply.

A shadow passed over the book's cover. He glanced up. His shoulders relaxed at the sight of Tamara—his love. Her golden hair lay in ringlets over her shoulders, and her plump ruby lips formed into a perfect bow.

"Tamara." He'd always enjoyed how her name rolled off his tongue.

Her brow furrowed, tension lines forming around her eyes. "Good, we're alone. We need to talk."

His breath caught in his throat. "What about?"

She crossed her arms. His qithan bracelet was markedly absent. That wasn't a good sign. "I... Craya, this is harder to do than I thought."

"What's going on?" Even as he asked, he already knew the answer. That she didn't wear his proffered gift, the promise to bond, was evidence enough. When he'd given her the bracelet, he'd expected her to accept, but she'd delayed, saying she needed time to think. He cracked his knuckles, the sound loud in the room.

She dug into the pocket of her dress and pulled out the silver chain. A knot formed in his gut.

"Here...I can't do this. I...I can't bond to you." She placed the bracelet in his palm and met his gaze.

The room suddenly seemed warm, and he loosened his collar. "Why? I thought—"

"There's someone else."

Her words were a dagger in his chest, ripping into his heart. He wanted to scream, fight this male for the right to claim her. Instead, he ground his teeth. "Who?"

"Quoron. He's a warrior..." She shrugged.

He cracked his knuckles again. Ever since the scourge devastated the population, wiping out more females than males, Tamara's selection of possible mates had increased dramatically. Warriors were the elite, most respected class in their society. She'd selected a warrior over him. It burned inside, flaring his heartburn. His status as a council member couldn't compare.

He curled his fist around the bracelet. "Of course."

"I'm...sorry." She shook her head, then turned around and walked away.

Females were cold and harsh, of that, he had no doubt. He threw the *bracelet onto the table where it skittered and landed against a pile of books. An ache built in his chest, leaving him empty and alone.*

Sweat beaded on Tanen's brow and a drop trickled along his hairline, pooling at the base of his ear. His breathing increased as the fever burned. Pinpricks of pain pounded in his head, beating a steady rhythm to match his thumping heart.

A soft female voice teased the edge of his consciousness. "...warm...fever..."

Her words were a rope just out of reach, and he couldn't wake, couldn't escape the delirium that raged, burning him on the inside.

"Need to...help..."

A small thread of lucidity floated by and he grabbed on for dear life.

So gentle and sweet, the female's soft voice faded and with it his tether to reality. His beast screamed inside fighting to break free. He wouldn't, no couldn't lose himself to the fever.

"Wake up!"

She shook him, and the headboard rattled against the wall.

Her touch reignited the fire between them, and his beast woke.

Tanen opened his eyes.

As his vision focused, soft strands of gold framed the beautiful female's features. Concern radiated from her hazel eyes. He raised himself to a sitting position, and the skin on his back screamed in protest.

"Oh, thank goodness, you're awake. You have a terrible fever. I can take you to—"

"No infirm—"

"Yes, I know. You don't want to go to the hospital. I could take you to a clinic, get you some medication to help fight this infection."

He'd forgotten about Gaetan's medication, the pills the old healer took to relieve his pain. Better yet, though, Tanen had the blue sunstone. The crystal had healed the Panthera leader, Demir. Maybe it would heal him as well. Even as the fever raged, a jolt of hope flitted along his nerves. "My coat...medication."

Her brow furrowed. "You have medication?"

"Yes, in my coat." He glanced around the room. Not seeing his jacket, he moved toward the edge of the bed. A wave of nausea hit him and a chill ran over his arms, leaving goosebumps in its wake.

She placed her cool hands on his shoulder, pinning him in place. "I'll get it for you."

He tried to focus on his surroundings, but his vision blurred. Along with the scratches on his back, the Gossum's venom had done a number on his nervous system. The fever—that was an added bonus. Fevers were a rare occurrence for any Stiyaha. Why was he unlucky enough to have one?

Soft footsteps approached and the attentive female returned. She held up his battered coat. "Is it in one of the pockets?"

The shredded remains of his sleeves bore the evidence of his brutal attack. How had he survived?

"Yes..." He reached for the jacket, but before he could grab it from her, she shoved her hand into one of the pockets.

Her eyes widened. She pulled out his weapon.

"What is this? A...a dagger?" Her mouth drew into a thin line.

Before he could respond, blood pounded at his temple, and the dagger blurred, morphing into two.

"Oh, damn. Stay with me." Her fingers trailed over his forehead. "All right, let's see what else you have here."

She returned the dagger and pulled the sunstone from his pocket. Even in the dim light, the gem resonated with an unseen energy, but its usual glow was gone.

In the back of his mind, a niggle of worry formed, perhaps over her discovery of the precious crystal, but he couldn't focus on the thought. He held out his hand. "Please..."

"This can't possibly help, but you can hold it while I continue searching." She handed him the sacred sunstone. He gripped the stone to his chest, but the crystal remained dark. Chills sent a shiver up his spine, and tiny dots of light filtered into his vision. The gem slipped through his fingers and disappeared over the edge of the bed.

"What about this?"

Concentrating on her voice, he focused on the object in her hand. Gaetan's old medicine bag. "Yes…three please."

She handed him three small white pills. He popped them into his mouth and swallowed.

"Let me get you some water." She took the satchel from him, put it in his pocket, and tossed his coat across the back of a nearby chair.

He ran his hand over his face. Blood pounded loud in his ears. Fortunately, the medication wouldn't take long to work.

"Here. Drink this." She handed him a glass of water.

As he took the proffered glass, their fingers touched. A small shock tingled his skin.

"Static electricity, sorry." A chagrined smile broke across her face.

As he swallowed the water, the pin on his lapel glinted in the light, stabbing like a knife into his brain. He raised his free hand to block the glare.

"Oh, wow, your pin. It's really bright. Here, let's move that for you." She reached for his most treasured possession.

"No!" He lurched, catching her wrist in his palm. Water dribbled over the glass's lip and down his arm.

She inhaled. Her eyes widened.

"I'm…sorry. Can't lose…my pin." He released her grip.

With a focused concentration, he aimed the glass toward the end table. The surface blurred, and he almost missed. Water spilled over the edge of the glass, pooling along the cracks of the wood grain. His brain fogged as the medication worked into his system. He leaned forward, easing his leg over the edge of the bed. The urge to leave, to get on with his mission, burned inside. "I…need to go now."

"You're in no condition to…" She pressed against his shoulders, pushing him back, and his head landed on the soft pillow.

Even as he fought to stay awake, his heavy eyelids drooped. Before he could protest, sleep dragged him under.

CHAPTER 10

$\mathcal{M}$auree picked up an old, half-rotten magazine and used the crusted paper to fan the heat away from her face. The decrepit cabin, the one the Gossum used as a safe house, was much warmer than the underground Keep. Even within the confines of the old building, the heat from the warm late-winter day made her skin clammy. She shivered. *I could use a bath.*

The door handle squeaked. She stood from the sole rickety chair and grasped the wooden back so tight her knuckles turned white.

The door swung open. A stream of sunlight grew across the floor, coming dangerously close to Mauree's leg. She jumped out of the way. "Would you watch it?"

Jakar turned to face her, one hairless eyebrow raised above the edge of his dark glasses. "What?"

"The sunlight!" She slapped her forehead. As one of Alora's characters, sunlight would kill her in seconds. The Gossum had no such restriction.

Jakar shrugged and shut the door. "Seems to me that's your problem, not mine."

She exhaled and tried not to let his irritating comment get under her skin. "Did you find it?"

"The stone? I searched the area. Nothing. Tanen must have it." He removed his cap and sunglasses and tossed them onto the counter. The dark glasses bounced against the Formica and rested on the edge of the sink.

Mauree huffed. "I'd like to know how Tanen ended up with the sacred blue sunstone, but that's beside the point. I wish you would've finished him when you had the chance."

He sauntered over to the table where the insides of an old mantle clock lay sprawled out like the remnants of a class dissection project. After pulling out the chair, he had a seat and started tinkering with the parts. "As I recall, humans arrived. Not up for getting in trouble with the boss."

She flinched. "Why? Are you afraid of him?"

His dark orbs focused on her and an uncanny smile tugged at the corner of his mouth. "Oh, I forget, you haven't met Zedron, lucky you."

Despite they were cohorts of a sort, she couldn't stop her lip from curling. "No I haven't and I don't want to, but I still don't understand. You turn humans all the time. Why were they any different?"

"Because there could've been more, and I couldn't take the chance they'd be missed. That's why we get our new members from Portland...in the seedy part of town."

Mauree placed her hands on her hips. "Speaking of seedy, I won't stay here another day."

The male turned his attention back to the clock on the table. Tiny bits of metal, nuts, bolts, and assorted other mechanical paraphernalia littered the worn wood. He picked up a screwdriver and focused on his work.

Mauree's face heated. She clenched her fists. "How dare you ignore me."

With determined strides, she crossed the small room and swiped her arm across the table's surface. The old clock crashed to the floor, the wooden case splintering into several pieces. The pendulum, a sprocket, various gears, and wheels scattered across the room. A small nail embedded itself in the wall with a quiet thud.

Jakar pushed his chair back, and the feet scraped against the cracked linoleum floor. He stood, his black eyes burning into her.

"I need new clothes, a decent shower, and a place with heat." She spit the words at him.

Jakar's tongue snaked out from his mouth, nearly hitting her on the arm. "Testy, aren't we?"

"You have no idea." She sneered and pointed at the wall. "Do you see that? Do you know what it is?"

Jakar's gaze followed her line of sight. He shook his head. "I fail to see anything significant."

Mauree gritted her teeth. "Those dark spots on the wall. That's mold. Do you know how disgusting that is? Not to mention bad for your health."

"You're worried about your health, out here?" He chortled. "Seems to me we're one step away from annihilation."

"…and you're fixing a stupid clock. What's wrong with you?"

"I need a distraction. Your incessant wailing is giving me a headache."

She gripped his chin in her palm, then quickly released him. A bitter tang filled her mouth. "Not only are you bald and ugly, but your skin is cold and clammy."

"Have you looked in a mirror lately?" His low words skated across her nerves, stoking her fury.

"Look. This isn't an easy alliance for either one of us, but we're all we—" She couldn't finish her sentence. Exiled from the Keep and everyone she'd ever known, a great loneliness settled over her shoulders. She bit her lip, holding back her tears. Anger was her best friend now, and she let her hatred for Noeh build inside her once again.

She narrowed her focus. "I'm not giving up. I want revenge against Noeh. Are you going to help me or what?"

He nodded. "We have the same goal, just different reasons."

She unclenched her fist and ran her hand over what remained of her grimy skirt and top.

"Maybe you should go into Portland and round up some new Gossum. We could use the extra backup around here."

"At this point, princess, that sounds like a great idea. Anything to get away from your bad mood. What else can I get for you while I'm out?" He gave an exaggerated half bow, but his gaze never left hers.

She evaluated him. Did he play games with her or did he truly bow down to her command? *Interesting...*

She glanced at the Smirnoff boxes stacked in the corner—alcohol, the Gossum's only source of energy. "How about some new clothes and some food. I still have to eat even if you don't, and if you really want to please me, find us a new place, one with a shower."

A slow, frightening smile formed on his lips. He steepled his fingers, and his long claws emerged from the tips.

Butterflies in her stomach fluttered around as if trying to escape. *Don't show fear.* She raised her chin. "Well?"

The skin around his eyes crinkled, and an odd chortle emerged from his lips. "You're a hard female to please. What will you give me if I am successful?"

She raised an eyebrow. "Besides a pat on the back?"

He smirked, then his gaze travelled down her body. "I'm sure you'll think of something."

A laugh bubbled up inside and she let it out. The sound echoed around the small room. "I didn't think Gossum could...perform. Keep trying, Jakar, but that is one thing you'll never get from me."

With an eerie grin, he grabbed his cap and glasses from the counter and headed for the door. "I'll be back with some new recruits...and a few of your requests."

She crossed her arms. "You do that."

CHAPTER 11

*T*anen's cheek rested against a soft pillow, his arms wrapped around the cushion as if it were a buoy. He opened his eyes. The outline of a dresser came into focus, a multitude of clothes strewn on top. He inhaled and her scent—the female who'd helped him, filtered into his senses stirring something deep inside. His body responded as it had before, blood rushing to his groin. In his grogginess he reached for her, but all he encountered was a cool sheet.

His thoughts cleared. He quickly rolled out of bed. A tightness pulled at the skin on his back. He glanced in the mirror. Pieces of white cloths attached with tape stretched over his back. The adhesive caused an irritating itch.

He reached behind and ripped one off, then another. Pink skin puckered around what would become a nasty scar. His pulse quickened, a rush of blood fueling his anger. He ran his hand over the one on his chest. Great, another reminder of his entanglement with his enemy. *You don't have what it takes to be a warrior.* His father's words tumbled through his mind, sending him back to the past.

Tanen ripped his shirt over his head and threw it against the wall. The cloth plopped on the stone floor in a small heap next to his dresser. The dirty shirt lying on the ground was out of place, and a sense of unease rippled under his skin. Before he could stop himself, he plucked the shirt off the floor and placed it in the hamper. The tension in his shoulders eased.

He clasped his hands together and raised them in the air, stretching out the muscles in his back. His shoulders screamed in protest, a firm reminder of his humiliation in today's training session. Heat raced up his neck and into his cheeks. He ran his hand over his face. Father—the great Altaire— wouldn't be pleased.

"Tanen!" Altaire's voice boomed from their main quarters.

Tanen grabbed a fresh shirt from the drawer and put it on. He smoothed the material over his chest and straightened the collar. Stalling was one of his few methods of protest and he used it often.

"Tanen!" His father's shrill call came again, scraping along Tanen's nerves like a sharp knife that knew right where to prick to cause the most pain.

Eager to bury himself in a book as soon as he could get away, he picked up one of the tomes he'd discovered in the Hall of Scriptures and emerged from his room.

His father sat at the small unused dining table. His large frame dwarfed the chair, his warrior's shirt stained with blood from a recent Gossum kill. With a rough grunt, he took off a combat boot and placed it next to his sword. The old male's gaze raked over the ancient text in Tanen's arms. A sneer formed on his lips.

"You called, Father?" Tanen couldn't quite keep the sarcasm out of his voice.

"Why you bother with those books is beyond me." His focused attention narrowed. "Did you practice today? That's a much better use of your time."

Tanen's gut twisted, sending a bout of heartburn up his throat. His recent run-ins with his father had inflamed the nasty ailment. "I attended training class."

"Did you win a match? Any match?"

No. Tanen fisted his hand, holding back the retort that would only inflame his father's irritation. He shook his head.

Altaire moved faster than Tanen thought possible. He gripped Tanen by the shirt, hefting him off the ground. The old text hit the stone floor with a loud bang.

"Newb, you are ever a disappointment to me." Spittle landed on Tanen's cheek.

He held his father's stare, refusing to give in to the elder male's tirade. Altaire was a formidable warrior and expected—no demanded—that Tanen follow in his footsteps.

"You don't have what it takes to be a warrior." With a rough push, his father released him.

Tanen's shirt ripped down to his breastbone, the sound mimicking the tear in his heart.

Altaire's attention narrowed on Tanen's chest, and he slowly shook his head. His piercing gaze burned into Tanen. "How a son of mine ended up with a marking like that I'll never know. Warriors have values like honor, duty, and conviction...not honesty, tenacity, and, and...prudence."

Fire burned inside Tanen, but he held his bitterness in check. Carefully, Tanen smoothed his collar, but the frayed ends remained rumpled, sticking out at an odd angle.

Altaire growled. "At least I can be proud of Remi. Why can't you be more like your brother?"

Tanen was more like his older brother than his father realized. Remi had introduced Tanen to the fine art of stealing. What started as a challenge soon became an obsession, one that eased the bitter ache of disappointment. Tanen met his father's hard stare. "I'll make you proud father, just like Remi. You'll see."

"I won't hold my breath. Now, off with you." Altaire waved his hand in the air.

Tanen grabbed his book and ran down the hall, toward his favorite room —the Hall of Scriptures. His only solace, the knowledge he acquired from the books...and his pilfered trinkets.

Tanen ran his hand over his face, wiping away the last of the memory. Over the years he'd learned to curb his compulsion through order and simplicity, but with all the stress lately, his obsession had flared to life. He cracked his knuckles. The sound reverberated around the room.

Strings of neck chains hung over the edge of the mirror. Light from the hallway glinted off one, blinding him with its glare. He flinched and closed his eyes, but his fingers...oh, they tingled. Curling them against his palm, he willed himself to look away. He wouldn't give in to his urge, not again. Yet, he took a step forward.

Soft footfalls from down the hall broke his concentration.

The female, his savior, strode into the room.

Their gazes met. She gave him a half-smile, a dimple forming in her cheek. "You're awake."

A swath of hair had escaped her bun and caressed her face. The ends moved as she breathed, and a part of him longed to brush them away from her eyes. Those beautiful hazel eyes—they bore into him, capturing him. Her mouth parted, and his attention riveted there. *Craya!* While in his fevered state, he'd kissed those delectable lips.

A niggle of worry grew in his chest. Although rare, Lemurians could transform a human into a Dren. The most recent turning— Melissa, the new Stiyaha queen. Transformed by the Panthera leader Demir's bite, saliva had filtered into her bloodstream through an open wound. Although Dren couldn't shape shift, each received a unique talent. Melissa had acquired an energy shield. As with all Dren, she needed to feed on the blood of the opposite sex regularly to keep her talent powered.

Tanen had kissed this female before him, nothing more. As long as his saliva didn't get into her bloodstream, there was no cause for concern. The tension in his shoulders relaxed.

Silence filled the air for far too long. The beautiful female had spoken, but he was so mesmerized by her, he hadn't responded. He held out his palms. "I...I don't know what to say...except thank you."

CHAPTER 12

*T*he man standing next to her bed was so much larger than Sheri remembered. His bare chest, from his sculpted pecs to his six-pack abs burned themselves into her memory. Smoldering blue eyes pierced her heart, weaseling their way in and setting up house. Her pulse increased along with her breathing.

She hadn't reacted to a man like this since...well, not since Ram. Life with her ex-husband had more than filled her need for excitement, but he'd always had a lurid side. The vibe from this man was intense, exciting, without the dark edge.

His brow furrowed, and she remembered he'd thanked her.

"You're welcome, but I couldn't very well kick you out given your condition. Is your fever gone?" As she approached, his unique scent of musk and pepper cascaded over her. A shiver of desire warmed her skin, and she bit her cheek. *Ow. Ugh. That's number two.* The slight taste of blood filled her mouth.

Wanting to let in a little air to cool her skin, she leaned toward the windowsill. "Let me open the window—"

"No!"

As she reached for the blind's cord, he grabbed her wrist in his firm grasp, pulling her to him.

Her hands landed on his broad chest, her fingertips grazing the raised skin around one of his tear-shaped tattoos. His heat seeped under her palms, warm, but not too hot. He no longer had a fever, but a whole new kind of delirium blazed between them. The sudden urge to run her fingers down his smooth chest and over his rock-hard abdomen prickled over her sensitive skin.

He inhaled through clenched teeth. As if on cue, his erection grew and pressed against her mound. Between his thin trousers and her sheer pants, desire burned the chemistry between them into a raging flame. She wanted to press against him, drive him crazy, fuel the fire even brighter. Nibbling her bottom lip, she looked at him.

"Please, tell me...how long have I been here? Is it still night outside?" His gravelly tone and the crisp scent of his breath sent a tingle of excitement along her nerves.

"It's just after midnight. You've been here several hours." Not that she'd counted the minutes, but she'd slept fitfully in the chair at his side.

With an intensity that caused her throat to constrict, his gaze roamed from her face to her lips and back again. His irises were pools of blue flecked with small bits of gold and seemed to deepen in color. Memories of their kiss flashed through her mind, and a desire to taste his lips once again sent a rush of blood through her body. Did he remember as well? He may not, given his fevered state at the time.

What am I doing? I don't even know him.

She broke from his embrace. Cold air replaced his warmth, and goosebumps formed along her arms. Turning away, she tried to catch her breath. Confusion fluttered in her stomach. Absently, she licked at the sore spot in her mouth. With a quick turn, she peered at him. "Tell me. Who are you and why were you in my shed?"

Somehow, the female had snuck under Tanen's skin and into his system. The sensual way she ran her hands over his shoulders and down his arms had driven him nearly insane with the need to take her, right here, right now. As much as he'd wanted Tamara and Mauree, they both paled in comparison to this fine female. That she was human mattered not to his beast. The need to claim her still ran through his veins despite she'd pushed him away. Her question pounded against his skull, trying to move through the haze of lust that consumed him.

"What is your name?"

She'd spoken again. He dare not ignore her further.

He gritted his teeth. "Tanen. My name is Tanen."

"Tanen? I've never known anyone with that name." She enunciated the last part like the English word "in." He rather liked the slight variation.

Her focus narrowed on him as she evaluated his ripped pants. She lingered for a moment on his groin, the material still tented from his erection. Her cheeks turned a perfect shade of pink. He wanted to stroke her smooth skin with his finger, but instead, he adjusted himself, covering his manhood as best he could.

She pulled her gaze up. Her dilated eyes spoke of her desire. His inner beast roared in response, but he clamped down on his animal, forcing it into submission.

She pursed her lips. "What happened to you?"

He exhaled, buying himself some time. What could he tell her? Certainly not the truth. *Yeah, I'm an alien from Lemuria here to fight over your planet's water. Just pretend you didn't see me.* There was no way he'd say those words. He closed his eyelids and rubbed the bridge of his nose. The first signs of a tension headache built behind his eyes.

"Yes, I'm fine. Why was I in your shed?" He peered at her. "It's...complicated."

Her attention focused behind him, on the mirror. She audibly inhaled and her eyes widened. "Your back, it's healed. How is that possible?"

It's not, in your world. He'd never seen the human realm before, always remaining in the Keep or the surrounding forests. The only details he'd learned about humans came from the Jixies. With their fast speech and animated gestures, some of their descriptions made sense, while others were vague. One thing was clear, although similar in appearance, humans were a different species. He swallowed, giving himself a moment before responding. "I have a fast metabolism." Wasn't that an understatement.

"That…can't be. Something's not right here." Her brow furrowed, and her gaze bore into him. "Okay, Tanen. Tell me what's going on or I'm calling the police." Her voice was terse.

The fire in her tone caused his beast to stand up and take notice. A strong pull to wrap her in his arms tugged at his chest. He fisted his hand and focused on her request. "I was caught in a bad situation, and…ended up in the losing end of a fight. Your small structure was a convenient place to hide."

She focused on him, eyes narrowed. He swallowed, hating himself for holding back the truth. His marking for honesty burned hot on his chest. Glancing around the room, he searched for his coat.

"That's not all, is it?" Her eyebrow rose slowly. He couldn't help but notice how her arched brow accentuated the spark in her eyes. "Did you steal something? Are you running from the law?"

A hard ball formed in his gut. *Yes and no.* "I'm not wanted by your law enforcement, if that's your concern."

"Well, I'm glad to hear that." She let out an exasperated breath. "All right, then, tell me about your back. Even a fast metabolism wouldn't have healed those wounds that quickly."

He clenched his jaw and looked into her eyes. Green flecks melded with the brown and he wanted to study them, learn more about the woman behind the lens, but the longer he stayed, the more risk he brought into her life. "I can't explain how it works, but my medicine was very potent."

She bit her lip, her gaze never leaving his. Would she trust him? Why did that matter? Still, he couldn't deny his desire to earn her confidence. He straightened his shoulders.

"I'm a nurse. I've seen a lot of people recover from some pretty heinous wounds, but never anything as bad as your back. Not so quickly anyway. So, Tanen, you're hiding something from me."

He clamped his teeth together so hard, a shooting pain lanced through his jaw.

She stepped back, assessing him with those beautiful hazel eyes. "But when I look at you, I can tell you have a sense of honor and integrity. So, I'm going to let your miracle medicine mystery slide, for now, but soon, I'll want an explanation."

He let loose a slow exhale.

After several long moments, the tension lines around her eyes visibly relaxed. "You are so not what I expected to find in my shed. I'm glad you are all right."

"I wouldn't be if it wasn't for you. You know, I don't even know your name." He approached, and the heat between them sparked anew.

"I'm Sheri, and I did what anyone would do." She licked her lips.

He focused on her delectable mouth. "Not everyone."

She took a step back, and he glanced at the curtain. There were several more hours before sunrise. His stomach tightened. He needed to leave, see if he could pick up Mauree's trail. With one long glance, he committed her features to memory. "I must go."

She visibly stiffened. "Oh, you're leaving?"

He placed his finger under the collar of his coat and tossed it over his shoulder. A loud rumble emitted from his stomach.

Her attention tracked from his jacket to his ripped pants. With a quick exhale, she crossed her arms. "Geez, I can't do this. It would be wrong to let you leave looking like that and hungry to boot."

He raised an eyebrow.

"You know… My ex-husband left a few things. I may have something that fits. Let me check."

The thought of an ex-lover touching her, making love to her, having her cry out his name on her lips, made him tremble with an unknown rage. Why did he react this way? She was human. The sooner he got away from her the better.

As she pulled on her closet door, the metal hinge squeaked in its track. She crouched and set a box lid against the wall. Her hair cascaded around her shoulders, and his fingers tingled with the urge to touch the fine strands. She rose, holding a white sweatshirt and a pair of grey pants in her arms. With his luck, they'd be two sizes too small.

She handed him the stack of clothes. "The bathroom is on your right. There's a clean towel on the rack and a spare toothbrush in the medicine cabinet. I'll make us a sandwich while you clean up."

He could use a shower and a good meal. Before he could change his mind, he took the clothes she offered. Her hand trailed over his fingers, leaving a tingle of energy in its wake. Fighting the urge to pull her close yet again, he gave her a nod.

Their gazes locked for several long seconds.

"I'll be in the kitchen." She peered at him one more time and left him alone in the bedroom.

He shook his head and glanced at the window. Even through the edge of the blinds, the night called to him. Why had he accepted her gracious offer? He should be out there, searching for Mauree. Deep inside, his inner beast growled. Staying here is what *he'd* wanted. With a quick head shake, Tanen stepped into her bathroom and closed the door.

CHAPTER 13

*T*anen toweled off his hair and glanced in the mirror. The paunch he used to have around his middle was long gone. The exercise and lack of food over the past week had done the trick. When Sheri had offered him a sandwich, he couldn't refuse her offer. That was the excuse he gave himself, anyway. The truth of the matter was he wanted to be near her, see her smile, soak up more of her warm scent. Unfortunately, she was human, and that was wrong on so many levels, but he couldn't leave, not yet.

Quickly, he dressed in the clothes Sheri had given him. The pants were a little too short, the shirt a bit too tight. To wear another male's clothes didn't sit well with him. His inner beast growled.

He picked up the toothbrush and squirted a line of paste onto the bristles. Working out a bit of his frustration, he scrubbed his teeth then spat the fluid into the sink. *Damn ex-husband.* He ran his hand through his short hair and exited the bathroom, returning to Sheri's room.

A pair of her trousers lay on the floor, and one of her sweaters draped precariously over the edge of a chair. The disarray in her room sent a thousand tiny bugs crawling over his skin. How she lived in such chaos was beyond him. The tips of his boots peeked from beneath the edge of her bed. He yanked them on and tied up the laces. With a quick tug, he grabbed his coat by the collar.

As he headed for the door, a glint caught his attention. A necklace hung from the edge of her dresser mirror, flickering in the light. He stilled. Freezing cold fingers of longing tickled the nerves in his arms. The old, familiar sensation wasn't welcome, but he couldn't stop the rush of adrenaline as it coursed through his veins. He took a step toward the dresser, then another, until he stood so close to the bauble he couldn't breathe.

Just one touch. He'd been down this road before. That's how he'd ended up with the blue sunstone. He didn't care. The lie gave him the excuse he needed. His finger grazed over the smooth round edge. Engraved on the front was a small symbol, the transposed curves beautiful, just like Sheri. *Perfect. He'd have something to remember her.*

Before he could stop and think about his choice, the necklace was in his pocket. He looked at his sweatpants in the mirror. The bulky material would hide his newfound treasure. He met his gaze. Torment and shame reflected in his blue eyes. His marking for honesty burned against his chest, hot and angry. He couldn't stare at his reflection any longer, so he turned to leave.

Coop met him in the hallway. He patted the canine on the head. "Take good care of Sheri, Coop."

Coop woofed and his tail beat against the carpet. The scent of bacon drifted into the hallway. Tanen's mouth watered.

As he entered the kitchen, he got a long look at Sheri. She stood at the counter, her back to him. Dressed in a fresh pair of pants and shirt, the loose material hid her luscious curves. His inner beast growled in frustration, and with a heavy heart, he cleared his throat.

She peered at him, taking in his attire. A smirk played along her lips. "Well, those clothes look better on you than they ever did on... um, never mind."

"I can never repay your kindness." *No, instead, I stole from you.* He clenched his teeth, hating himself for his weakness.

"I'm glad I could help. Here, take this." She handed him a sandwich, bits of bacon and lettuce protruding from beyond the crust. Even through the paper napkin, the toast warmed his fingers. He didn't deserve her generosity.

She stepped past him into the living room. He couldn't help but follow.

"Aren't you having one?" Despite the rumbling of his stomach, he wouldn't eat his sandwich. To do so, alone, would be rude.

She blinked. "I'm not hungry, but please, eat."

A sour taste rose in his throat. He shook his head. "Please, share this with me."

～

The sincerity in Tanen's voice seeped under Sheri's skin, worming into the inner reaches of her heart. The loud grumble from his stomach was evidence of his hunger, but this proud, cultured man wouldn't eat in front of her. She couldn't refuse his kind gesture. "All right. Let me get a knife—"

He stepped into her path, wrapping her in his personal space. The heat radiating from him warmed her, and against her will she leaned in, eager for his touch. He brought the sandwich close to her lips.

"Here. Take a bite." His whispered words were sensuous, soothing in their cadence.

This seemed like so much more than an offer to share his sandwich, and suddenly, she was caught up in a hunger all her own. She swallowed. Before she could stop herself, she bit into the crust. The taste of mayonnaise and bacon woke her taste buds.

A satisfied grin formed on his lips, and she had a strong desire to kiss them. Instead, she watched, mesmerized as he, too, bit into the sandwich. A soft groan eased from his chest, and he closed his eyes as he chewed.

What is wrong with me? Why am I so attracted to him? To put distance between them, she headed for her bookcase. The old paperbacks brought much comfort on those long, lonely nights. She trailed her finger across the spines, purposefully turning her back to him.

"This sandwich is very good. Would you like more?" His deep voice resonated into her chest, tickling her.

Yes. No! She brought her fist to her mouth. "Please, you have the rest."

"As you wish." The crunch of the toast filtered across the room. She couldn't look at him for fear she'd want to kiss him again. Instead, she studied her paperbacks.

"You have a large selection of books." She hadn't heard him approach, but a tingle of awareness spread over her shoulder. Something in her chest fluttered. "I have a library, too. So much knowledge between the pages." The tenor of his low, gravelly voice settled deep inside her.

She glanced over her shoulder. He studied her collection, his eyes gleaming with appreciation. She'd never met someone who loved books as much as she. A crack formed in the armor around her heart. Using her index finger, she pulled an old paperback from the stack, *The Mists of Avalon.*

"I picked up this book several years ago in Powell's bookstore." She flipped the book open to the title page. "See, it's even signed by the author."

"You love your books."

She had the sudden urge to put her arms around him and continue what they'd started not long ago. Instead, she put the book back on the shelf. "Yes, I do. I love fantasy, horror, and science fiction. The thrill of going to other places, other worlds, excites me."

He moved away from her and closer to the bookshelf. His finger grazed over several of the spines, straightening a couple along the way. With rapt attention, he focused on a few titles. "These are remarkable."

She peered at him. "Most of them are everyday paperbacks, but I have a few classics."

He met her gaze. "Tell me. Which is your favorite?"

The intensity in his eyes drew her in, and she responded before she could think. "*The Hobbit.* Tolkien does a fabulous job with description. Have you read it?"

He shook his head, and a few stray hairs covered the tip of his ear.

She reached for the top shelf, scanning the titles with her fingers. The books were in disarray, stuffed into whatever space was available. Long ago, she should've cleaned up this mess, but there was always something else to do. She huffed. The elusive book seemed to hide from her. "It's here somewhere. It has to be."

"What does it look like?" He hunched down and straightened some of the books on the middle shelf.

"It's a small paperback with a picture of Smaug on the front."

He peered at her and his brows furrowed.

"Smaug, the dragon? I take it you haven't read the book."

The sheepish look on his face endeared him to her.

"You have to read that book. So good." She spotted the worn paperback shoved on top of the second row. With tender care, she pulled her favorite novel from the stack and caressed the cover.

She pointed to the picture of an orange dragon protecting his golden treasure. "See, that's Smaug."

"A dragon indeed. It's good they aren't real. Would you read me something from it?"

She held out the book to him. "Here, why don't you read some?"

The muscle in Tanen's jaw clenched. Sheri had asked him to read from her book. How could he? All he could read was cuneiform.

She lowered the old paperback. "What's wrong—"

He clasped his hand around hers, the book in their combined grasp. Her warmth radiated up his arm, rekindling the flame between them. "I'd rather you read me something. Perhaps a favorite passage?"

She licked her lips, and his gaze dropped to her mouth. He wanted to kiss her, ravish her mouth until she begged for more. Instead, he released her, lowering his hand to his side.

With her free hand, she gripped the bookshelf. Her lips quivered as if she sensed his interest. "Um…sure."

He nodded. "I look forward to hearing you read the passages. Words are so compelling, don't you think?"

Her chest heaved with quick breaths, and he couldn't help but notice how her breasts filled out her blouse. She opened the book.

An audible crack rent the air.

Dust fell from the pages.

"Oh, the spine broke." Her soft words were filled with anguish, and he wanted to comfort her, take away her pain. His hand jerked with his sudden impulse to caress her cheek. The thought made him still. He couldn't allow himself to get too close to this female.

She flipped through some of the pages. A single sheet slipped from the book and danced like a feather on its way to the floor.

Tanen picked up the torn page between his fingers. The aged text danced before his eyes, and the softness of the paper took his breath away. He handed it to her. Their fingers brushed, fanning the flames brighter between them.

He studied her for a long moment before she spoke. "I love this book so. I've been meaning to repair the spine, but haven't had time." Her attention focused on a small bottle of glue atop the windowsill. She shook her head.

Placing the sheet back in the book, she turned to a page, one with a bent corner. "There is nothing like looking, if you want to find something. You certainly usually find something, if you look, but it is not always quite the something you were after."

The melody of her soft and reverent tone washed over him, sinking into his soul. He could listen to her read for hours.

She glanced at him. He needed to hear more. "Please, continue."

Her cheeks turned that pretty shade of pink he'd already grew accustomed to, and she flipped to another page. "Here's a riddle for you. Tell me what it is."

"It cannot be seen, cannot be felt,
   Cannot be heard, cannot be smelt,
   It lies behind stars and under hills,

And empty holes it fills,
It comes first and follows after,
Ends life, kills laughter."

"That's a tough one." He tapped his finger along the side of his chin. "Hmmm…death?"

"You're close. The answer is darkness." Her eyes brightened. Happiness radiated off her in waves with almost a physical energy. "How about one more?"

He couldn't help but smile, caught up in her magnetism. "Sure. Another."

"This is my absolute favorite." She turned her attention to the text. "There is more in you of good than you know, child of the kindly West. Some courage and some wisdom, blended in measure. If more of us valued food and cheer and song above hoarded gold, it would be a merrier world."

As the meaning behind her words hit home, his chest clenched. *War.* That was why he was here. The humans were but a pawn in their game. He cracked his knuckles and stepped away.

"Hey, what's wrong?" She grasped his arm.

The lines around her eyes drew together, and her delectable mouth turned into a frown. He winced knowing he'd caused it. With a quick head shake, he peered out the window. The night called to him. His beast stirred. He tore his attention away and focused on Sheri. "I have to leave."

She blinked, and even he could see how her energy deflated. "Of course. Let me get you some water."

Before he could respond, she raced into the kitchen. He gave her a moment, then followed. When he found her, she faced the open fridge, her shoulders stiff, blinking her eyes.

A heavy weight settled into his stomach. She didn't need his kind of problems.

She shut the fridge and turned around. As she handed him the water bottle, their fingers touched. The spark between them reignited, but she shuttered her features and pulled away. As much as he wanted to comfort her, tell her everything would be normal, good in her life, he couldn't make that promise. The longer he stayed, the more risk he brought to her.

He let out a slow exhale. "Thank you for your kindness."

He walked away before he could change his mind. A part of him didn't want to leave, and as he closed the front door, the bitter realization stung him worse than any Gossum bite.

CHAPTER 14

*T*anen stood outside Sheri's home. The cool night air burned into his lungs, but didn't ease the ache in his chest. When Sheri had handed him the bottle of water her eyes had glistened with unshed tears. He hardly knew her, but he couldn't deny the attraction between them. With a quick swig he took one long drink, crushed the bottle in his fist and tossed the empty container in the trash can.

As he left, his boots crunching against the gravel driveway, he forced himself to concentrate on Mauree. The distraction was a welcome relief. That the traitor could bring him any kind of solace was an odd sort of irony, but he couldn't dwell on Sheri, not now.

He crossed into the woods, the scent of cedar and pine filtering into his senses. The night was quiet, only his ragged breaths and the sound of his boots on the wet underbrush filled the air. He returned to the scene of the fight. The broken and crushed ferns were a reminder of how close he'd come to losing his life. His heartburn flared, sending hot, fiery bile into his mouth. He spat the fluid onto the ground and followed Jakar's astringent scent.

Rumors abounded in the Keep over the location of the Gossum's safe house. So far, none of the warriors had found the elusive place. Tanen wracked his brain, searching through his knowledge of the ancient texts for any clues, but there was nothing. The building must be protected somehow. Frustration lit a fire under his feet, and he increased his pace.

An hour later, the soft gurgling of a stream caught his attention. The soothing and comforting sound should've calmed him, but it only fueled the anxiety skating along his nerves. His delay had given his quarry a significant head start, and his inability to find Mauree stuck in his craw like a burr.

He glanced into the sky. Despite the clouds covering the moon, darkness waned, giving way to the soft orange glow of brightening dawn. He'd have to hole up for the day, continue his search again at nightfall. A low growl eased from his throat.

Not far away, blackberry bushes covered the entrance to a dark cleft in the ravine. He shoved the brambles aside and peered into the small outcropping. Roots dangled from the dirt and hung like sharp, pointy fingernails similar to a Gossum's claw. He curled his lip. Staying here was not his idea of fun, but the lightening sky left him little choice. He needed to find shelter, now.

As if on cue, the first rays of the rising sun crested over the tree tops. If he were ever caught in the sunlight, his skin would burn. Exposure for more than a few seconds would kill him. The hairs at his nape rose. *Goddess Alora, may I never suffer such a fate.*

He shoved aside a few stray vines and entered the small enclosure. Leaning his shoulder against the earthen wall, he exhaled. Against his will, thoughts of Sheri invaded his mind. Her sweet kindness in the way she cared for him, the soothing sound of her voice as she read from her favorite book, the look of innocence in her eyes.

He stilled, tension tightening the muscles in his shoulders. *I'm a thief, plain and simple.*

Raising his fist, he pounded the earthen wall, his fingers scraping against dirt and small bits of rock. The scent of his own blood didn't slow him down. Only when the froth of his anger abated did he relent. Ragged breaths eased in and out of his lungs.

Unable to resist, he reached into his pocket and pulled on the thin chain, releasing the necklace from its hiding place. He held up the simple charm. The small circle twisted back and forth, glinting in the brightening daylight.

He caressed his finger over the monogrammed symbol. *Sheri...* Loathing, deep and powerful, burned inside. His heartburn flared to life, adding to his self-contempt. He'd never felt such remorse. While his stolen treasures used to give him such comfort, this trinket was different. This necklace belonged to Sheri, the sweet, innocent female who had helped him recover. She had no knowledge of his war and the evil that dogged him. He palmed her necklace in his fist. *Sheri...I'm sorry.*

His symbol for honesty burned hot on his skin. He tugged on the sweatshirt collar, revealing his markings. The small teardrop closest to his heart pulsed and darkened slightly, but it was barely visible. If he didn't change his ways, the mark would disappear. Then, he'd start the slow descent into madness.

He released the material and leaned his head against the wall. A deep rumble echoed through the trees—thunder. Even through the overgrown underbrush, rain drops pelted the ground outside his makeshift home. He pulled his knees closer to his chest, but the bitter wind pushed the rain into his shelter, soaking his boots and pants.

He uncurled his fist and glanced at Sheri's necklace. If he got the chance he'd return it to her, but he'd never see her again. She was human. To be with her would be...unimaginable. The best gift he could give her would be to keep himself and all his problems far away. With tender care, he placed her necklace deep into his pocket, stared out at the rain, and waited for nightfall.

CHAPTER 15

The wall clock beat out a steady rhythm, like a resting heartbeat, but Alora's favorite timepiece didn't provide any comfort. Instead, the constant tic-tic-tic only tightened her tense muscles. After the meeting with Zedron and Radnor, she'd fled the council leader's chamber. The tears hadn't stopped until she was almost home. As she headed to the window, she stole a quick glance in the mirror. The image of her red-rimmed eyes brought the anger back in full force. She fisted her hand and smashed it against her palm.

"Zedron, I hate you. Why did you have to challenge me for Earth?" She already knew the answer. He'd wanted to lash out at her for turning down his bonding offer. That she'd picked Veromé, his former best friend, only added to his determination to win this war.

Veromé. She glanced out the window. The faint light of impending dawn filtered through the canopy of leaves from the Etila and Rolmdew trees. He'd be here soon. Her heart leapt into her throat. She wasn't sure if she wanted to see him, tell him about her latest sanction. Not that she had a choice…now.

He materialized, pixelating, growing from lighter to darker until his entire form solidified. His scent, the smell of the ocean, salty and fresh, filled the room. The skin around his eyes crinkled when he saw her, his mouth forming into his telltale grin. She melted at the sight and ran into his embrace.

He wrapped his arms around her, holding her tight. She felt safe, wanted, and a tear slid over her cheek, wetting the skin on his neck. With a warm gentleness she knew so well, he tugged at her chin to gaze into her eyes. His smile faltered, and his brows creased. "My love, what is it? Why the tears?"

He cradled her head in his palm and wiped her tear away with his thumb. His thoughtful demonstration brought forth another and she pulled away, wiping the traitorous thing with the back of her hand.

He let her go. The hurt look in his eyes just about broke her. "You're upset. Please, tell me what's happened."

"I'm so angry." She ground her teeth so hard, her jaw ached.

"At what...or whom?"

Unwilling to admit her guilt, she turned around. "I met with your father tonight."

"I take it this wasn't a family visit."

She rubbed the end of her nose and snuffled. "Nope. Radnor summoned me."

Veromé wrapped his arms around her, easing her shoulders against his chest. His breath tickled the base of her neck, and she longed to have more than a few minutes with him. She'd be gone as soon as the first rays of the sun crested over the horizon, punishment for the first time she'd cheated.

"Alora." Veromé's voice was low and sensual, yet firm. "Something tells me I'm not going to like what I hear. What did you do?"

She turned in his embrace, facing him. "Why do you assume I've done anything?"

He raised an eyebrow. "Because I know you so well."

She pursed her lips and tried to push away, but not very hard. "You don't trust me."

"I never said that."

A buzzing noise started in her ear as her pulse picked up. The echoing ping receded as quickly as it started. "I...Zedron...I did something I shouldn't have."

She pushed her palms against him harder this time, and he let her go. With quick strides, she headed toward the window, eager to put distance between them.

"Zedron." His bitter tone carried across the room. "Why am I not surprised your mood involves him."

A sudden coldness hit her in the chest. She turned toward him. His shoulders were visibly tense, his mouth pursed.

She blinked. "You're upset."

He furrowed his brow, a pained expression crossing his handsome features. "Tell me, Alora. What do you do at night when I'm not around?"

She inhaled. The pounding in her ears resumed, and she couldn't speak for several long seconds. "You think...me...and Zedron... together. N...no, absolutely not."

His gaze roamed her face. She didn't like his scrutiny and her cheeks heated.

She took a step back and another until the back of her knees crashed into a side table. The flower vase tipped over, water spilling onto the wooden floor. She gripped the flowers by the stems, bringing the delicate petals close to her chest. Her heartbeat pinged so hard, it thrummed in her veins. "How could you think this of me?"

He flinched. His features softened for a brief moment, but then he regained his composure. He pointed to her bracelet, the one he'd recently given her for their anniversary. "I ran into Zedron not long ago. He mentioned your bracelet—said you wouldn't wear it. Tell me, why would he say such a thing?"

She froze, her mind unable to process what Veromé had said. Against her will, her mouth fell open. She shut it so fast, her teeth clanked together. "I have no idea what you're talking about."

He raised an eyebrow. "Really?"

Her hand tightened around the flower stems and the petals wilted over her fingers. She tossed them to the ground. "He goaded you to cause problems between us. Are you going to let him succeed?"

As he narrowed his attention on her, the skin around one of his eyes twitched.

She'd wait him out. Let him come to his own conclusion Zedron was the issue here, not her. The problem was she didn't have time. As the first rays of the sun peeked through the trees, the familiar tug pulled at her. Before she could say another word, she disappeared, heading to her dark place, the one she went to during the day, leaving Veromé to stew alone.

CHAPTER 16

Sheri walked to the nurses' station and scanned the current list of patients. No new arrivals in the past two days. *Good.* The facility was already at maximum capacity and they didn't hire enough staff to keep up with demand, placing extra pressure on the existing nurses to fill the gap. She picked at the skin around her nails, her anxiety bringing back the old habit with a vengeance. Hopefully, she'd land the new job in Seattle, and soon.

"Hey, Sheri!"

Sheri glanced down the hallway. Olivia strode toward her at full speed. As she approached, she wiped back a strand of hair that had freed itself from her short ponytail. "Hey girl, am I glad to see you."

Sheri gave her a quick hug. "What's going on today?"

"Mrs. Alton, bless her heart, has been asking for you, along with the new guy, Michael."

Michael. Sheri's heart skipped a beat. The last time she'd seen him, he'd tracked her every move, as if he were on death row and she was his final meal. "What do you think of Michael?"

"I feel sorry for him. All alone. No one to visit. Why do you ask?"

Sheri shrugged, uncertainty and apprehension crawling over her shoulders and down her back. "There's something about him. He seems a bit creepy."

"Huh, I don't get that vibe from him."

Olivia's eyes were red-rimmed. She had her own problems. "How are you and the kids holding up?"

Olivia exhaled a long breath, but her eyes gleamed with determination. "I refuse to let Ben and the divorce rule our world. On my day off, I'm taking the kids to a movie, relax a bit. We'll get through this."

"Of course you will." Sheri had gone through her own trying divorce with Ram. A memory from Sheri's past surfaced—the day when she'd left her ex-husband.

The doorknob jiggled in Sheri's hand. She pushed against the door and the latch gave way. The smell of rancid bacon and beer filled the air. Fighting off the nausea, she held her breath, and peered at the kitchen counter. Where her mother's antique silver tea pot used to reside was now an empty space. She clenched her teeth and muttered under her breath. "Damn you, Ram."

This wasn't the first cherished possession he'd stolen from her and sold to feed his addiction, but it would be the last. Her gaze flitted to the "Eat at Sam's" chipped mug, the one Ram had given her on their first anniversary as a memento of where they'd met. Anger sent a rush of heat to her face. No, I can't stay here, not with him, not anymore.

"Strike three." Over the television's tinny speakers, a cheer rose from the crowd. Ram was home, watching sports, yet again.

She rubbed her eyes and exhaled. After tossing her keys into her purse, she hung her shoulder bag and coat on the wall hook next to his jacket. The scent of the well-worn leather brought back memories of better days, and a pang of guilt tightened her chest. At one time, she'd loved that coat, or at least the man who used to wear it. He wasn't the same, not since he started the trip down heroin lane.

Her pulse raced, but she fisted her hands and headed for the living room. Ram sat on the sofa, his focus on the baseball game. A discarded needle lay on the coffee table next to a wad of tinfoil, a lighter, and a cotton ball.

His gaze tore from the TV screen to her face. She raised her chin, steeling herself for the impending confrontation.

"Sheri, my bug." He glanced at the clock, then returned his attention to her. "Glad to see you could...eh...make it home."

The muscles in her arms quivered and she fisted her hands. "You're high, again."

He shrugged. "Care to join me?"

The skin on her arms tightened, like a thousand ants had crawled over her nerves. With determined strides, she headed into the bedroom and yanked her suitcase from under the bed. Tears, hot and fast, streaked down her cheeks. She jerked open her dresser and snatched bras, underwear, socks, shirts, anything she could grab and shoved them into the bag. When the case was full, she zipped it shut and gripped the handle. Her knuckles turned white from the strain.

Ram grabbed her shoulder, and spun her to face him. His tiny round pupils were the telltale sign of his addiction. "What's going on?"

"You said you'd quit, but you haven't. I...can't do this anymore."

He trailed a finger down the side of her face.

She flinched.

His shoulders visibly shook. He wrapped his fingers around her wrist, trapping her. "You're not leaving."

The flight impulse she'd learned from her father fluttered in her stomach. She ripped her arm free and grabbed her suitcase.

He caught her around the waist, pulling her to him. With a firm grip behind her head, he kissed her. The taste of bacon and beer infiltrated her senses. Disgust roiled in her gut. Her gag reflex kicked in and she choked, pushing his face away. With a loud exhale, he shoved her. She stumbled and caught herself, but not before her hip whacked against the edge of the dresser. A sharp pain bloomed from the bruised tissue.

"I'm sorry, bug." Creases formed around his eyes, and he frowned. He placed two fingers against his lips and patted his chest, right above the heart. "I love you, Sheri. I'm a good man. Let me prove it to you."

He'd always said he'd wanted to please her, but his selfish, self-destructive nature got in the way. A hot dose of anger had her spitting the words before she could stop herself. "I need someone I can rely on, Ram. Someone who doesn't steal from me to buy drugs. I need someone who cares about my well-being." She picked her fallen suitcase off the floor and brushed past him.

He followed her into the hallway. "Please...Sheri. Don't go. Don't leave. If you want me to stop, I will. I...I promise."

She stopped, her hand on the doorknob. I'm just like my father, running away. A lump formed in her throat. Part of her still cared for Ram, but she couldn't stay, couldn't deal with his problems. Her pulse pounded at her temple. Without a glance, she walked out of his life.

Sheri shook her head to clear the unwanted memory. Ram was a part of her past, not her future. An image of a tall, handsome stranger entered her mind—Tanen. *I wonder where he is...*

Olivia touched her arm, pulling her back to reality. "Hey, you okay? You seem kind of...I don't know, tired?"

Tired? Try exhausted. After her encounter with Tanen last night, she hadn't had much sleep. Before work she'd napped for a few hours, forcing herself to relax, but all she could think about was his penetrating gaze and the gentle way he'd held her, not to mention their kiss. She traced her forefinger over her bottom lip, the way he'd done with his thumb. An ache built in her chest, and she longed for more.

"Wait a minute," Olivia's eyes widened, "...are you...are you seeing someone?"

Heat raced up Sheri's neck and into her face. "Shhh...not so loud."

"Oh, so there is someone in your life." Olivia clapped her hands. "I'm so happy for you. After everything you went through with Ram, I wasn't sure you'd ever get back in the game. Tell me, what's his name? Do I know him?"

"Olivia, quit. It's not what you think."

"Well, then, tell me. I'm dying to know. Is he cute?"

Out of the corner of her eye, Sheri caught sight of Matt. He approached with quick strides.

Sheri plastered on a smile. "Good morning, Matt."

Olivia turned to face him. "Hey, Matt. I was on my way to check on Mrs. Alton." Her gaze darted to Sheri. "We'll chat more later."

Sheri squeezed her friend's arm. "Thanks, Liv."

Matt rubbed the stubble on his chin. "Sheri, Michael needs his bandages changed. Would you take care of that before you start your rounds?"

She exhaled and gave Matt a quick nod. As much as she didn't want to see this patient, she couldn't disappoint her supervisor. "Sure, I'll see him now."

"Thanks." He nodded and headed down the hallway.

A couple of nurses passed by on their rounds. Against the far wall, an elderly male patient held on to the railing, taking one tentative step at a time, his physical therapist right at his side. At mid-morning, the place seemed alive and well with the buzz of phones and muted conversation, despite the number of sick and broken people hidden in its depths.

A shiver ran over Sheri's shoulders. She shook herself and headed to Michael's room. He lay on his bed, a pile of pillows supporting his back and neck. The television was on, but his attention was riveted to the window. A late-winter storm raged outside, rain tinkling the glass with a fierce intensity.

He seemed gaunt and pale, his skin slack against his cheekbones. For a man in his mid-thirties, he appeared ten years older. The boot from his broken leg stuck out from beneath the sheet, and his good hand gripped the channel controller. He must've sensed her nearby for he glanced her way.

With a deep breath, she put on a smile and walked up to him. "Good morning, Michael. How are you today?"

A smile formed on the good side of his face, pulling his mouth into an odd grimace. Strangled sounds emerged from his mouth, and then a word burst from his lips. "H...h...hi."

She smiled. "My goodness. You're making progress already."

"H...hi, Sh...Sherriii..."

Goosebumps formed along her arm. *Stop it!* He was just a man recovering from an accident-induced stroke.

Shaking her head, she headed for the cabinet. Her palm itched. An odd redness marred her skin, and she scratched the inflammation with her nails, easing the irritation. She opened a drawer and pulled out some gauze, tape, antiseptic cream, and a pair of scissors. "Looks like it's time to change your bandages. You ready?"

He nodded. As she rounded the end of his bed, his gaze tracked her every move. The hair on the back of her neck rose. *Just get this over with.* She'd dealt with difficult patients before.

After pulling up a nearby chair, she sat next to him. "Let's take a look at your arm, shall we?"

"Mmmm...hmmm." A spot of drool dripped from his crooked smile.

"Oops." She grabbed a tissue from the box on his table and wiped the spittle from his chin.

His eyes gleamed in appreciation.

She forced a smile and patted his hand. His grin widened.

"I'm going to peel off the bandage, clean your wound, and put a fresh one on. Okay?"

He nodded.

She pulled on the edge of the bandage and gently removed the dressing. The gash was still visible, covered with a thin scab. She wiped the wound with the antiseptic and opened new gauze. After placing the clean bandage on his arm, she looked at him. "There, all done. Does that feel better?"

He smiled and reached out to her with his good hand. The movement caught her off guard and she froze. He trailed a finger down the side of her face and along her chin.

A chill swept over her arms.

"There you are. I'd hoped to catch you again." Olivia's voice broke the spell, and Sheri stood so fast the back of the chair hit the floor with a loud bang.

"Liv...you startled me." Sheri placed her hand over her chest. Blood pounded at her temple, clouding her vision.

"Oh, sorry. Hey," Olivia glanced at Michael before returning her attention to Sheri, "can you step away for a moment?"

With shaking hands, Sheri righted her chair, giving herself a chance to catch her breath. "S...sure."

"Oh, good." Olivia gripped Sheri's arm, leaned in, and whispered, "I'm on a quick break, but wanted to hear about the guy you were with last night."

CHAPTER 17

Guy? Last night? Ram's chest constricted and a wave of adrenaline coursed through his veins. *Nooooo!* Sheri belonged to him! He fisted the sheet in his good hand. The need to pull her to him, tell her he'd changed, that he would prove himself worthy, festered inside.

Olivia glanced at him. "You can spare her for a minute, can't you, Michael?"

He wanted to lash out, yell at Olivia for taking Sheri from him. Instead, he gritted his teeth so hard, his broken jaw ached.

Sheri's forehead wrinkled slightly before a forced smile formed on her lips. "I'll be right back."

Sheri... When she'd sat next to him, her unique scent had engulfed him, bringing back all kinds of memories, yet, his Gossum senses, the ones that had followed him to this human body, picked up a slight difference. Her fragrance was tinged with something familiar, but he couldn't quite place what it was. Unable to resist his need to touch her, he'd run his finger over her soft cheek. She hadn't pulled away. His heart raced. Maybe he had a chance yet.

The two women left his room, but didn't go far, standing outside his doorway. Using his Gossum's extra-sensory hearing, he listened to their conversation.

"All right, Liv. Yes, I was with a guy—"

"I knew it. Spill."

Ram's fist knotted tighter around the sheet.

Sheri lowered her voice. "I found a strange man in my shed. He was injured and I helped him...get better."

"What? You took him in like one of your strays? You're kidding, right?"

"No. He was really tall and muscular. His clothes were odd, different, handmade and he had a strange accent. He said he'd been in a fight and hid in my shed. I cleaned up the worst of his injuries."

Ram's stomach clenched. *Odd clothes, strange accent, a fight. Was it possible? Had she run into a Stiyaha, his old enemy?*

Olivia inhaled. "Were you scared?"

"Surprisingly, no."

"Good looking? Nice package? Out with the details."

"Blond hair, blue eyes, muscular. Yeah, a nice package."

"Your cheeks are red. Oh, honey, did you sleep with him?"

Ram's heart skipped a beat, and he held his breath.

"No, oh no, but...we kissed."

Olivia squealed and her laughter grated on Ram's nerves. He wanted to grab the male that had kissed his Sheri and beat him to a pulp. How he longed for his Gossum claws.

"What's his name? When are you seeing him again?"

"Tanen, and I'm not seeing him again. He's gone."

"What? You let a cool drink of water like that get away?"

Sheri huffed. "It's not like that...it's complicated."

"Uh-huh. If he's a hot as you say, maybe he'll come back for more of your *special* attention. Look, I gotta go, Matt's giving me the evil eye from the nurses' station, but I'm glad for you." Olivia's soft shoes swished on the tiled floor.

Sheri peered around the edge of Ram's door. A chagrined smile crossed her face. The knot in his gut loosened. He remembered that look—he'd seen it when she was about to cave in to his demands. A slight, painful smile curled his lip.

She approached and picked up her tools. As she walked around the bed, her thin slacks hugged her sexy backside and her bottom jiggled ever so slightly with each step. He wanted to give her cheeks a gentle squeeze to see how she'd react, but he didn't have the strength.

She threw away the empty bandage package and put the scissors and tape back in the drawer. When she was done, she glanced at him. "I'm sorry for the interruption."

He opened his mouth, but the sincerity in her voice stalled the words in his throat. Their marriage had been filled with ups and downs. He was to blame. In many ways, he was surprised she'd stayed with him as long as she had. Perhaps this man she'd met, this Tanen, would make her happy in a way he never could. *Maybe she's better off without me.* He fisted his hand. *No...I won't give up.*

"Rest now." With a quick smile, she ran her hand from his shoulder to his elbow. Static electricity popped loud in the room and his skin tingled. "I'll come back in a bit to check on you."

As she headed for the door, his need to keep her here with him burned in his gut. He forced the words from his mouth before he could stop himself. "I pr...promise t...to...make it...up...t...to you."

Her back visibly tensed. She looked over her shoulder, her hazel eyes penetrating into him. "W...what did you say?"

He struggled to repeat his words, but his tongue seemed two sizes too big. "I...p...p..."

"I have to go, Michael." She turned away and left him in her wake, abandoning him once again. A raw pain tightened his throat. He'd never felt so alone.

CHAPTER 18

*M*auree applied the last swipe of mascara and studied herself in the mirror. Gone were the dark circles and bags under her eyes. She pursed her lips and blew a kiss at her reflection. A sense of giddiness filled her chest, and a laugh bubbled up inside. The sound reverberated off the walls of her new bedroom, soaking into the king-sized bed as if she'd marked it as her own.

The chair creaked as she stood, almost in protest of having to bear her weight. A Stiyaha, she was a large female and damn proud of it. Her expanding lungs filled her with an odd sense of contentment. She headed into the hallway, her bare feet sinking into the plush carpet. After reaching the top of the circular staircase, she peered over the railing.

Jakar stood in the middle of the fancy living room, staring out the large picture windows. Several cushioned chairs and leather couches filled the space. The earlier storm clouds had dispersed, and the late afternoon sunlight cut a shaft of light onto the dark green carpet, turning the beam an emerald green. She huffed.

"Jakar, be a dear and close the blinds for me, would you?" Even to her ears, her voice sounded too sweet, but she was in a good mood. She'd savor the small comforts and enjoy herself while it lasted.

Jakar's gaze tracked from her feet to her head, lingering on her thighs beneath her short skirt.

A sour taste filled her mouth. *He's so disgusting.*

Turning quickly, he pulled the curtains shut. The rings racing across the bar rang like small chimes. He faced her once again, and his smile revealed his serrated teeth. "Do the clothing and makeup meet your expectations?"

"They're adequate." They were more than adequate, but she wouldn't say that out loud, that would only encourage him. With purposeful strides, she descended the stairs.

He chuckled. "You look fabulous, for a Stiyaha."

She pursed her lips. "Enough, Jakar. We agreed to be partners, nothing more."

As she walked toward him, he studied her every move.

He smirked. "So, the clothing is acceptable. What of the house?"

Jakar had broken into the deserted home. Deep in the forest on the edge of a lake, the humans didn't typically visit their resort houses until summer. They should be safe here, at least for a while. She stepped around him, careful to avoid the bits of light streaming between the gap in the curtain. "You've impressed me. That's not easy to do."

"I didn't complete all your requests. Ran out of time. The new recruits will have to wait."

Her stomach rumbled.

The skin on his bald head crinkled. "I acquired some groceries from a local market. Went through three stolen credit cards before I found one that worked, but you shall eat. Come, see what's in the kitchen."

She hadn't eaten much in the past week and her stomach was so flat, her hip bones protruded. With a small skip in her step, she followed him, eager to satiate her hunger.

Pots, pans, and an assortment of utensils hung from a rack over the cooking island. A coffeemaker, toaster, and finely crafted ceramic canisters lined the counters. The tiles gleamed, reflecting the light from overhead spotlights. Through the north-facing window, deck chairs sat on the large patio. A slight breeze wafted in through the opening.

Against the far wall, the fridge stood out like a beacon, calling to her. She covered the distance in an instant and ran her fingers over the smooth handles. With a quick tug, she opened the doors. A waft of cool air caressed her cheeks.

Three solitary items sat on the top shelf—a head of lettuce, an apple, and a square carton of milk. Her mouth went dry. She grabbed a box from the frozen section. A round pizza with small chunks of some unnamed substance graced the picture. Jakar's idea of a decent meal—so not up to par.

She held up the package. "You call this food?"

He cocked his head, and the hairless skin over his eyes furrowed. "Are the groceries not to your liking?"

Before she could respond, the temperature in the house plummeted. Their breaths formed into small clouds of steam.

"Oh, no." Jakar's already pale face grew more ashen.

Tiny pinpricks of fear crawled up her back as she closed the fridge doors. "What's happening?"

"Zedron…"

A blue mist wafted through the open window. The haze grew larger, molding into the shape of a man. Brown, shoulder-length hair cascaded over his tailored jacket. Clean-shaven, his smooth jaw accentuated his full lips. His handsome features made him appear gentle, caring, until his gaze riveted on her. Cold blue eyes pierced into her, rooting her in place. A knot grew in her stomach, hardening under his scrutiny.

"Lord Zedron." Jakar bent to one knee.

Mauree swallowed, her muscles stiff with tension.

A slow, predatory grin formed on Zedron's face. "Mauree, so nice to meet you."

Adrenaline pumped through her veins, and a bead of sweat moistened her upper lip. She opened her mouth to speak, but no words came out.

Zedron winked. "My dear, you don't need to fear me. I am your new master."

Her knees gave way, and she steadied herself against the kitchen island. "Wh…what did you say?"

A low chuckle eased from his throat. "I think you heard me, but a little explanation is in order."

Zedron glanced at Jakar. "Stand, Gossum."

Jakar rose, but kept his gaze on the floor.

The god refocused his attention on Mauree. She met his stare and raised her chin.

A smile crossed his face. "Very good. I think you will do well as my new leader."

She blinked as the words sank in. "Leader?"

He waved a hand in the air. "Since Ram is no longer with us, I need someone with enough hatred, enough contempt, to continue this war against Alora and her minions. You seem more than qualified."

Noeh…I should've been queen. Anger built to the point she wanted to scream, and she fisted her palms. "I seek vengeance against Noeh, but I'm a Stiyaha. Technically, I'm supposed to fight for Alora."

"Not anymore. You're on my team now."

She frowned. "How is that possible?"

"Alora…erred in judgment, and…let's just say the tide has shifted in the war. You now work for me." Determination gleamed from his eyes, and his perfect white teeth accentuated the gemstone piercing in his nose.

"What do you want *me* to do?" Despite the tremble in her fingers, her words were forceful.

Jakar shuffled his feet. Zedron peered at him and curled his lip. When he returned his attention to her, his smile reappeared. "I have much for you to do."

He scanned the kitchen and glanced into the large living room. "These accommodations will suffice. Expect a group of Ursus to arrive in the next day or so. They also work for me now."

The tension in Mauree's shoulders abated and new purpose steeled her resolve. "Ursus?"

"Bear shape-shifters. They come from the north and bring a band of Gossum with them." He shrugged. "The two used to be enemies, but now, we're all one big happy family. With the Ursus's strength and the Gossum's resilience, you shall have more than enough warriors to battle the Stiyaha and the residents of the Keep."

"So, you want me to lead them?" Mauree licked her lips, giddiness and hope growing inside.

"I expect you will do a fine job." The smile on his face didn't quite reach his eyes. "Some of the Ursus may retain some misguided allegiance to Alora, but to ensure your success I've programmed into them the inherent need to protect you."

Mauree bowed her head, but didn't break eye contact. "As you wish, Lord Zedron."

"A piece of advice, if you will." He raised an eyebrow, and flecks of silver flashed through his irises. "Tanen's blue sunstone—obtain it. Like many things in life, the crystal has both light and dark tendencies, depending on the user. If your heart is black enough, Mauree, you can ignite its penchant for evil."

She blinked. "Is my heart black?"

Zedron's mouth curved into a grin. "Perhaps not yet, but I suspect you'll have the...*opportunity* to prove yourself worthy."

Mauree had started down the dark path, and there was no going back for her now. Resolve hardened in her chest, darkening her soul. "Consider it done."

He nodded his approval. "There is one other benefit for you and the Ursus. Unlike Alora, I have not been sanctioned by the council. Since you are now on my team, you can go out in the sun."

Mauree's chest expanded. She glanced out the window. To feel the warmth of the sun on her skin—what would that be like?

Jakar cleared his throat. "What of my role, my lord?"

Zedron placed his hand on Jakar's shoulder. "You work for Mauree. Serve her as you did Ram. Just don't disappoint me."

Jakar bowed his head.

Zedron started to fade, his skin and clothing disintegrating into the air. The blue mist swirled between the pots and pans, moving them in an odd breeze before wafting out the window. Loud bangs reverberated around the room long after the god was gone.

A sudden rush of adrenaline lightened Mauree's chest. This was the opportunity she needed to obtain revenge against Noeh, but first, she wanted to experience the sun. "Jakar, let's go outside."

CHAPTER 19

Sheri's palm itched, and she scratched at the red welt that had worsened over the past couple of days. Before she could stop herself, she absently picked at her fingernail. Blood welled into the crevice of her cuticle, and a dull ache throbbed in her finger. "Perfect."

She rummaged through the drawers at the nurses' station until she found a box of bandages. After ripping open the paper, she wrapped the gauze around her finger. If only she could cover the wound in her heart so easily. After her divorce from Ram, she'd become wary of men. Did they all have a mean streak or did she just pick the rough ones?

She shook herself and logged on to the computer to check her email before leaving for the day. The security screen popped up, and she typed in her password. A long list of emails displayed on the monitor. She tried to focus on the words, but her previous encounter with Michael haunted her. A sour taste formed in her mouth. The way he'd drawn out the "I" in her name reminded her of Ram.

They'd met at Sam's Hof Brau near Portland State University when they were both young—and ignorant. The place had become their regular hang out and during their college years they'd collected several "Eat at Sam's" trinkets—mugs, glasses, ashtrays.

Ram had seemed so nice and had showered her with attention. She'd soaked it up like a dry weed, eager for any drop of water. It wasn't until after she'd divorced him that she saw on the final decree he'd had a previous marriage and in fact, was married at the time they'd met.

She bunched the bottom of her shirt in her hand, and the words on the screen blurred through her moist eyes. She would've never dated a married man—to think she'd spent eight years of her life with him was a blemish she could never erase. He'd taken advantage of her kindness, using her. Good thing they didn't have kids.

Originally, "Eat at Sam's" had been a personal joke between them. Now, these items were a constant reminder of her bad choices and naivety. She refused to let them go for fear she'd make a similar mistake. A pang of guilt caused her throat to go dry. Maybe she was like her father, unreliable and shallow.

With a quick sniff, she tugged on her resilience, the toughness she'd needed to pull through her messy divorce. A bowl of candy with its brightly colored wrappers sat on the edge of the counter. Some sugar would do her good. She grabbed one of the small wrapped chocolates, removed the foil, and popped it into her mouth.

As she chewed, her jaw ached from the sugar rush, but the bitter-sweet taste eased some of her anxiety. Rolling the candy from one side of her mouth to the other, her teeth clamped down on the inside of her cheek.

"Ow!" *Third time's the charm.* Her mother's voice echoed in her mind.

Sheri swallowed what remained of the candy. Her tongue explored the raw gash in her mouth and she tasted blood. *Great. Just perfect.*

She stood and was about to head for Mrs. Alton's room when her phone vibrated in her vest pocket. Pausing, she pulled it out and glanced at the display. The number was a 206 area code—Seattle. A rush of adrenaline raced through her veins, quickening her heart.

She peered around, searching for a quiet place she could take this call, away from the other nurses and staff members. A small conference area was right next to Michael's room. Before she could think of a better spot, she entered the space and closed the door.

She accepted the call and placed the phone next to her ear. "Hello?"

"May I speak with Sheri Lockwood, please?"

Sheri looked out the window. The sun peeked through what remained of the dark clouds. "Speaking."

"This is Cam Newton, the manager at Firwood Estates in Seattle. You applied for a job with us."

Her pulse rose, pounding loud in her ears. "Yes...yes..."

"The panel was very impressed with your interview. Your references gave you rave recommendations, and your background check came back clean. We'd like to offer you the job."

She leaned her shoulder against the wall and rolled onto her back. Looking up at the ceiling, she blinked away tears. "Th...thank you. I'd love to work at your facility. I accept."

"Perfect. We've had a few people retire sooner than expected. Would you be able to start Monday? I know it's not much time, but we're really in a bind."

She bit her lip. Today was Thursday. A two-week notice was standard protocol, but she sensed the urgency in his voice. "I'll see what I can do. Can I call you back at this number?"

"Of course, and welcome. I'm so happy to have you on board. Call me as soon as you know."

"Thank you, I will. Bye."

A soft click echoed through the line.

I got the job! A well of excitement expanded her chest and she let out a relieved breath. She could finally escape Portland and leave behind the sad memories of her mother...and the bad ones of Ram. A new lease on life was what she needed. With a renewed sense of purpose, she opened the door. Time to give notice.

CHAPTER 20

"This is so not going to work." Mauree pulled off one high-heeled shoe and lost her balance. Her bare foot landed on wet moss growing along the base of a tree. The soft, spongy lichen cooled her skin and her shoulders relaxed. Not even the wrong pair of shoes would bring her down today. She clutched the pump to her chest and faced the late afternoon sun. The brightness was more than her sensitive eyes could handle and she squinted, but the warmth on her skin was heavenly.

With a firm grip, she snapped the heel from the shoe and threw it behind a rhododendron bush. The other shoe suffered a similar fate. A couple of sparrows hopped from branch to branch in a nearby pine tree, their song filling the air. To be outside during the day—such a treat! Mauree's spirit lifted at her newfound freedom. Who knew switching sides would have such a benefit?

Mauree placed the heelless shoes back on her feet. "Jakar, why you couldn't have picked me up some hikers instead of these pumps—" her stomach clenched at what she'd done to the lovely pair of shoes, "is beyond me."

Ahead of her on the trail, he turned to face her. His gaze wandered from her breasts to her thighs. "They seemed to go along with the skirt. Practicality wasn't on my mind."

Her fingers twitched with a flash of irritation. She placed her hands of her hips. "Window shopping, Jakar, that's as far as you go. How much farther?"

He smirked. "We just passed the spot where we battled with Tanen. When those humans arrived, sunrise was nigh. He couldn't have gone far."

"Funny...the hunter has become the hunted. Never would've thought I'd be the one to track him." She waved Jakar forward. "Continue, continue."

Today's earlier rainstorm had washed away Tanen's scent, at least to her nose. Jakar, on the other hand, had a much finer sense of smell. He flared his nostrils and his chest visibly expanded. His speed increased, forcing Mauree to run.

Her gait was awkward, a result of her broken shoes. Combined with the late afternoon sun warming her back, perspiration gathered under her armpits and along her hairline. "Ugh. I'll need a shower when we're through."

Scattered on the ground nearby were pieces of a small wooden fence in disrepair. Visible through the trees—a yellow house with a small outbuilding. Other homes appeared in the distance, but all seemed quiet. Mauree crept up behind Jakar. His unique astringent aroma permeated her senses and she gagged. "Even after a shower, you still smell bad."

He peered over his shoulder. "You'll get used to it."

She returned her attention to the structure. "Is this the place?"

He chuckled, the sound low and menacing. "What do you think? Can't you smell Tanen?"

"Not after the pounding rain and certainly not over your aroma."

He curled his lip, displaying his serrated teeth. "He was here."

"Was?"

"His trail leads that way." Jakar pointed deep into the woods. "But he stayed here a while."

She tapped her finger against her chin. "Perhaps he holed up in the small structure to avoid the sun."

"That's my assumption. Shall we investigate?"

Jakar looked to her to take the lead. She straightened her shoulders. *I'm a queen after all.*

"Before we barge in, are there any humans around?" Her pulse increased. What would it be like to meet one? Her life had been in the Keep and the safety of the forest.

His gaze roamed the surrounding area. "The house seems quiet."

A small bird buzzed around her head and she squealed. The creature returned, fluttering in mid-air. As she reached to touch the small animal, it flew away. She pursed her lips.

Jakar laughed. "Even the hummingbirds avoid you."

Heat raced into Mauree's cheeks. "Let's check the small building."

Jakar studied her for a moment. "With Ram, I could never speak my mind. You never knew when he'd get a taste for torment. At least with you…" He shrugged.

"Be careful, Jakar. Just because you haven't seen my bad side, doesn't mean I don't have one. Do you think Zedron selected me for my beauty?"

He visibly swallowed.

"Let's go before I lose my patience…what little I have."

She stepped over the fallen fence and headed into the backyard. Her shoes squeaked on the uncut lawn, the grass cool against her ankles. When she reached the small building, she grabbed the door handle and pulled. Light filtered through a broken pane in the grime-encrusted windows. Shadows hugged the corners, casting strange shapes on the objects hidden within.

Jakar pushed in behind her, and she stumbled forward. He gripped her hips, holding her against him back to front. Despite his shorter stature and build, he was stronger than she'd expected. His closeness and his smell made her cringe. She stomped on his foot. The cutoff edge of her heel bit into the leather of his running shoes.

A muffled groan escaped his lips. He released her. "What was that for?"

She glared at him. "Don't touch me again."

"You shouldn't rush blindly into places you don't know." His breath heaved in and out of his mouth.

She narrowed her gaze. "Search the place."

A low hiss eased between his lips, but he did her bidding.

He threw empty pots into the air, overturned bags of potting soil, and tossed garden tools off the workbench. In his frenzy, a bottle fell over and a liquid spilled onto the floor. The scent of pine and licorice filled the air.

Mauree pressed her lips together. "Have you found anything?"

Jakar knelt in the far corner. With a quick swipe, he ran his fingers through a dark spot on the wooden floor. He rubbed the tips together and brought them to his nose.

Mauree's pulse increased. "What is it?"

"Dried blood. Tanen's."

Mauree peered through the hole in the broken window. The yellow paint on the house shimmered, the setting sun's rays encasing the place in hues of gold. Something in her stomach fluttered. "Perhaps we should search the house."

Jakar stood, and the scales at the back of his neck flared. "Indeed."

CHAPTER 21

*T*anen adjusted his legs, stretching them out, easing the tension from his muscles. Pressed against the rough earthen edges of his shelter, his back ached. The last rays of the setting sun crested over the tree-tops. Darkness would arrive soon. Thank the gods.

Time seemed to pass at a snail's pace. He'd tried to sleep, but his thoughts kept returning to the beautiful human female—Sheri. He growled, letting the sound build until it reverberated off the trees. The forest creatures quieted, as if aware of the great beast in their presence.

He glanced into the sky. The setting sun coated the clouds in beautiful shades of pink and orange. The shelter had protected him from the sun's rays, but not the rain. Oh, no. Rain had pelted him several times during the day. The dampness soaked through his socks and into his skin. A shiver ran over his arms, and he yanked his coat tighter around his shoulders. Despite its torn and ragged appearance, he couldn't abandon the old garment or the precious pin on his collar.

Dusk turned to night, and he emerged from his makeshift cave. He stretched his arms over his head and loosened his muscles. *Onward.*

He needed to forget about the beautiful little human and concentrate on his task—find Mauree.

This time, he wouldn't fail. He couldn't face Noeh, see the look of disappointment in the king's eyes. At this point, he'd rather die than return without Mauree. His marking for tenacity tingled against his skin, giving him a boost of energy, a sign of hope.

A bitter wind kicked up, blowing strands of his hair against his cheek. He inhaled, but the cleansing rain had washed away her scent. If he couldn't track her and find the elusive safe house, he needed to determine her next move. Motivated by revenge, she'd want to attack Noeh.

Ostrum... She wasn't stupid, was she? No, but reckless, crazy. She'd already proven the lengths she'd go to seek revenge when she'd attacked the queen and her unborn child.

The spring equinox and the sacred ceremony were tomorrow night. Many of the Keep's residents would attend the celebration, including Noeh. This would be her opportunity to attack him. Determination formed in Tanen's gut, flaring his heartburn. *I must go to Roan's Rock.* This time, he wouldn't hesitate to use force to capture Mauree.

He raced through the trees, his boots slipping and sliding against the wet ferns and grasses. After cresting a small hill, he gazed over the horizon. In the distance, the outline of Roan's Rock loomed in the moonlight. His chest clenched. He hadn't attended an Ostrum ceremony in several years, electing to stay inside the Keep. *Mother Alora, I've neglected my tribute to you for too long.* He pulled on his inner strength and continued on his way.

Several minutes later, he arrived in the small clearing. Tall blades of grass blew in the wind, none broken or trampled. No one had been here for several days, including Mauree. He looked at the sky and let loose a slow breath.

A small stream ran through the meadow, leftover from the recent storm. He sloshed through the wet grass and approached the stone. Mesmerized by the sight, he placed his hand against the sacred boulder. Notched into the rock were several crevices, used during the ceremony to hold offerings to Alora. The crowd would circle the stone, holding hands, chanting their praises to the goddess. The boulder tapered to a dull point at the top. During the spring ceremony, the tip aligned with the stars and Lemuria, their home.

Runoff from the rain had followed a path around the edge of the stone, clearing bits of plant material, cleansing the surface. Carved in the edges at the rock's base were strange, handmade, etched lines. Tanen's heart skipped a beat. *That looks like cuneiform.*

He bent down, his left knee squishing into the soft mud. In awe, he ran his fingers over the images. The rough edges tingled his skin. Carved into the surface was the symbol for Lemuria or "Mu" and life everlasting.

He touched the matching silver emblem on his coat, the one that signified him as council leader—his most treasured possession.

His heart pounded. He searched his mind, trying to recall anything in the ancient scriptures about an inscription on Roan's Rock. Nothing...not that he'd ever seen. His chest expanded, and he pulled at the bits of weeds and grass still stuck to the stone. Was there more?

Another symbol appeared. Something fluttered in his chest... hope? With a speed he'd long forgotten he possessed, he wiped at the dirt, digging his fingernails into the soft loam, unearthing more and more markings with each handful. He didn't stop until he'd circumnavigated the entire stone. He stood, his heart pumping with excitement.

He took a step back and circled the perimeter, reading the ancient text that had remained buried under the soil for countless ages. Some of the characters he recognized, others were unfamiliar, undecipherable. He pieced together the message as best he could.

Lemuria. My homeland.
   Energy...
   Strongest...equi...
   Beware blue...warp...power.
   Those...spill blood...falter.

...pure of heart...stop...wrath.

Tanen's heartburn flared. What did the words mean? A headache built behind his eyes. Walking the perimeter again, he reread the glyphs, trying to decipher the unfamiliar ones. How was this possible? He knew all the symbols in the old language. Over the years, he'd read many of the ancient texts and all of the journals from the great warrior, Roan.

He cracked his knuckles, but that didn't ease his frustration. He reached into his coat pocket, searching for the blue sunstone. Hopefully, the bauble would calm him enough so he could concentrate, figure out the meaning behind the ancient text.

His fingers grazed over his knife and Gaetan's satchel. No stone. He tensed.

With shaking fingers, he checked his pants pocket. Where was the sunstone?

Panic welled inside, and he couldn't breathe. He traced his hands over his jacket, searching for the familiar bulge. Nothing...the blue sunstone of legend was gone.

His throat constricted and he choked on his own saliva. Several coughs wracked his body before he regained his composure. His pulse pounded behind his eyes. A vision formed in his mind. While in Sheri's bed, in his sick, fevered mind he'd clutched the stone to his chest, hoping against hope it would heal him. The legends said the stone would heal someone who'd sacrificed himself for another. He'd learned firsthand he hadn't deserved its power. The stone had tumbled from his fingers.

Mauree will come for the stone.

He held his breath. The old legend mentioned the stone could be used by the enemy to cause great harm. In her effort to obtain the blue sunstone, Mauree would follow the path he'd taken after their fight— straight to Sheri's house. Blood pounded at his temple. Sheri wasn't safe. *I must go to her.*

CHAPTER 22

*L*emuria's dual moons lit up the sky, filtering through Alora's window. She placed her arms along the sill and gazed across the Rolmdew trees, listening to the quiet creak of the limbs in the breeze. Goosebumps rose along her skin. How she longed to feel the warmth from the sun, but that wouldn't happen until the war over Earth was won. *Damn Zedron.*

She stepped away from the window and glanced at the war map on the wall. Situated above the dining room table, it was a constant reminder of what was at stake—Earth's precious water, something Lemuria desperately needed. Lights blinking on the holograph displayed characters in the game with their current location—green for Alora's, red for Zedron's. The area surrounding the Keep was a sea of crimson. Many represented the Ursus and not so long ago, she would've been thrilled to see them there, but not now. She fisted her hand. "I hate you, Zedron!"

With more force than she'd intended, she swiped her fingers over the map. The tiny dots scattered, and in its place, a categorized character list lit up the screen. She scanned her options—active, expired, new. A lump formed in her throat and she couldn't swallow. Her list of actives continued to decline, moving to expired with each death.

Under the "new" category, a single entry blinked. She caught her breath. She hadn't had new characters on the board for centuries, not until Melissa became a Dren and Anlon was born.

With shaking fingers, she hovered her finger over the shimmering screen, pulling up the character's name—Sheri.

Sheri? Who was that? Alora's pulse rose. She tapped on the name to get a visual.

A young human female appeared on the screen. She was in her early thirties with shoulder-length blonde hair and hazel eyes. A wave of dizziness peppered Alora's vision with white spots. Sheri was Ram's ex-wife. Who changed her and why?

Tapping on the holograph once again, Alora traced her finger over Sheri's history. A single name rose on the screen—Tanen.

Alora blinked. Of all her character species, Stiyaha avoided humans the most, electing to remain hidden in the forests. To think Tanen had interacted with humans was a big surprise, to say the least. The last time she'd seen him, he'd tracked Mauree to a small waterfall near the edge of the forest. Where was he now?

She swiped at the hologram, scattering the legend into tiny particles of light and returned to the map. With careful scrutiny, she zoomed in on the area near the waterfall, searching the green lights for Tanen's unique signature. There...in the woods by Roan's Rock. He was alone.

Alora stepped back and studied the board. "Okay, Tanen, why isn't Sheri with you?"

She tapped her finger against her chin, her mind whirling with possibilities...and implications. A ball of fear clutched at her chest.

Alora ran her fingers over the map, faster and faster, searching for her new character's light. At last, she spotted the faint green radiance, shades lighter than her other characters. Sheri's new icon was several miles away at a human institution. She was a Dren, but remained in her human world.

That was against the rules.

The coil inside Alora tightened. Of all the people to break the rules, Tanen, the Stiyaha council leader and keeper of the ancient texts, would've been her last guess. She swiped her finger over the hologram, returning the map to its original state. With a quick turn, she paced the small space between the table and her front door. *What to do...what to do...*

The Calorin vines crept through the window, their soft, lulling murmur beckoning to her. She wanted to let the vines wrap around her arms, enjoying the sweet fragrance from the yellow blooms, but she was too uptight. By all rights she should remove Tanen from the game and return him to the character board for breaking the rules, but she understood all too well what it was like to be punished for transgressions.

She slapped her palm against the table's hard surface. Pain radiated up her arm and pinpricks of tears coated her eyes.

"Tanen, come through for me. Bring Sheri into the game." She longed to tell him those words, but he had to make his own choice. Non-interference was the number one rule, and she wouldn't break it again. What she could give him, though, was a small bit of time. "Hurry, Tanen."

If he didn't bring Sheri into his world, and soon, Alora would be forced to pull him from the game. To let Tanen go unpunished, Alora would break another rule. She couldn't go there, not again, for if she did, she'd lose the war.

A tear slid over her lash and splashed against her cheek. She didn't bother to wipe it away. It was a reminder. This was more than a game.

This was war.

CHAPTER 23

*S*heri tapped on the brake pedal and a high-pitched squeal pierced her ear. She flinched. The car needed new brakes. With her odd hours and busy schedule, she hadn't had time to deal with the issue. She'd do that before she left for Seattle.

Seattle...

After shoving the gearshift into park, she relaxed in the seat and leaned against the headrest. A new job, a new life, a chance to start over. A feeling of weightlessness lifted her spirits, and she couldn't suppress the smile that tugged at her lips.

When she'd given her notice, Matt had reacted better than she thought he would. One more shift was all he'd asked of her. To ease her conscience, she'd stayed late to help him clean the break room. It was dark now, but if she hurried, she could make dinner and start packing before she called it a night. She got out of the car and with an extra bounce in her step, headed up the small walkway to her front door.

The moon peeking through the clouds cast strange shadows along the ground, turning the tree tops into long pointy claws. As she flipped through her keys, the slippery bunch fell to the ground. With a groan, she bent over to pick them up. From inside the house, a small thump echoed.

"Oh, Coop, what are you doing in there, boy?" She couldn't wait to see her pet.

A strange silence emanated from the house. *Why didn't he greet her?* She tensed.

Goosebumps rose along her arm.

"Coop?"

She remained in her crouched position, and she tightened her fingers around her keys. The wind in the trees and her own heartbeat were the only sounds.

After several seconds, she shook her head. Maybe she'd imagined the noise and Coop was still asleep in his bed. Still, her hand shook as she placed the key in the lock. With a quick turn of the handle, she opened the door and stepped inside.

The bitter tang of rubbing alcohol assailed her nose. She flicked on the light.

Her home was in shambles. A broken chair leg protruded from under the love seat. White stuffing sprung from gashes in the over-turned cushions. Books and papers were strewn across the floor.

Coop's still form lay partially hidden behind the upended coffee table.

She gasped. Her keys slipped from her fingers. They jangled as they bounced on the carpet.

A torrent of fear rippled over her skin. *Oh, Coop!*

Something moved, catching her attention. A scream bottled up in her throat.

She took a tentative step toward the door, her legs nearly giving out underneath her.

"Stop." A woman's rough voice ground Sheri to the spot.

She held her breath, her muscles aching with tension.

"Where's the stone?" Dressed in a short skirt and tight blouse, a woman emerged from the kitchen. She sauntered into the room as if she owned the place. Tall, with long blonde hair, she was beautiful—

until an unearthly grin spread across her face. "Give me the stone and I'll let you live."

"S...stone?" Sheri shook her head, taking another step toward the door.

The woman eased closer, her hands loose at her sides. "Of course, the stone. I'm sure Tanen must've mentioned it to you."

Sheri's heart skipped a beat. "Tanen? Where is he? Is he okay?"

The woman's forehead creased. "Don't play games with me, little girl. I could crush you in my palm." She curled her hand into a fist.

A rush of adrenaline coursed through Sheri's veins. An unfamiliar need welled inside—to fight this female, rip at her hair, kick and tussle until one of them was victorious. Although this woman was taller and bigger, Sheri wasn't a waif, her own frame large and strong.

The woman smiled. "Jakar, please, join us."

She has a partner. Great.

A man emerged from the hallway leading to Sheri's bedroom. He was bald, his head as hairless as a newborn babe, but his most noticeable feature were his black, inhuman eyes.

Her throat constricted, cutting off her scream. She bolted for the open door.

He crushed her against the wall, slamming the door shut before she could escape. The clammy skin on his arms rubbed against her, and the sharp astringent scent intensified. She gagged.

"Were you leaving? No, I don't think so." His deep voice resonated into her chest, chilling her.

He grabbed her wrists and yanked them behind her back. Pain radiated up her arms and she cried out, but he only snickered. With a quick pull, he flipped her around to face him.

His breath reeked of alcohol, bitter and tangy, adding to his awful smell. Except for his dark eyes, he seemed human, that was, until he smiled. Serrated teeth gleamed white in the entryway light.

Her adrenaline spiked. This time, her scream tore from her throat, continuing on and on until she ran out of breath.

He raised an eyebrow. "Are you done?"

"Jakar, bring her here."

"As you wish, Mauree."

Twisting and turning in his grasp, Sheri couldn't break his hold. Before she knew what had happened, she was face to face with the woman. Her blue eyes flickered with madness.

"So, this is what a human female looks like." Mauree's gaze raked over her face and down her body. "You're not much different in appearance, but the word "weak" comes to mind."

"What did you do to my dog?" Sheri blurted the words before she could stop herself.

Mauree gripped the front of Sheri's shirt. "He got in the way... attacked Jakar. He's only unconscious, for now. So, where is the stone?" Face to face, Sheri stared into this crazed woman's eyes. Gold flecks swam in her irises, reminding Sheri of Tanen.

"I...I don't know..." A memory flashed before Sheri's eyes. Tanen had gripped the stone to his chest during his fever. It must still be in the bedroom.

"Tanen's been here. I can smell him." Mauree's lips drew into a thin line. "Knowing that weasel as I do, I'm sure he would've gloated over his bauble. Such a pretty blue stone—now, tell me. Where. Is. It."

With her hands behind her back, Sheri didn't have any leverage. Jakar's grip was firm, and his fingernails bit into her skin. She could only shake her head.

Mauree yanked Sheri free of her captor. Sheri's hands landed on Mauree's biceps. The skin on skin contact lit up the sensitive nerves in her fingertips. Hot and powerful, anger roiled in Sheri's gut, building, growing until a strong tingle rippled down her arm. A short, intense spark radiated from her fingers.

"Ow!" Mauree shoved Sheri aside. Her eyes widened for a moment before her focus narrowed once again.

"You seem...attached to your little pet." Mauree smiled and gold flecks danced in her eyes. "If you don't give me the stone, I'll kill your dog."

"No!" Sheri's legs shook, yet a part of her wanted to strangle

Mauree for threatening Coop. Her fingers curled into a fist, and her warm palm itched.

"Jakar." Mauree nodded toward Coop. "Take care of that animal."

Jakar turned toward Sheri's little companion, and her chest clenched. "Wait. I...think I know where the stone is."

Mauree licked her lips and took a step forward. "Ah, much better... and where would that be?"

"In my bedroom, on the floor or under the bed." Sheri hated herself for giving into their demands, but she wouldn't let them hurt Coop.

Mauree motioned to Jakar and he raced down the hall. Moments later he returned, the blue sunstone wedged between his thumb and forefinger.

"Give it to me." Mauree held out her hand.

Jakar hesitated ever so slightly, but then handed the gem to his companion.

Sheri edged toward Coop, putting more distance between herself and these two intruders.

"Well, looks like we're through here. We'll be going now." Mauree headed for the door, then stopped. With exaggerated flair, she placed her finger along the side her chin. "Oh, wait. One last thing... Jakar, change her. Turn her into a Gossum. We could use the extra help."

He snickered. "I can't."

"Why not? She's human."

"Females don't survive the transition to Gossum."

Sheri's mind spun. She didn't understand their words, but the intent behind them was clear. If she stayed, she was dead. She sprinted for the door.

Mauree grabbed her arm, but Sheri slipped through her fingers only to trip and land on her hands and knees. Skidding on the carpet, the rug burned into her skin.

Mauree gripped a fistful of Sheri's hair, using it as leverage to haul Sheri to her feet. Her scalp burned.

"I'm afraid you've seen too much, my dear." Mauree shoved Sheri toward Jakar. "Kill her."

As Jakar's grip tightened around her waist, Sheri's chest clenched and she couldn't breathe.

Outside, loud footsteps approached on the walkway. The ground shook from the force. Before she could blink, the front door burst open, slamming against the wall. A large figure loomed in the doorway. *Tanen...*

CHAPTER 24

Tanen stepped over the threshold and into Sheri's home, his dagger gripped in his palm. An acrid, astringent scent filled his nose. He scanned the room and his vision pinpointed on Sheri. Jakar held her in front of him, his hand wrapped around her waist, pinning her arms to her sides. His free hand was at her throat, claws extended.

Tanen froze.

Mauree's laughter bubbled into the air, thick with acid. She smiled, her once beautiful features morphing into something dark, something evil. Tanen's gut twisted.

"My, my, Tanen. Your timing," she waved her hand in the air, "...is perfect, shall we say."

A low growl emitted from his throat, his beast pounding against his will, eager to attack and fight against the threat. He preparing to strike, the muscles in his arms and legs tensed.

"Don't move...that wouldn't be a wise choice." Mauree's low tone skated over his nerves, pinning him in place. A bead of sweat rolled down his cheek and dripped onto the carpet.

"Tanen..." Sheri's voice quivered.

He glanced at her and his chest constricted. All of this was his fault. Sheri was caught in the consequences, the undertow of his choices. His grip tightened around his dagger. "Let. Her. Go."

Mauree tittered then her features hardened. "Silly Tanen, you are in no position to make demands. Jakar, we have what we came here for. Kill her and be done with it."

"Noooo!" Tanen launched himself toward Jakar.

Time seemed to slow.

Flashes of light pulsed from Sheri's fingers. Static electricity sparked in the air.

Jakar flinched, releasing his hold on Sheri. She slipped through his fingers.

Tanen tackled his enemy and they rolled across the carpet. Jakar's back slammed into the wall and a picture frame fell, nailing him in the face. His tongue lashed out, barely missing Tanen's ear.

Tanen thrust his dagger at Jakar's chest, but the wily creature squirmed under Tanen's weight. The weapon missed its mark, embedding into the Gossum's shoulder. He hissed.

Mauree approached Sheri, her blue eyes flecked with gold.

A sour taste formed at the back of Tanen's throat. He ripped the dagger from the creature's shoulder.

Jakar's tongue snaked from between his serrated teeth, the barbed end connecting with Tanen's wrist. The venom worked into his hand, numbing his fingers, and he couldn't maintain his grip. The dagger slipped to the carpet.

With his free hand, he clawed the scales at the back of Jakar's neck —the Gossum's weak spot. Jakar screamed, his shrill screech piercing the air. The evil creature writhed beneath him.

"Tanen!" Sheri's shriek pulled his attention to her.

Mauree wrapped her hands around Sheri's throat.

Sheri scraped at Mauree's fingers, her face reddening.

A surge of adrenaline coursed through Tanen's veins. *Sheri!* He pushed away from Jakar and rose to his feet.

A bright blue flare burst from Sheri's fingers. Mauree screamed, releasing her hold. She stared wide-eyed at her hands. The smell of burnt flesh filled the room.

Tanen tensed. *What just happened?*

Mauree punched Sheri in the jaw. She fell to the floor—lifeless.

His chest constricted so tight he couldn't breathe, his scream of rage bottled up in his throat. *Sheri...* He raced toward her.

Before he could get there, a heavy weight landed on his back. Claws tore into his shoulders.

He lost his balance. One knee crashed to the ground.

Jakar's teeth snapped at Tanen's neck.

Tanen couldn't take his eyes off Sheri. She lay on her back, motionless. Her blank stare bore into him.

The scream he'd held on to burst from his lips, morphing into a howl. His beast took over, pumping blood through his veins, fueling his anger, his need for retribution.

He lashed out at Jakar with his uninjured hand, punching the creature in the face, again, and again. The hair on his arms grew long and thick, and his bones cracked as they expanded.

A deep growl rumbled in his chest.

His beast was loose. Tanen couldn't stop the change now. A moment later, he was eight and a half feet tall. His clothes disappeared under a thick pelt of fur covering his bulging muscles. Tusks burst from his mouth, the ends sharp as a razor. The need to kill welled inside, and he poured all his aggression into his attack, his focus solely on the Gossum behind him.

He reached over his shoulder and grabbed Jakar by the nape. With a quick jerk, he tore the evil creature from his back, and threw him against the wall. At the impact, a grunt burst from Jakar's chest. He shook his head and glared at Tanen, spittle dripping from his mouth.

Tanen roared. His beast couldn't wait to rip into the enemy.

Movement out of the corner of his eye caught Tanen's attention. As he turned, the bottom of a high-heeled shoe, the tip missing, slammed into his face. *Mauree...*

Pain blurred his vision. Blood trickled from his nose. He shook his head, trying to clear his thoughts.

"Hurry, Jakar! Let's go. We have the sunstone." Mauree's voice floated through the fog in Tanen's brain. "Now that I have the blue sunstone of legend, I'll have my revenge on Noeh. Thank you, dear Tanen, for your contribution."

The sunstone...Noeh. Tanen's breath caught in his throat. With his beast in control, the need to protect his king drove him forward.

As the two disappeared through the doorway, he raced after them. Before he crossed the threshold, he stilled. He turned toward the female sprawled on the floor. *Mine...* His beast's declaration reverberated through Tanen's mind, the truth in the words settling into him. He released a low, baleful roar.

He rushed to her side. Was she alive? He couldn't swallow, his mouth suddenly dry. With as much care as he could muster in his beast form, he wiped a few stray strands of hair away from her face. She didn't stir, but her soft breaths against the back of his hand tingled his skin.

She was alive.

His shoulders slumped, and the weight on his chest lightened. The beast sat and pulled her onto his lap, wrapping her in his embrace. Her dark lashes caressed her cheek, and her lips were rosy from her fight. A few cuts marred her skin along with a red spot on her chin, but he didn't see any other wounds. As he cradled her against him, his beast growled softly. A possessiveness he'd never experienced before washed over him. Her soothing breaths calmed him, relaxing him.

He rocked her until the beast slept.

CHAPTER 25

A short canine whine filled the air, and something warm and wet nuzzled Tanen's cheek. As he woke, a headache pounded behind his eyes. Coop barked, and his tail beat against the carpet. Fogged memories flooded Tanen's mind—Mauree, Jakar, the fight— Sheri. He tensed. *Sheri...*

Awareness of her weight in his arms and the warmth of her skin brought him fully awake. He was in his human state, his sweat pants and shirt clinging to his body. *I must've transitioned back to human while I slept.* He didn't want to think about how that happened, his concern for Sheri forefront in his mind. As he cradled her close, her magnificent hair covered her face, hiding her features from him. The fine tresses tickled his arm, and her soft skin tingled his nerves. His need to touch her, hold her, protect her, burned a bright flame in his chest. He swallowed, and his throat constricted.

"Sheri," he whispered.

She didn't rouse.

Coop whined. He stood and barked, again, and again.

"Shh...Coop."

With a soft caress, Tanen wiped a few stray hairs away from her cheek, uncovering her gorgeous features. Long, luscious lashes graced her skin, and soft, even breaths escaped between her parted lips. He longed to kiss her, the pull so strong, his chest ached. Instead, he trailed a finger down the side of her cheek to her jaw. A couple of cuts and a small gash, inflamed and red with a dried spot of blood, was the only indication she'd been injured.

He glanced around the room, assessing the damage. Magazines and papers from the overturned coffee table were strewn across the carpet. The sofa cushions and pillows lay haphazardly over the couch, the floor, the chairs. In the corner, tilted at an odd angle was the bookcase, its contents scattered across the rug, as if a giant wave had taken the books out to sea.

At least Mauree and Jakar were long gone. He curled and uncurled his fist. His rage, his need to protect Sheri had brought his inner beast to the surface. The beast had elected to stay with Sheri instead of pursuing his enemies. *He was protecting his mate.*

Tanen returned his attention to the beautiful female in his arms. With a gentle nudge, he rocked her in his embrace, rousing her. "Sheri, wake up."

A soft moan eased from her mouth.

Coop barked, the loud noise piercing Tanen's ears.

Sheri's eyelids fluttered. She peered at him. The tension in his chest released, and he let loose a slow exhale. He couldn't help but smile. "Sheri."

Her brow scrunched together. "Tanen?"

She sat up, pulling away from his embrace. Her gaze darted around the room. She tensed, the muscles in her legs and arms instantly rigid. "What…oh, no!" A high pitched scream emerged from her lips and she scrambled out of his arms. "Where…where are they? Are they gone?"

Coop barked, again and again, adding to the confusion.

Tanen stood and wrapped her in his embrace. "It's just you and me, Sheri."

She latched on to him, her trembles reverberating through their connection, worming into his heart. He held her tight until her shivers ceased.

"Tanen..." She leaned back and peered into his eyes. "Wh...What happened? Who were those...people?"

The muscles in his jaw clamped tight. "Not anyone you wish to know."

Coop jumped, placing his front paws on Sheri's hip. He gave her a few soft woofs, his tail wagging back and forth.

"Oh, Coop." She wrapped her arms around his neck, burying her face and hands in his fur. The adoration and love she displayed for her pet melted Tanen's resolve. Despite they were from different worlds, literally and figuratively, he couldn't deny what was in his heart. He cared for her, more than he should.

"Sheri..."

She released Coop and glanced around her home. Although her fingers shook, her hand fisted at her side. She turned her focus on him, and a fire burned in her eyes. "Tanen...tell me. What's going on? Who were those people and what were they doing here? Why did they want your blue stone? Are you in some kind of mob?"

Heat raced over his shoulders. He exhaled, forcing his heartbeat to slow. "Sheri...there's more to this—"

She brought her fist to her mouth, and held up her other hand. "Stop, don't tell me. I don't want to know what kind of trouble you're in. Besides, it doesn't matter. I'm moving to Seattle." With short, quick movements, she picked up a cushion and tossed it on the couch. Bending over, she grabbed the edge of the coffee table, returning it to a standing position. Her frantic pace increased and she raced to her bookcase.

Her head jerked back and forth as she assessed the damages. She dropped to her knees. With tears streaming down her cheeks, she grasped book after book.

Tanen couldn't take anymore. He wrapped her in his arms, tugging her to him. "Shh...Sheri. Calm down."

A short sob escaped her lips then she relaxed into his embrace.

"That's better." He trailed his fingers over her hair, trying to quiet her as best he could. *She's moving away?* The words haunted him, but his need to care for her outweighed the sudden ache in his chest.

She pulled back to look at him. A tear slipped over her lashes. Tanen cupped her face in his palm and gently trailed his thumb over her cheek, wiping away the wetness.

"Sheri..."

Coop shoved his way between them and issued a short bark. Sheri stepped back, wiping her hand over her face, drying the remaining moisture from her eyes. "Oh, Coop. I'm so glad you're okay."

She gave her companion another hug. "Good boy. Go lie down."

After a quick finger snap, she pointed to his bed. He tilted his head, woofed, then headed for his spot.

She scratched at her chin, the skin red and swollen.

A tendril of worry skittered over his nerves. "Does your jaw hurt?"

"It's nothing, just burns now and then..." The lines around her eyes drew together and her delectable mouth turned into a frown.

He winced, knowing he'd caused her such pain. "May I take a look?"

She bit her lip, and he had the sudden urge to bite it, too. The pull, the magnetism between them, drew him to her and he couldn't stop himself. He traced a finger over her brow, placing a few stray strands of hair behind her ear.

"You've been through a lot in the past few hours. You seem fine, but please, let me look at your wound." She met his gaze and he concentrated on her features, memorizing the intricacies in her hazel eyes. The brown melded with the green in a unique pattern and he'd never seen anything so beautiful. He wanted to dive into their depths and please her, please this female he'd come to care for so much in such a short time.

She nodded, the brief gesture a victory as much for her as for him. A resolve built in his chest. He wouldn't let her down. With thoughtful attention, he tilted her head and trailed his finger to the red spot on her chin.

She flinched ever so slightly.

"I'm sorry you were injured."

Mauree's fist had left a small welt and a tiny scratch, but it was already well on its way to healing. Good thing Jakar hadn't bitten her. She wouldn't have survived.

"How does it look?" Her voice was soft, shaky.

"Not too bad. The redness will disappear in a few hours. Are you hurt anywhere else?"

"N...no, I'm fine." She straightened her head and glanced into his eyes. "Thank you. If you hadn't showed up when you did..." She inhaled. "You saved my life."

His chest constricted at the sincerity in her voice. "You wouldn't be in this mess if not for me."

Her brow creased, and her eyes shifted back and forth as she studied him. "I'll be honest. I don't know what's real and what isn't anymore and I'm scared out of my mind right now, but with you, I feel safe."

His heart pounded double time. That she trusted him, felt protected by him, lifted his spirits. "I...I thought you were dead. You have no idea how much that scared me."

"Tanen..." The affectionate way she looked at him shredded his insides, her eyes boring into his soul. His inner beast woke and a low growl started in the base of his chest. The vibration rumbled between them. An answering moan eased from her parted lips.

He cupped her head in his palm, and traced his thumb over her bottom lip. She audibly inhaled and licked her lips. Holding back was no longer an option. With deliberate intent, he glanced from her eyes to her mouth and brought her close. Their lips met and sparks ignited, tingling the inner lining of his mouth.

She mewled in acceptance, and he deepened the kiss. He wanted more, and blood rushed to his groin. His growl turned into a moan of pure need. Leaning into him, her body molded to his, her breasts pressing against his chest. His shaft filled with his desire, and he stroked his free hand over the dip in her waist to her full, rounded hips. He tugged her to him. She gasped, breaking their kiss.

He cradled her nape in his palm, holding on, not ever wanting to let her go. Leaning in, he pressed his lips to her forehead. "Let me clean you up, care for you as you did for me."

She peered into his eyes, trust and faith radiating from their depths. All she gave him in response was a quick nod.

That was all the encouragement he needed. He grasped her hand and led her toward the bathroom, only stopping long enough to lock the front door.

CHAPTER 26

$\mathcal{T}$anen pulled Sheri into the bathroom and shut the door. He scanned the counter, looking for the small box with the red cross on the front. A myriad of bottles, tubes, and assorted containers lined the countertop, but nowhere did he see her medical kit. Restlessness tingled his nerves, and he glanced at her.

She touched his arm, his skin lighting up at the contact. Her gaze was focused on her reflection in the mirror. "Oh, my..." Her lip quivered.

Wanting to distract her, he placed his hand on her shoulder. "Why don't you sit?"

She nodded, and he helped her perch on the toilet seat lid.

"Where's your medicine box?"

At the sound of his voice, her attention tracked to him. She pointed at the cabinet under the sink. "D...down there."

He opened the door and a slight squeak issued from the hinge. There, on the bottom shelf, was the little white box. Next to it was a bottle of what looked like ointment. He couldn't read the label, and an irritated flush raced over his shoulders.

Quickly, he grabbed both items and placed them on the counter, scooting some of the bottles out of the way. He eased open the metal latch, revealing her medical supplies. An assortment of bandages, cotton balls, ointment, scissors, and tape filled the small box.

He stole a glance at her. Her gaze was focused on the floor, her shoulders shaking. The last thing he wanted was for her to go into shock. Gripping the bottle, he held it in front of her, forcing her to pay attention to him. "Is this an antiseptic?"

She peered at him then focused on the container in his hand. "Yes."

He unscrewed the cap and moistened a wad of cotton. Bending on one knee, he leaned into her and placed a hand on her arm. His fingers tingled at the skin-on-skin contact and reminded him of her battle with Mauree. Sparks had radiated from Sheri's fingers.

Craya. She's no longer human. Somehow, he'd changed her. She was a Dren now, and would soon need to feed from him. Her special gift had something to do with the electrical energy in her fingers. He needed to help her ease into her transition.

He moved a stray strand of hair away from her eyebrow and looked into her eyes. "I'm going to take good care of you. I promise."

Her eyes flicked back and forth as she evaluated him. Then, her full mouth, still red from their kisses, pursed. "Tanen...my mother used to say people come into our lives for a reason. That sometimes, we have to take a leap of faith."

He studied her. "Do you believe that?"

She shrugged. "After what I saw tonight, I think anything is possible. But what I do know, is you came back for me."

His chest tightened. A warmth for this female spread through him, searing her into the very fiber of his being. He swallowed and leaned forward. With attentiveness, he dabbed the moist cotton onto her cut, wiping away the bit of dried blood.

She trailed her fingers up his arm until she latched on to his, holding on as if for dear life. "Tanen, kiss me."

He wanted to oblige, please her until she couldn't remember anything except his touch, his kiss, his love, but he wouldn't take advantage of her, not in her current state of mind. "You've been through a lot..."

With an ache in his chest, he stood, put the cap back on the bottle, and returned both it and the medical kit to the cabinet.

She rose from her seat and trailed her hand down his arm. A shiver of pure need trembled through him. His beast wanted what she offered and so did he, his shaft hardening.

"Tanen, I meant what I said. Please, kiss me." Her soft words tore into him, breaking his resolve.

Her eyes glistened with unshed tears, melting his heart. He couldn't deny her request, not now. Wrapping his hand around her waist, he drew her to him, pouring his love for this tender-hearted female into his kiss, showing her what she meant to him. She'd given him the one thing he'd always wanted—faith. There wasn't anything he wouldn't do for her now.

Their kisses took on a frenzied tone, her need fueling his own. When they stopped for a quick breath, she bit her lip and stared into his eyes. "Did you mean it when you said you'd care for me?"

A tinge of unease travelled along his nerves. "Of course. What—"

"I want to bathe, get rid of all the dirt and... Please, would you bathe with me?" The plea in her tone was something he couldn't refuse. His beast growled in agreement.

Eager to rid them both of their clothes, he tugged at the waistband of her pants, pulling her close. Her fingers landed on his chest. A soft squeal eased from her lips. With deliberate slowness, she trailed her hands between them and undid the buttons on her blouse, her fingers tickling the skin on his chest.

He eased the blouse from her arms, and the material landed on the tiled floor in a heap. The smooth skin of her neck trailed into the "V" of her cleavage, and her rounded breasts swelled with each breath, taunting him, teasing him. With mindful attention, he slipped one bra strap over her shoulder then the other. She took a step back and undid the clasp. As the material slipped from her fingers, her tight little nipples peaked.

He groaned, the sound low and needful. Unable to resist, he trailed a finger over her shoulder and around the edge of her breast. As he took her weight in his hand, he gently flicked the sensitive tip with his thumb. A soft gasp escaped between her lips. He'd never heard anything so alluring.

She eased her fingers over his coat, pausing for a moment to study his emblem. "Your coat is a mess. I'm afraid it's not much more than a tattered rag."

He shrugged out of it and left it on the counter. "It's all I have and will have to do."

She ran her hands over his shoulders and down his sweatshirt. With a quick pull, she yanked at the base of his shirt. He raised his hands and the cloth landed on the counter. Her gaze traced over the healed scars on his chest and shoulders.

His erection tented his sweatpants and she gripped him, squeezing him tight. A low hiss slid from his throat, and the need to claim her churned deep inside. She tugged at his pants, stretching the waistband over his hips. Quicker than he thought possible, he removed the restraining material along with his shoes. As he straightened, his shaft strained toward her, longing for her touch. But he would have none of that, not yet. First, he wanted her naked.

He pulled the string on her thin scrubs. She slid them over her hips, and tossed them into the corner with one foot. Scattered around the small room, the bits of clothing seemed right at home. For some reason, the familiar urge to straighten the mess no longer seized him.

He leaned into the shower, gripped the handle and turned. As the water poured from the shower head, the sound of the spray hitting the tiles filled the room. He turned to face her and became lost in everything that was Sheri. Her warm skin, the gentle shape of her curves, and the desire in the depths of her eyes.

"Come, be with me." He extended his hand in invitation. She placed her fingers alongside his until their palms touched. He squeezed her hand, sending all his comfort and support through their connection. As she joined him in the shower, he couldn't help but think her acceptance meant more to the both of them then either would admit.

CHAPTER 27

e with me. The deep timbre in Tanen's voice was gentle and soothing, calming her and drawing her to him. She accepted his proffered hand, letting him guide her into the shower and into his arms. He wrapped her in his embrace, holding her close. Leaning against him, she soaked up his strength.

Deep lines formed along his cheeks and his intense focus left little doubt of his intent. He ran his hand over her hip and over her waist. His fingers skimmed along the curve of her breast, coming dangerously close to her nipples. The taut peaks ached, and she longed for him to touch her, bring her some relief, and make her forget about everything that had happened.

She stroked her fingers over his shoulders and down his biceps. Tenderness and affection reflected deep in his eyes. This man had wreaked havoc with her life, but there was something about him she couldn't resist, something that called to her at a level so deep, she couldn't ignore it. Right now, nothing mattered except Tanen.

He leaned into her, his hot length pressing against her abdomen. Although he was a big man to begin with, the length and breadth of him made her pause. Could she take him? She wasn't a small woman, but even still, a niggle of worry built in her chest.

He pressed soft kisses against her forehead, her cheek, her chin, then gave her another bruising kiss, sending a jolt of electricity all the way to her toes. He flicked her nipple, and her clit pulsed along with her heartbeat. She couldn't stop her needy moan.

He kissed the tender spot behind her ear. When she cried out, his smile stretched the stubble on his chin, tickling her skin. He played her like he was a conductor of his own orchestra and each of her nerves was his instrument. She shivered in his embrace, wanting more.

He slathered the bar of soap between his hands and rubbed his fingers over her shoulders, down her sides and between her breasts. The slick, soapy water ran along her legs, pooling at her feet. With exquisite grace, he kneeled and washed her calves and thighs, pausing for a moment at the junction between her legs.

A shiver of anticipation traveled over her shoulders.

A hungry smile graced his features as he rubbed his hand between her legs, careful not to get any soap between her folds. She moaned as his hand teased the fine hairs on her mound.

The warm gleam in his eyes bore into her, cracking the protective shell around her heart. He stood, trailing his fingers up her thigh, his hand coming to rest at her hips.

He gripped her leg and placed it over his hip. A short squeal of delight escaped her lips. His member lay against her thigh, warm and firm. She grasped him, squeezing her fingers tight. A growl born of masculine frustration rumbled in his chest. "You drive me crazy."

His quiet taunt lightened her mood, relieving some of her earlier stress, and she melted under his onslaught. He teased her, circling his fingers over her mound, stoking her need.

She arched her hips and bit her lip. "Oh, yes please."

Pure male pride graced his features. With attentive devotion, he eased his finger between her sensitive folds. "You are so wet. I could make you come right now."

He circled her lips with his finger. At every turn he gave an extra swirl to her sensitive bud. Her hips moved in rhythm with him as he worked her into a frenzy. He inserted his finger into her cleft, and she gasped, the sensitive skin flaring to life. Little lightning bolts of desire traveled along her nerves.

He chuckled and his shaft jerked, the end pressing harder against her thigh. Increasing the intensity, he rubbed her clit with his thumb while his finger slid in and out of her sheath. She couldn't hold on, and she bucked against his hand as she came.

Her frantic breaths eased in and out of her lungs. "I want you inside me."

The muscles in his arms tensed, and his brow furrowed.

"Don't worry, I'm on the pill. I won't get pregnant, and I don't have any diseases."

"Pregnancy? That didn't even cross my mind." His gaze roamed her face and his features tightened, as if with longing. "I don't have any diseases. Are you sure this is what you want?"

"I do...want you."

The smile that played on his lips caused butterflies to flutter in her stomach. Focusing on her once again, he placed the head of his cock at her entrance. He circled the tip around her clit, just like he'd done with his finger. She gripped his behind. "Please."

"Anything for my lady." With a gentleness she'd never known, he peered into her eyes, further cracking the shell around her heart. He eased into her, inch by inch, waiting for her to adjust to his size. When his balls tickled her skin at her entrance, she held her breath. This man filled her, heart, body, and soul.

They fell into a rhythm, slow at first, but gaining tempo with each thrust. He cradled her in his embrace, preventing her from pounding against the tile. Water cascaded over her back and dribbled over her shoulders, pooling where they joined. The warmth flowing between them melded together and she became lost in his gaze. *I'm falling for him...*

An orgasm exploded within and she clenched him, squeezing his shaft with each pulsing heartbeat. He stilled, pulling her closer, tightening his hold until his own climax receded. His warm breaths teased her cheek. All she wanted to do was stay in his embrace.

A fierce ache in her teeth sent a shudder down her back. She cried out from the pain.

Tanen gripped her shoulders. "Did I hurt you?"

The vein in his neck pulsed with his heartbeat. Her attention riveted there, and she swore she heard the fluid rush through his blood vessel.

The throbbing in her mouth grew. Her canines elongated.

She screamed.

Tiny white dots filled her vision.

"...Sheri...Sheri..." As if far away, Tanen's voice echoed, growing softer as each second passed.

He held her close, and trailed his fingers over her shoulders, stroking her, caring for her. She trembled, unwilling to believe what had happened. Her pulse pounded and before she lost her nerve, she ran her tongue over her teeth—normal—the elongated canines were gone.

Had she bitten him? She glanced at his throat. His smooth skin was blemish free. Her legs gave out and she lost her balance.

Tanen caught her before she tumbled into the curtain, sweeping his arm under both of her legs. Instinctually, she wrapped her arms around his neck, holding on. He shut off the water with his knee then yanked open the curtain. The scraping of the rings against the metal rod echoed against the tile, hurting her sensitive ears. She cringed.

He stepped out of the tub and cradled her in his arms.

"P... Put me down."

He hesitated, holding her tighter. She longed to stay in his arms, but the fear-driven adrenaline coursing through her veins had her in its grip. As he set her feet on the rug, his hand remained on her waist.

She grabbed a couple of towels from the rack and shoved one into his hands. "What's happening? This is crazy..."

"Sheri..." He gripped her arm, forcing her to look at him. "We need to talk."

"Please...I can't deal with this..." She pulled on her underwear and clasped her bra. As she moved, her body ached in all the right places, reminding her of the way Tanen had made love to her. A throb built in her chest and tears blurred her vision. She couldn't stay here, not with him.

He hadn't moved, so she glanced at him. The creases in his brow tightened and his eyes, oh, his beautiful blue eyes, they tore into her, making hers prick with tears once again. She opened her mouth to speak, but her throat constricted. Swallowing the lump, she squeaked, "Get dressed...please."

He stood rigid, his face a mask of emotion.

She couldn't look at him, so she concentrated on her task.

The slight sound of rustling clothes indicated he dressed. As he pulled on his sweatpants, a small chain fell from the pocket and bounced on the rug.

The round metal disc with the letter "S" was unmistakable.

My necklace.

She inhaled.

"Sheri...I..."

A surge of adrenaline spiked through her veins. She gritted her teeth and glared at him.

"You...you...stole my necklace?" She fisted her hands at her sides, the muscles in her legs trembling, threatening to give out. "How could you?"

He raised his hand. "Sheri, please...let me explain."

A flood of emotions washed over her—anger, disappointment, sadness—and she couldn't process them. So, she'd do what she'd done before, what she'd been taught to do by her father—bury her feelings and run away.

She raced for the door, but he gripped her arm, stopping her.

"Sheri, we *need* to talk... "

"Let me go!" She pushed against him. Tiny sparks flicked from her fingers. *More static electricity?* Deep inside she knew better. She was different, altered somehow. Dizziness threatened to pull her under. This was all too much, she couldn't deal with it.

His brows furrowed and the pained look in his eyes almost broke her resolve. She swallowed, but the dry lump wouldn't go down. He's just like Ram...and my father...no good. *Sheri, you sure know how to pick 'em.*

She pulled on her inner strength and raised her chin. "I should've called the police the first time I saw you. I should do it now. Leave, before I change my mind."

He cracked his knuckles, and the tic in his jaw pulsed to life. "Sheri, you need to hear—"

"I don't want to hear another word from you!" The tense muscles in her arms and legs shook with her rage. "You like book quotes? How about this line from *The Hobbit*—'You have nice manners for a thief and a liar,' said the dragon."

He flinched, and his mouth drew into a thin line. "I shouldn't have taken your necklace, but I wanted something to remind me of you. There's more we need to discuss, though, like what's happening here, to you...and between us."

The back of her throat ached and moist, unshed tears stung her eyes. She gripped the doorknob and flung open the bathroom door. "Get out!"

A low growl filled the air. Coop stood in the hallway, his legs stiff with tension. Several short warning barks erupted from his throat.

That her pet had come to her defense solidified Sheri's decision. "Leave, Tanen, before I sic Coop on you."

Tanen's gaze flicked between her and Coop. "I'll wait outside, give you a few minutes to calm down, but we will have that conversation."

Grabbing his boots and his jacket, Tanen turned to leave. He hesitated at the door, the muscles in his shoulders and back tensing.

A moment later he was gone.

He took her heart with him.

CHAPTER 28

*A*lora pulled the heavy bag over her shoulder and a melon whacked her in the ribs. She adjusted the strap and headed up the stairs. Stars twinkled between the upper branches of the Rolmdew trees, and a strong breeze blew across Alora's cheeks. The market had been crowded tonight, patrons squeezed into the small store pushing and shoving to obtain the limited supply of fresh fruit recently imported from the Matronin colony. To obtain a melon was a treat, and Alora's chest expanded at her good fortune.

Alora's best friend, Bellamy, walked ahead, her grocery sack clutched in her arms. Her ponytail bobbed as she stepped onto the suspension platform connecting to the nearest Rolmdew tree. She glanced over her shoulder. A sly smile pulled at her lips. "You're awfully quiet. Are you still fretting over the war on Earth?"

Alora exhaled and gripped the railing, using the wooden rods to steady herself. "Yes, I can't believe I was sanctioned, again. To top it off, I had to give up one of my character species, the Ursus, to Zedron."

A sudden pang hit her in the chest. "Bellamy, remind me to visit Noeh on Earth. I need to warn him about the Ursus." To tell him his expected reinforcements now worked for the enemy would be a diffi-cult conversation.

"Sure. No problem." Bellamy adjusted her grip on her grocery sack and kept up her pace. Stray strands of hair from her ponytail whipped in the wind, as if glad to be free. "I'm sorry this has been so tough on you. What ever happened to your character-turned-traitor, Mauree?"

"She's on the loose, working with Jakar, but Tanen is hot on her heals. I didn't think he'd actually go after her given his unease of the Gossum, but his sense of self-worth is wrapped up in the scriptures. He enforces them at all costs." Alora took a deep, satisfying breath. He wasn't a warrior, but she had a certain affinity for the Stiyaha council leader.

"By the way, did you see the guy in the green tunic at the market?" Bellamy's question broke through Alora's thoughts. "Nice eyes, cute smile. We made eye contact and I about melted on the floor."

Alora suppressed a laugh. "I'm surprised you didn't hunt him down, and—"

Bellamy halted. Alora bumped into her friend. The shopping bag slid off Alora's shoulder, catching in the crook of her elbow. She placed her hand on Bellamy's arm to steady herself. "Hey, why'd you stop?"

A loud screech filled the air, echoing off the trees. The hair on the back of Alora's neck stood on end. The branches swayed in the breeze, as if they also feared the sound. A young woman on a separate plat-form several feet away stepped closer to her male companion. He wrapped his arm around her shoulder, pulling her close.

Bellamy gripped Alora's arm. "Rhondo beasts."

"Close by," Alora whispered.

Light from the hanging globes cast strange shadows on the ground below. The tree branches dancing in the breeze added to the eerie sight. Rhondo beasts were the most feared creatures on Lemuria and part of bedtime stories told to children. Their deadly claws and sharp teeth were the reason the Lemurians stayed in the trees. Visions of a similar creature, a Gossum, flared in Alora's mind. Her characters fought these abominations on a regular basis on Earth. Alora's hand tightened on the railing.

"Do you see anything?" Bellamy leaned over the edge, tilting the small walkway.

Alora gripped her friend's arm. "*Craya*, Bell, don't do that."

"I've always wanted to see a rhondo beast. Not up close, of course, but just one little peek."

"No, you don't. Keep moving." Alora gave Bellamy a gentle push.

Bellamy took a few steps forward, her ponytail bouncing back and forth with each step.

A wind gust burst through the trees and the walkway swayed.

Alora's pulse spiked. She gripped the railing.

Bellamy fell to one knee. "Ah..."

A melon, bread, and green Antorro stalks tumbled from her sack. The melon rolled between the suspension bridge's ropes and disappeared over the edge.

Caught in the breeze, the wooden span swung back and forth, gaining momentum.

Alora spread her legs apart to maintain her balance. Her bag slid off her arm and landed on the floor. She glanced at each end of the walkway, gauging the distance. They were well along the fifty foot suspension bridge. Continuing forward was the best option.

Bellamy grabbed the rail's edge, and pulled herself to a standing position. "Alora—"

A crack rent the air.

Several boards beneath their feet split apart, a weak spot in the wood giving way.

Alora's throat constricted, bottling the scream.

Bellamy's foot fell through the broken board. A shrill shriek escaped her lips.

Pops and cracks from the disintegrating wood were audible even above the wind.

Bellamy yanked her foot, but couldn't free herself from the imprisoning planks. Fear reflected in the deep lines around her eyes.

Alora took a tentative step forward and stretched out her fingers. "Bellamy, take my hand."

Bellamy's fingertips grazed against Alora's.

A low creak split the air followed by a loud snap. Splinters showered over Alora, prickling the bare skin on her arms.

The floor fell out from under Bellamy.

She disappeared through the hole.

Her scream echoed into the night.

Alora lost her balance. Her knees and palms slapped against the wooden floor. Terror sent her heartbeat thrashing through her ears. She backed up on her hands and knees, away from the hole.

A roar bubbled up from below. The sounds of flesh tearing and bones breaking echoed into the night.

"Bellamy!" Alora let out an anguished cry.

A man gripped Alora under the arms and dragged her from the walkway. When they reached the safety of the wooden platform, he released her. "Are you okay?"

"Bellamy..." she whispered.

"I'm sorry for your friend. I...couldn't save you both." Regret reflected in the depths of his brown eyes.

Alora's stomach clenched, and as she dry heaved, an ache deep inside engulfed her. *Oh, Bellamy...*

Bellamy was not the first friend she'd lost to the rhondo beasts. Mitan, her best friend since childhood had disappeared one day. His betrothed, Ophea, had found him—or what was left of him. Over the broken deck railing at his home, his dismembered arm lay on the ground below, the only evidence of his fate.

With shaky hands, Alora covered her eyes. The rhondo beasts were her worst nightmare.

CHAPTER 29

*S*aar bent to one knee and brushed his finger along the broken branch. A bit of brown material hung from the end, blowing in the soft breeze. The crescent moon peeked from behind a cloud and enough light filtered through the pines to illuminate the downed tree and the aftermath of a violent fight.

He pulled the cloth from the branch and the material ripped, a few splinters woven into the fabric. With interest, he brought the bit of clothing to his nose. Even after the fierce rain, the scent was unmistakable. *Tanen...*

"Whoever battled here didn't fare well." Revin, one of Saar's best warriors, held up the remnants of what looked like snake skin. "Gossum."

"Looks like we found Tanen, or at least evidence he was here." Saar shook his head. Seems the traitors had run into the enemy.

"Quoron, any sign of Mauree?" Saar's other warrior who'd elected to go on this recovery expedition stood several yards away. He ran his fingers over the bark of a fir tree. "Nothing yet, but I'd swear this was a knife wound."

Revin laughed. "Perhaps Tanen lost his dagger during the battle."

"Yeah, aimed...and missed!" Quoron snickered.

The warriors' taunts brought up unpleasant memories of a time when Saar had been the target of ridicule. As he pursed his lips, the scar on his face pulled tight. "That's enough. Show a little respect for our council leader."

Revin quieted, but a small smirk played at his lip. "Do you think Mauree and Tanen are still together?"

Saar pulled his toothpick out of his pocket and put it in his mouth. "I do. Despite his overt loyalty to Noeh, I've always questioned whether Tanen is as he seems."

Quoron approached Saar. "What's that supposed to mean?"

"Have you ever noticed things sometimes disappear when Tanen's around?" *Like the blue sunstone.*

"Naw, I don't know him that well. Don't sit in the same circle...you know what I mean?" Quoron winked at him.

Tanen often kept to himself, only associating with others during required events and rituals. Most of the warriors avoided the council leader. His failure to become one of their own tarnished their image of him. Besides, his arrogant knowledge of the ancient laws and scriptures didn't sit well with many of them. The old texts and the knowledge they contained were unfamiliar and foreign among the warrior ranks.

"From council leader to traitor. Seems he finally fell under Mauree's spell. He's wanted to bed her for as long as I can remember." Revin walked past Saar and started examining the ground amid some ferns.

Quoron shook his head. "She'd never take him. Been after Noeh too long."

"Seems she changed her mind." Revin waggled his eyebrows.

Saar rolled the toothpick to the other side of his mouth, but even the familiar movement couldn't calm him. "Enough. Until we find either one of them, speculating on why he left is futile."

Revin whistled. "Hey, look what I found." He held up the heel of a woman's shoe. The red painted wood gleamed even in the dim light.

Saar's pulse spiked. "Mauree's?"

Revin nodded. "Her sickly sweet rose scent is all over it."

Perfect. They were together. Now…time to track them. "If Tanen or Mauree are injured, they couldn't have gone far."

"Here are a few more bits of Tanen's jacket. Looks like he went this way." Quoron pointed down the hill.

"Excellent. Let's go." A jolt of adrenaline fueled Saar's muscles, propelling him over the small bushes and scrub brush between the dense trees. He didn't want to return empty-handed, again, and face Noeh's disappointment. A new resolve built in his chest, and he used the added energy to drive him onward.

A man-made path came into view. Saar slowed and raised his hand. "Beware. Humans."

Using his extra-sensitive hearing, he homed in on the sounds of the forest. A snake slithered between the leaves, a small rodent dug in the soft loam, and a bird chirped. The lightening sky held the first hint dawn. He clenched his teeth. They didn't have much time.

"Night is ending." Revin's skyward gaze echoed Saar's thoughts.

"We follow the path for a few minutes, see if we can find them." Saar removed the toothpick from his mouth and placed it in his pocket. "Stay alert."

Saar ran along the trail, Quoron and Revin close behind. Blood pumped through his veins and his need to complete his task flared inside.

Over the edge of a broken fence, a small, yellow house came into view. *Humans…*

To get this close only to be stopped by the threat of human intervention…so not right, but his kind had avoided humans for centuries. Saar wouldn't break that code, yet his need to capture Tanen was one he couldn't ignore. He fisted his hand.

Quoron's brow furrowed. "By the smell, Tanen and Mauree were here—recently, along with a Gossum. Neither has a chance against our enemy."

Saar raised an eyebrow. "I wouldn't make that assumption."

A squirrel ran up a nearby tree, its feet skittering on the bark. The small creature paused, its beady eyes glaring at the strangers in its territory. The animal's nose quivered before it continued to a higher branch and out of reach. Tiny squeaks and titters emerged from its mouth.

Rays from the rising sun colored the scattered clouds in shades of pink and orange.

The tense muscles in Saar's back and shoulders burned with unspent energy. Returning to the Keep without the traitors didn't sit well with him, but the brightening sky made the decision easy. He glanced at his two warriors. "We call for a portal and resume our search tomorrow."

They each nodded, but Quoron's mouth pursed and Revin rubbed the back of his neck. As they blended into the forest to find the nearest clearing, Saar peered over his shoulder at the human home. *Tomorrow, Tanen...tomorrow.*

CHAPTER 30

*T*anen paced at the edge of Sheri's property, his boots crunching over the gravel driveway. Even from several yards away, he heard Sheri moving around in her home. He glanced at her front door, willing her to open it and invite him back in so they could continue their conversation. "If I could take it all back, Sheri, I would."

His marking for honesty burned against his skin, darkening at the truth in his words. Not since he'd held her necklace while in the small shelter had the trinket crossed his mind. Not, that is, until the bauble had fallen out of his pants pocket. An ache built in his chest. As much as he regretted stealing her necklace, what really bothered him was how he'd upended her life, traumatizing her, bringing her into this war. That she was no longer human was another complication altogether. The sparks that had radiated from her hands weren't natural. Somehow, his saliva must've gotten into her bloodstream, changing her into a Dren.

Anxiety raced through his bloodstream. *She must be scared.* Given the events over the past few nights, and despite her anger toward him, how could she be anything but? Soon, she wouldn't be able to handle the sun and would need to drink blood to stave off the madness.

There was no way she'd want to go with him, not after what he'd done, but he'd find a way to convince her—or die trying. As much as he wanted to race back to her this instant, he'd give her a few minutes to calm down before he returned.

"If not for Mauree..." The muscles in his legs tensed.

The evil bitch had the sacred blue sunstone. A tendril of fear raced over his nerves, and the hair at his nape stiffened. She planned to use the crystal against Noeh at the Ostrum ceremony. He needed to warn Noeh, but he couldn't move, his legs locked firmly in place. There was no way he would leave Sheri.

Light from the impending day coated the clouds in shades of orange and red. He didn't have much time. If Sheri didn't let him in soon, he'd have to spend another day in the shed. *No...absolutely not.* With a new determination burning in his veins, he headed toward her house.

The front door opened, a creak issuing from its hinge. Sheri peered at him. Their gazes met, and her brow furrowed. Before he could speak, she bolted for her car.

A shot of adrenaline propelled him forward. He wouldn't reach her before she enclosed herself in her vehicle. Panic welled in his chest.

As he lunged past the rear bumper, the slam of her car door reverberated off the trees. He gripped the handle and pulled—locked.

Sheri looked at him through the window. Anger and fear radiated from her hazel eyes. The car's engine rumbled to life.

"Sheri, wait. Don't go—"

The car lurched, yanking him forward. He tightened his grip on the handle. Even his Lemurian speed was no match for a racing car, but he refused to let go. With blood pumping through his muscles, he ran at her side, his boots pounding on the gravel.

His breaths came hard and fast. He couldn't maintain this pace.

His fingers slipped.

As her car sped down the driveway, all he could do was watch her leave. His inner beast clawed to get free, continue the chase, but that would be pointless. A growl born of frustration burst from his lips. She was gone.

Worry tightened his chest. *Be safe, my love.*

With a quick glance into the lightening sky, he headed back the way he'd come, electing to cut through the forest instead of following the curve of the driveway. The pointy ends of tree branches pricked his face and long vines pulled at his legs, as if the Earth tried to keep him from his task.

He approached the house. Sheri's front door was wide open. Coop stood in the doorway. He barked once and wagged his tail.

"Ah, Coop. I'm glad to see you, too." Coop whined, and Tanen stroked the animal's fur. That she hadn't taken her pet was a good sign. She'd be back. "Good boy, Coop."

With the sun cresting over the horizon, Tanen had little choice but to seek shelter in Sheri's home. Hopefully, she'd return soon, and he'd get his chance to explain everything—who he was, where he lived, what she'd become. Then after sunset, he'd convince Sheri to go with him to Roan's Rock and warn Noeh about Mauree and the blue sunstone. He exhaled a long, slow breath. To wait out the sun tortured his mind. He needed something to do, anything to occupy his time.

The devastation in the living room was worse than he'd remembered. Heaviness settled over his limbs. Several long gashes marred the back of the couch. Shards of glass from a broken flower vase littered the carpet. Although Sheri had righted the coffee table, the magazines and papers were strewn throughout the room, some on the chair, some on the couch, some lying on the floor. The topper, though, was the bookcase.

It tilted against the wall, the books scattered across the floor. Her precious books. He understood her love of the treasured tomes. The skin on the back of his neck heated. *Sheri, sweet Sheri.* He couldn't change the past and how he'd ruined her life, but he'd clean up the mess. Resolve cut deep, tightening the muscles in his chest. He cracked his knuckles and started on his task.

CHAPTER 31

*M*auree trailed her fingers over the carved footboard and admired the deep green and blue pillows atop her bed. The opulence matched her old quarters at the Keep, and she let out a satisfied exhale. Still damp from her shower, a few wet hairs tickled the back of her neck. After a quick rub behind her ears, she tossed the towel onto the back of a nearby chair. The material hit the bedside table in the process, knocking a small frame to the carpet.

In the picture—a human male with a baseball cap and a quirky grin held up his hand. A large fish dangled from the end of a line. Thanks to Jakar's internet skills, seems the solitary owner had died and the place was tied up in the human legal courts. They could stay here for months without fear of discovery. Mauree curled her lip and kicked the frame under the bed. So much for the prior owner.

Mauree crossed the large room and entered the walk-in closet. She slid on a clean skirt, the hem several inches above her knees, and pulled a tight sweater over her head. Turning, she glanced into the mirror and paused before her reflection. The material formed perfectly to her well-rounded hips and ample breasts. She took a deep, satisfying breath and winked at her reflection. *Who could resist her?*

Mauree returned to her room and yanked open the drawer of the small bedside table. *Ah, the blue sunstone of legend.* The crystal pulsed with a soft glow, mesmerizing her. She couldn't resist its allure.

With attentive interest, she traced her finger over the stone's edge. The light brightened, and a careening sound buzzed in her ears. She gripped the gem, cradling it in her palm.

An unnerving warmth traveled up her arm and into her chest, fueling her bitterness and rage, deepening her desire for destruction and pain. Caught in its web, she could only stare at its beauty. A tiny scream echoed in the back of her mind. She acknowledged the cry for what it was—the loss of her soul. She didn't want to see what was in its place.

"Mauree!" Jakar's call brought her out of her trance.

The stone tumbled from her fingers and landed back in the drawer. The light extinguished, and her bitterness and rage ebbed.

"Mauree. We have company." Jakar stood in the doorway, his hands clasped behind his back. His gaze traveled over her body.

She curled her lip. "Stop staring. Who's here?"

"The Ursus and the new Gossum."

She inhaled. "How many?"

"Forty-three Gossum and thirty-one Ursus." He shrugged. "Good thing there's a few small cottages on the property."

She grabbed the stone and shoved it between her breasts. Warmth filtered along her skin, and her stomach fluttered. "Where are they?"

"Downstairs." He tilted his head. "Can't you hear them?"

She'd been so engrossed in the stone, she hadn't heard a thing. The quiet sound of chatter filtered through the doorway. She raised her chin, smiling. "Well, let's not keep them waiting."

He gestured with his hand. "After you."

She stood at the top of the circular staircase and peered at the crowd. Below, clustered in groups of three or four were her new fighters, her soldiers in this battle over Earth's water. Some sat on the cushioned couch and the recliner chairs, others congregated by the windows.

The Gossum were easy to distinguish—all male, all bald, all with black eyes. What set the Ursus apart was their muscular build. Both male and female alike had massive shoulders, thick torsos and burly arms and legs. Many were covered in thick coats made of leather or animal hide. Their dark pants and shirts seemed thin in comparison. A few had brown hair, but most had long jet-black strands that accentuated the deep brown of their eyes.

Mauree inhaled at her strong and impressive warriors. "Ah-hem."

Conversations quieted, then ceased altogether. She puffed out her chest and raised her hand. "Welcome, Gossum. Welcome, Ursus. I am Mauree, your new leader."

She wasn't sure what she'd expected, but deadly silence wasn't it. A heavy weight settled into her stomach. She narrowed her eyes. "Who is the Ursus leader?"

A large male strode forward, his dark, penetrating eyes focusing on her. By his side was a female with a gold stud over her eyebrow. "I am Arbane, and I lead the Ursus along with my mate, Entrania."

Mauree raked her gaze over him, then glanced at the female. "I suppose you'll do."

Taking her time, she sauntered down the circular staircase. As she approached, the others stepped aside.

She faced the Ursus leader and they locked eyes in a battle of wills. He narrowed his focus, and a loud rumble burst from his throat. "I must battle for Zedron, but you, I will *not* follow."

Mauree's stomach fluttered, but she held her ground, fisting her hands at her side. "Zedron placed me in charge." *...and as much as you despise my authority, you can't hurt me.* Zedron had ensured the Ursus would protect her at all costs, but she wanted to win their loyalty on her own.

He chuckled. "You think that matters to me or any of my kind?"

Shouts and murmurs of agreement raced through the group. The tension in the room electrified. Several Gossum hissed.

Mauree laughed, a long hearty chuckle.

Silence stretched on for several seconds.

With deliberate intent, she reached between her ample cleavage and removed the blue sunstone. The gem reflected in the overhead lights, but didn't illuminate.

Gossum and Ursus alike inhaled, the quick intake of breaths loud in the room. Arbane took a step back, shielding his mate.

Mauree raised the stone for all to see. "The magical blue sunstone belongs to me. Have you heard of it?"

Frantic whispers filled the air.

Entrania placed her fingers over her mouth. "H...how did you get that?"

"Irrelevant. What matters is I will use the crystal to win this war."

Arbane shook his head. "I am leader of my tribe. They follow my lead, not yours."

A male stepped behind Arbane and gripped his shoulder. "Please, brother. Not here. Wait for a better time."

Arbane shrugged off the male's hand. "Theron, enough."

Mauree clutched the stone to her breast. The crystal darkened her heart, blackening her soul, but she didn't care—not anymore. Her heartbeat sped, flushing heat through her body. The gem brightened until the glow hurt her eyes. Cries of discomfort and muffled shouts filled the large living space.

As if the stone had a will of its own, Mauree had the sudden urge to lash out, hurt Arbane. A small light burst from the stone, piercing the male in the chest. Entrania gripped his arm, and the glow engulfed them both. A moment later they disintegrated, leaving only a pile of dust.

The light extinguished.

A scream of pure anguish rent the air.

"My parents—you killed them." An Ursus female, with a long dark braid, strings of gold twisted in the plait, emerged from the group. She pressed her lips into a tight line. Her eyes blazed.

She shifted, her form growing into a large bear. The clothes she wore disappeared under dark fur and claws extended from her fingertips. A loud, pitiful roar burst from her throat. She bolted for Mauree, her thundering steps shaking the floor.

Theron stepped in her path. His strong arm gripped her around the waist, halting her progress. She strained to get around him, but the large male held her tight. "Calm yourself, Kaelyn. Patience."

The Ursus female returned to her human form, her clothes reforming to her body. Hatred burned in her eyes, but she stopped fighting against Theron's grip. She fisted her hands. "I hate you." Spittle flew from her lips.

Mauree smiled. "But you'll do as I say."

Above the sobs and wails of the Ursus, Gossum grunts echoed.

Pointed words pierced the din.

"She killed one of our own."

"Dark…evil."

Mauree's heart thudded, the black core hardening.

Theron's face reddened. "You…you…"

"Would you like some?" Mauree held up the stone.

He gritted his teeth, and his mouth pulled into a thin line.

"I didn't think so." She raised her chin and evaluated the group. "Anyone else want to question my authority?"

Only the sound of shuffling feet filled the air.

Perfect. Mauree had her new warriors, now all she needed was an opportunity.

CHAPTER 32

*S*heri peered through the windshield at the Columbia Rehabilitation Center. Angry and scared out of her mind, she'd driven without a planned destination. Anyplace to get away from the craziness that had invaded her home. Somehow, she'd ended up here, at work. Maybe her brain had been on autopilot.

Memories of Tanen flitted across her mind—his tender touch, the longing in his gaze—and her necklace falling from his pocket. A sharp jab hit her in the chest. "Damn you, Tanen."

She retrieved her phone from her purse and glanced at the screen. Her hands shook so hard she could barely read the time—8:50 a.m. Ten minutes until her shift started. All she needed was to get through the day, then she could pack and head to Seattle. Starting over in a new city was a way out of this nightmare. She held on to that thought for dear life.

She caught her reflection in the rearview mirror. Her haunted, red-rimmed, puffy eyes were the look of a stranger. Was she a vampire? Her pulse fluttered. Gingerly, she ran her tongue over her teeth. Nothing but ridges. She let loose a relieved breath. Using her fingers, she swept her hair into a tight bun and some semblance of normalcy, whatever that was anymore.

With purse in hand, she headed into her last day of work. As she rounded the building's corner, bright morning sunlight pierced her eyes. She raised her hand to shield herself from the hot, almost painful, glare. The sliding glass doors whooshed open and she stepped into the air-conditioned building. Her shoulders shook with relief.

Several staff bustled around the nurses' station, going through the daily routine of life at the rehab center. The normality seemed strange, foreign, and Sheri's vision swam. *Get a grip, Sheri.* With a quick turn, she headed for the break room.

The aroma of fresh roasted coffee filtered into her senses. A good dose of the strong elixir was what she needed. She put her purse in her locker and headed for the coffee pot. Pouring herself a cup, she took a sip. The bitterness left a sour taste in her mouth, and she dumped the rest in the sink. As the brown water drained from the cup, the remnants reminded her of the men in her life. They used her up until there was nothing left but the sludge.

"Hey, Sheri." Olivia touched her shoulder. "I hear you're moving to Seattle. Why didn't you tell me?"

Sheri turned to face her friend. "I'm sorry, Liv. Everything happened so fast—"

Olivia pulled her into a hug. "I'm sure gonna miss you, but, wow, Seattle. This sounds like a great opportunity."

Sheri's chest ached at her friend's sincerity. "I'll miss you, too. Keep me posted on your situation with Ben."

Olivia released her, and peered into her eyes. "That bastard? I try not to dwell on him, but sure, I'll keep you up-to-date. Don't worry."

The friendly banter helped calm Sheri's nerves and her muscles relaxed. "You're too much, Liv."

A mischievous smile pulled at Olivia's lips. "Hey, I've got some info you won't believe. Curious?"

Olivia's contagious smile eased some of the ache in Sheri's chest. Maybe this would help her forget about Tanen. "Sure, tell me."

"Michael's broken jaw is a lot better, and he's had a vast improvement in his speech. Blew Matt away with how far he's come in the past couple of days." Olivia winked. "Michael asked about you."

Goosebumps formed on Sheri's arm. "What did he say?"

"He was afraid you weren't coming back. We assured him you'd stop by today to say goodbye."

A lump formed in Sheri's throat and she couldn't speak, so she nodded.

Olivia gently touched her elbow. "If I didn't know any better, I'd say he has a crush on you."

Sheri shook her head. "N...no. Don't go there."

"Well, I've got to make my rounds. Fetch me before you leave, okay?" Olivia raised an eyebrow.

"Of course...and call me. Maybe you can come to the Emerald City for a visit sometime."

"I'd love that." Olivia winked once more before heading down the hall.

Sheri's stomach quivered. She didn't want to see Michael. *Gah, he's just another patient.* She pressed her lips together. Time for her rounds.

Several hours passed and after helping with the dinner rush, she looked through the dining hall's window. The late afternoon sunlight streamed through the panes, cascading a brilliant rainbow of colors onto the carpet. As she passed through the beam, the sunshine seemed a bit too warm, causing an uncomfortable tingling on her arm. She flinched and rubbed the red spot on her skin. *I didn't think it was that hot today.* A slow sigh eased from her lungs.

She picked at the skin around her finger and glanced at the clock on the wall. Its thick hands covered the large numbers—6:25 p.m. She'd avoided Michael all day. There was always another patient to visit first. Maybe that was the excuse she'd told herself. She'd even volunteered to give Mrs. Alton a sponge bath, but the time had come, and she couldn't ignore her final patient.

Steeling herself for the task, she took in a large breath and left the dining hall. As she walked down the corridor, her soft-soled shoes skated on the linoleum. A couple of her co-workers chatted at the nurse's station, but caught up in their conversation, they didn't seem to notice her. Approaching Michael's room, her stomach fluttered.

Michael sat in his bed, his eyes focused on the TV—a comedy.

Although she couldn't pick up the specific words, the laugh track cued, the contrived chortles filling the room. She stood in the doorway, taking the brief moment to evaluate her patient. His face wasn't as pale as when he'd first arrived, and he appeared relaxed, his hand gently grasping the remote.

He must've sensed her, for he glanced her way. The gleam in his eyes brightened. "Sh...Sheri."

Her scalp prickled. Putting on her best smile, she forced her feet to move. As she approached, he studied her with his intense gaze. She placed her hand on his shoulder and gave him a gentle squeeze. "How are you today, Michael?"

"G...good. Glad...to...s...see you...Sheri."

"How about we take a look at your arm, see if we can remove the bandage." She gripped the edge of the chair, pulled it close, and sat next to him. Her heartbeat raced, but she wouldn't show him her unease.

His gaze roamed her face, his crooked smile beaming. She unwound the bandage, and when her finger brushed against his skin, a small spark crackled.

He flinched.

The hair at her nape rose.

"I'm...I'm sorry, Michael. There's been a lot of static electricity in the air lately." An uneasy chuckle escaped from her, and unwilling to look at him, she focused on her task. "I hear you've kept Jason busy with your speech therapy. It's working, I can tell."

"Made...progress, yes." His deep voice skated over her nerves leaving a trail of goosebumps along her arms.

Just finish this and get out of here. She forced a smile.

"Let's see how your skin looks." As she ripped the bandage off, part of the scab came with it. A drop of blood pooled in the wound.

Sharp pain lanced through her teeth.

Blood pounded in her ears.

She pushed against the chair, her knees knocking against the armrest in her haste to stand. The muscles in her legs shook.

What's happening to me? She ran her tongue along the edge of her teeth. Sharp points. A scream bottled up in her throat. The urge to flee rippled through her.

Michael gripped her arm, surprisingly firm for a man in his condition. "Don't...r...run."

She met his gaze.

"I know...what's...h...happening to...you."

She froze. *How could he know?* Adrenaline spiked through her veins. She yanked against his hold, but he was too strong. "Nothing's happening to me. Why would you say that?"

"Sam's...Hof Brau. Eat at...S...Sam's."

Her legs trembled, and she plopped into the chair. The pounding of her heart echoed in her ears.

"Sheri, my bug...listen...t...to me."

Her heart skipped a beat. Breathing became difficult, her lungs refusing to expand. A million thoughts exploded in her mind, confusing her. "Ram?" she whispered.

His eyes lit up. "Sheri, don't...go to...S...Seattle."

Her need to flee overwhelmed her. She yanked against his grasp. He released her, and she stood once again, her legs wobbly. "How is this possible? This isn't real, none of it. I'm losing my mind."

"Not cr...crazy...you—"

She turned and bolted for the door.

Michael raised his voice. "Tanen..."

She stopped.

Her shoulders tensed. Slowly, she glanced behind her.

He frowned. "He isn't hu...man...and now...n...neither...are you."

Ram held his breath. Sheri stood in the doorway, poised to flee, her arms and legs visibly tense. At the mention of Tanen's name, she'd halted. When she'd turned to face him, he'd seen the yearning in her eyes. She cared for Tanen.

Ram's heart clenched as if she'd stabbed him with a thousand knives. He couldn't blame her for leaving their marriage, messed up psychopath that he was, but he wasn't that man anymore. For so long he'd wanted to prove to Sheri he was honorable, and here he thought he'd get a chance to win her over.

At this point, that no longer mattered. She wouldn't take him back, not now, not ever.

When the blood had pooled in his wound, her eyes had dilated, and with his old Gossum senses, he'd picked up the slight change in her scent, the tinge of something...more. She was a Dren. This male he didn't know, this Tanen, had changed her.

Fate had turned her into one of the Lemurian warriors, his old enemy, but he'd never see her that way. To him, she would always be Sheri, the love of his life. A part of him had known all along that winning her back was a long shot, but that would never happen, not now. All he'd ever wanted was to be the one to make her happy. To do that he'd have to give her up, convince her to be with Tanen. Losing to the enemy yet again in this intimate way crushed his soul, but he couldn't deny his love for Sheri. He'd do what he could to help her.

"What do you mean—I'm not human?" Her wide, disconcerting gaze bore into him.

He'd said the words on impulse, anything to prevent her from leaving. She needed to know what she faced, yet his inability to speak clearly hampered him. A ball of frustration coiled in his gut. He concentrated on his mouth, forcing his tongue and lips to bend to his will. "I...can...h...help you."

Her brows creased, her lips pursing. He recognized that look— fearless determination. *Good.* She'd need it.

The desire to touch her again, feel her warmth, caused the fingers on his good hand to twitch. He motioned for her to return to the chair. She hesitated, and he held his breath.

On unsteady feet, she approached. Instead of sitting as he'd requested, she stood alongside his bed.

He'd take what he could get.

He gripped her hand. Another small jolt of electricity raced up his arm. All Dren received a unique gift after the transformation. She seemed to have a powerful one.

"Sheriiii..." He tapped two fingers against his lips then touched his chest over his heart.

She blinked. "Ram...how is this possible?"

His chest expanded. "Sheri, love...you s...still. Go to...Tanen. He w...will help you."

"How do you know about Tanen? How could you?"

"I...know of him, his kind. You must go...to him—"

She tugged on his grip and a hot, powerful jolt of electricity rippled along his nerves, breaking their contact. The air fizzled with static electricity. A bone-chilling agony radiated from his chest into his brain, reigniting his age-old passion with pain. A shiver rang along his arms and he smiled.

She backed up until she bumped into the empty chair. "I...I have to go to Seattle."

He shook his head. "Go to...Tanen. He's your best...chance...to s...survive."

"I'm so confused."

"You...love him."

Her brow wrinkled and she bit her lip.

That was all the confirmation he needed. Tears threatened in his eyes as his love for her burned deep inside. "I...love you. Be strong, bug. Believe in...him...and yourself."

"This isn't possible. I'm human, I tell you, human! I can't handle this, not any of it." Shaking her head, she took a tentative step backward then bolted from the room.

Running when things got tough was Sheri's natural response. He knew that all too well. Ram closed his eyes and leaned his head against the pillow. A sense of detachment worked its way into his mind, relaxing his shoulders. He'd never see her again, but he'd given her the opportunity she needed to find herself, find a love that could be everlasting.

The pain in his chest expanded, pressing on his lungs. His heart skipped a beat, then another. A wild keening sound echoed in his room, the steady noise bringing a gauntlet of people.

"Call an ambulance, stat."

"I've got the chest compressions."

One of the nurses placed a mask over his face. She squeezed an attached blue-colored bag and oxygen forced its way into his lungs. Someone pressed against his chest, again and again, pumping blood through his veins. It didn't matter. The desire to live no longer burned inside. He'd accomplished his goal by putting Sheri's needs above his own, thus proving to her, and himself, he was worthy. That was all he needed. As the sounds faded, he left his broken body behind and headed to Lemuria.

CHAPTER 33

*S*aar glanced at his king, and a bead of sweat dampened the base of his neck.

"Did you find Tanen and Mauree?" Noeh's deep voice echoed through the Throne room.

Quoron shuffled his feet.

Revin coughed.

Heat radiated from the sunstones lining the chamber, and the bead of sweat rolled down Saar's back. The carved owl perched over Noeh's desk seemed to glare, as if mocking Saar for his failure.

Saar cleared his throat. "We came close—"

Noeh slammed his hand into his fist. "Close isn't good enough. We have to find that traitorous bitch."

Both Quoron and Revin took a step back, their attention focused on the stone floor.

Saar stared at his king. A niggle of worry tightened his chest. Noeh's reaction was so out of character.

"Ah, *craya*." Noeh ran his hand through his hair and leaned against his chair. The ornate wood creaked as he settled into his seat. "Quoron, Revin, leave us, please."

Quoron bowed.

"As you wish, Your Majesty." Revin glanced at Saar before both he and Quoron exited the room.

Jax closed the double doors, then stiffened. He looked at Noeh. "Oh, Your Majesty, oh, dear, not sure what to do, no, not at all. Am I to leave? Or would you rather I stay—"

"Jax—"

"I really don't—"

"Jax—"

"—know what do."

Noeh chuckled. "Jax, the day I kick you out of my chamber would be a sad day indeed. Please, stay."

The little Jixie's shoulders visibly relaxed and a smile lit up his eyes. "Oh, thank you, Your Majesty, thank you."

Noeh stood and placed his hand on Saar's shoulder. "Forgive me, my friend. With Mauree still on the loose, I'm a bit on edge."

The tension in Saar's shoulders released. "For a minute there, I thought something had happened while I was away."

Noeh raised an eyebrow. "All is fine in the Keep. Now, tell me, what of Mauree and Tanen."

"We tracked them to the outskirts of the forest...to a human home." Saar pulled a toothpick from his pocket and stuck it in his mouth. "Seems we weren't the only ones who'd found them because the place reeked of Gossum."

Noeh inhaled. "Are they dead?"

Saar met Noeh's gaze. "Not Mauree, for her trail led back into the forest. Quoron and Revin suspect that Tanen is dead."

"You don't believe that."

Saar removed the toothpick from his mouth and paced. His frustration built along with his blood pressure. "He may be injured, but I don't believe he's dead."

"Saar. Look at me when you speak." Noeh's voice was low, even.

Saar turned to face his king.

Lines formed around Noeh's eyes. "I can't read your lips with your back turned."

Saar's stomach clenched. "Forgive me, Your Majesty."

Noeh gripped Saar's shoulder. "No need to apologize, my friend. Just be aware. Now, what did you say?"

"I think Tanen may be alive. I'd like to return to the house this evening."

Noeh shook his head. "Tonight is the Ostrum ceremony. I need you to lead the warriors and provide security for the event."

Ostrum. Saar had lost track of time and forgotten about the spring ritual. A numbness crept into his veins, turning him cold. "Mauree. I still think she may show."

A tic pulsed in Noeh's jaw. "As we discussed, that is a possibility."

"I hope she does, then we will recapture her." Saar's pulse pounded, conviction winding its way into his chest.

Noeh's brow furrowed.

Saar's gut twisted into a tight knot. "Tell me your concern."

"Council members, merchants, and civilians alike will be at this ceremony. Everyone in the Keep, including Mel—" Noeh clamped his mouth shut, and the tic resumed in his jaw.

"Melissa and Anlon will be there." Saar closed his eyes on a slow exhale. He tensed and peered at his king. "You could forbid them to go, make them stay at the Keep."

Noeh snorted. "Yeah, right. Not if I care to live."

Saar's heartbeat picked up. How he envied Noeh's relationship with Melissa. He'd always wanted a mate, but he'd avoided females, or rather they'd avoided him. The familiar pull of the disfiguring scar on his cheek as he curled his lip was a stark reminder why.

"Mauree has a vendetta against me. I wouldn't put it past her to take this opportunity to attack me where it would hurt the most."

Saar straightened and raised his chin. "I will notify the warriors. Melissa, Anlon, and anyone else will be well protected." *Including you...*

Noeh's alert gaze focused on Saar. "I have no doubt of your conviction. Ensure that it is so."

Saar bowed low before his king. "As you wish, Your Majesty."

CHAPTER 34

*M*auree closed her eyes and leaned her head against the chaise lounge's soft cushion. After breakfast, she'd come out on the master bedroom's deck to relax. Smiling, she pushed up the sleeves on her robe and let the warmth of the late winter sun heat her arms. *I could get used to this.* So far, switching sides in this war had been the best move she'd ever made.

She trailed her palm over the robe's soft fabric until her fingers ran across the lump in her pocket. *Ah, the blue sunstone.*

She peeked through her lashes at her first lieutenant. Jakar sat in one of the patio deck chairs, elbows on his knees, head in his hands. His intense gaze focused on the training exercises on the massive home's lawn. Loud voices, grunts, and battle cries bubbled from the activity below.

Suddenly, he stood. He gripped the deck railing and his fingers tightened over the wood. "Hey! No claws!"

Mauree slid off the soft cushion and padded over to him in her bare feet. Her soldiers fought in pairs on the mock battlefield—Ursus versus Gossum—learning each other's strengths and weaknesses, preparing for the upcoming battle.

A rush of adrenaline left her breathless, and she patted her chest. "What's your assessment?"

"The Ursus resist our training protocols." Jakar peered at her, then returned his attention to the field. "I wish you hadn't killed their leader."

Mauree clenched her jaw, and a sharp pain radiated from the joint. "I don't regret what I did. Besides, the Ursus will come around."

Jakar's gaze tracked down her body. "What are your plans?"

A sour taste filled her mouth and she curled her lip. "The spring equinox is tonight along with the Ostrum ceremony. At nightfall, Roan's Rock will be the center of a large celebration. The Stiyaha believe it is good luck to worship Alora on this night, pray for her support, and receive encouragement in this war."

Jakar smiled, revealing his serrated teeth. "You wish to attack during the ceremony. Good choice."

Mauree fisted her hand. "Not only will the warriors be there, but many of the merchants and civilians as well. This is my best chance to get revenge on Noeh—take out the ones he cares about, prey on the innocent."

"...and I thought Ram had a black soul. You, my dear, are evil to the core."

I suppose I am. Her heart hardened, and she slapped her palm against the railing. "Noeh humiliated me in front of the entire Keep by selecting Melissa as his queen. He *will* pay."

"I shall prepare the soldiers." He bowed, his black gaze never leaving her face. The edge of his lip curled into an odd grin. "Is there anything you need?"

Mauree watched the warriors on the training field. Theron, the male that had almost challenged her lobbed a make-shift mace at a nearby Gossum. The creature spun out of the way, but not before the wooden prop beaned him on the head. Theron spread his stance, ready for another blow, the mace dangling from the chain.

The way his muscles bunched beneath his tight shirt sent a shiver over Mauree's arms. Her fingers tingled, and she had the sudden urge to run her hands over those smooth shoulders. She glanced at Jakar. "Send Theron to me."

Jakar's lips tightened. "As you wish." As he left, his long strides shook the deck with each step.

Mauree smiled and returned her attention to the training session. One female Ursus stood out, the one with the long black braid. She raised her mace and attacked, the force of her blows raining down on her opponent. Her features were drawn, her mouth set in a thin line. Mauree had killed her parents—the Ursus leaders. Her skin prickled. She'd have to watch this female.

For several minutes she studied her warriors, observing as they trained. The strength and aggression on display would come in handy in the impending battle. Noeh wasn't stupid. He'd bring warriors to the ceremony, but he had no idea of the size of her army. A shiver of delight raced over her arms.

"You called for me." Theron's low voice rumbled through her chest.

Mauree's pulse sped, and warmth spread over her skin. With a sense of giddiness she hadn't felt in a long time, she turned to face him. His brown eyes narrowed beneath his furrowed brow. He crossed his arms, his biceps bulging under the edge of his black T-shirt.

She purred in admiration. "So glad you could join me."

"What do you want?" His attention never wavered.

"The question is—what do you want?" She uncoiled the rope around her robe and slowly opened the folds, exposing her nakedness.

The muscles in his arms and shoulders visibly tensed. His focused attention roamed from her breasts to her feet before returning to her eyes. The lines around his pursed mouth indicated his distaste, but his dilated pupils said otherwise. "I'm not interested," he rasped.

She laughed, rewrapping herself in the robe. "Well, now. I like your spunk."

She tapped her finger against the side of her lip, then peered at the battlefield once again. An idea formed in her mind, and a wicked smile pulled at her lip. "Come here. I have something to show you."

He raised his chin, but didn't move.

Her smile faded. She placed her hand over her shawl's pocket. "Do I need to pull out the stone?"

A tic started at the corner of his eye.

Good, I got to him. She raised an eyebrow and crooked her finger.

He placed his hands at his sides, yet took a step forward. Anger radiated from him in waves, the heat burning straight to her core.

When he was close enough, she pointed to the warriors below. "That female warrior, the one with the braid. Kaelyn...is that her name?"

She looked at Theron. His gaze was on the female in question, a tic pulsing in his rigid jaw.

Mauree trailed her finger down his arm. "I think she'll be a fine warrior, fighting against Alora's troops. I'd hate for something to happen to her, wouldn't you?"

He turned on her faster than she thought possible, pulling her to him. One hand held her around the waist, the other gripped her throat.

A tendril of fear coiled in her chest. She pushed against him. "Let me go!"

The tendons in his neck flared and his arm shook, but he didn't squeeze her throat. His eyes widened. He released her and stepped back.

She rubbed her neck. Her skin was unharmed. *Zedron's protection... he can't hurt me.* The proof left her breathless. She smiled. "So, about Kaelyn—"

"What do you want?" His rigid body shook, and with his arms firmly at his side, his hands clenched into fists.

"I think that's obvious." She ran her fingers over his chest and down his arms, stopping to squeeze his firm biceps. "Let's go inside, shall we?"

His lips pulled into a frown, but he complied. Her chest expanded as she escorted him through the doorway into the master bedroom. *Time for a little fun.*

CHAPTER 35

*T*anen bent down on one knee, sinking into the soft carpet. One by one, he picked up Sheri's books, placing them back on the shelf. She'd had neither rhyme nor reason for her organization, and normally, that would've driven him crazy, but instead, warmth filled his chest. Her disarray and clutter were a part of her. Maybe a bit of chaos was good for the soul. Despite the niggle of worry that gnawed at his heart, a well of love for her rose inside.

Coop sat down next to Tanen and cocked his head.

Tanen stroked Coop's fur. "What do you think, boy? Are these in the right place?"

Coop barked, as if in agreement, and his tail beat against the rug.

Coop's happiness wore off on Tanen and he relaxed. As he inhaled, the scent of the aged paper reminded him of the Hall of Scriptures at the Keep. His mind wandered to the strange cuneiform writing he'd discovered on Roan's Rock and the mysteries within.

Lemuria. My homeland.
  Energy...
  Strongest...equi...

Beware blue...warp...power.
Those...spill blood...falter.
...pure of heart...stop...wrath.

What was the message? Something tickled the back of his mind. He picked up another book and ran his hand over the cover. The words on the front were meaningless, but they reminded him of an old text he'd read in the Keep when he'd looked for the scripture on treason. In the ancient text it was something about... He strained to remember, but the elusive passage teased him, the connection just out of reach. His blood pressure spiked, flaring his heartburn.

Coop nudged his nose under Tanen's elbow.

"You're a good boy, Coop." Tanen ran his palm over the dog's head and down his back. Tanen understood why some people preferred animals over human companions. Pets never judged, were loyal to a fault, and loved you no matter what. He longed for the same. Coop woofed, as if in agreement.

Sheri, come home. She'd fled in her car. Unable to slow her, he could only watch as she drove away. After everything she'd been through in the past few days she was scared, and rightfully so. He clenched his jaw. This was his fault. For a fleeting moment, he wished he'd never sought shelter in her small shed, but deep inside he knew that was a lie. In confirmation, his marking for honesty pulsed. With a quick exhale, he peered around the room.

A small book partially hidden under the couch caught his attention. He slid the work out of its hiding spot. His heart picked up speed. The small brown cover with the dragon on the front was the one Sheri had read to him—*The Hobbit.*

Burned into his memory, she'd handled her precious book with a look of reverence. With care, he riffled through the pages, remembering her sweet voice as she'd read. A page slid from between the sheets and floated to the floor. He picked it up, holding the treasured page between his fingers. A new resolve built in his chest.

He glanced to the window. The tiny glue bottle sat on the sill. A beam of morning sunshine passed through the vial, turning the adhesive a vibrant shade of green. In order to obtain it, he'd have to reach across the sunlight. Without a second thought, he headed for the window.

The warmth of the sun beat on the sill and heat resonated from the pane. The hair on his arms rose.

Coop whined.

"She's worth the pain, Coop, so worth the pain."

As his hand crossed through the sunlight, pain radiated up his arm, smoke curling from the wound. The stench of burnt flesh seared his nose. With clenched teeth, he focused on the bottle, his tie to Sheri. His fingers grazed against the glass, and he clutched the prize in his grasp. He jerked his hand back and raised the bottle in the air.

A shot of adrenaline coursed through his veins. *Success!*

Red and raw, a swath of scorched flesh marked a path across the back of his arm. With his Lemurian blood, he'd heal in a matter of hours, and the pain focused his mind.

Tanen looked at Sheri's companion. "Now, we can get started."

With the book in one hand and the glue in the other, Tanen sat at the kitchen table and fixated on his task. He glued the spine, repairing each torn and tattered page. Coop watched his every move, a soft whine easing from his throat now and then.

The consuming task didn't deter Tanen, and he noted the passage of time by the waft of sunlight as it moved across the carpet. During the day a scab formed over the burn, easing the misery to a dull throb. When he was done, he straightened the rest of the room, replacing the couch cushions, picking up every last shard of glass, and situating the papers and magazines on the shelf under the coffee table. As he assessed his handiwork, a passage from an old text filtered through his mind.

Alone at the rock that bore his name, Roan kneeled in the wet grass. "Alora, save us from ourselves. I came upon the carnage too late. We lost twenty warriors. When in the enemy's hands, the power in the blue sunstone can..."

Tanen stilled.

The passage from Roan's journal jolted his memory. While searching for the scripture on treason, he'd glossed over the small section. Unfortunately the ending was gone, the bottom of the page torn, but its meaning hit him between the eyes, and he put the pieces together. *The blue sunstone...Mauree...Roan's Rock...the Ostrum ceremony.*

A massive weight settled onto his shoulders. If Mauree could harness the power of the blue sunstone, she wouldn't just go after Noeh. She'd kill them all. *That can't happen.*

He peered out the window. Dusk settled among the trees, the waning rays of the sun showering the clouds in rich copper tones. The Ostrum ceremony would start in a few hours. Acid burned up his throat. As much as he wanted to stay, he couldn't wait any longer for Sheri to return. Every minute he delayed put the Keep and all its residents at risk. He needed to beat Mauree to Roan's Rock and warn Saar and Noeh of the danger.

He ran his hand over his lapel, tracing the engraved silver emblem. The pin defined him, but meant nothing compared to his love for his female. He took off his coat and tossed it onto the couch, where it hung precariously over the back. With both hands, he unhinged the tough clasp, removing his most treasured piece of jewelry.

The book...

He glanced at the kitchen table, where he'd left Sheri's favorite story, the one about a hobbit, a dragon, and the goodness in the human spirit. He picked up the worn paperback, placed it on the coffee table, and laid his pin on the cover.

As he headed for the door, Coop issued a short bark and followed. "No, Coop. Stay here. Take care of Sheri."

Coop tilted his head, and a short whine rumbled from his chest. A lump formed in Tanen's throat, but he forced it down. He loved Sheri like he'd never thought possible, but King Noeh and the Keep's inhabitants took precedence. *I'll come back for you, Sheri. I promise.*

When he saw her again he'd convince her to go with him, help her acclimate to her new world at the Keep. Did he think he had a chance for something more? No. He wasn't worthy, not after all the chaos and havoc he'd brought into her life. She'd never bond to him as his mate, but somewhere along the way, she'd stolen his heart, and wasn't that fitting? Before he could change his mind, he opened the door, welcomed the night, and raced to save his kind.

CHAPTER 36

*S*heri killed the motor and turned off the lights. Soft pings echoed from under the hood as the engine cooled. She gripped the steering wheel, her fingers turning white from the pressure. Leaning her forehead against the back of her hand, she closed her eyes. Her arms shook, the tremor increasing until her whole body hummed from the movement. Somehow, she'd put up a front and said goodbye to Matt before racing from the building. Lucky for her, she hadn't ended up in a ditch.

She took in several deep breaths until her muscles relaxed. This was crazy. Michael couldn't be Ram, could he? Yet, he'd known about Sam's Hof Brau, and had called her by his special term of endearment, "bug." Goosebumps raised the hairs at her nape.

The soft glow from the entry light lit up the front door and the small steps that graced the entrance to her home. When she'd left before sunrise, Tanen had raced alongside her car, running until she'd sped away. *Tanen...*

Memories of his low, husky voice, his deep blue eyes, and his endearing smile caused her chest to clench. She ran her tongue over the smooth surface of her teeth. Normal. Yet, she couldn't forget how the urge to bite him had overwhelmed her. Tears filled her eyes, blurring her vision. She hit her palm against the steering wheel, once, twice, three times.

"No. I don't believe it, any of it. I'm fine, perfectly fine." She had to reach Seattle, start her new life. Everything would work out, it must. A few rain drops pelted the windshield, and the wind rustled the nearby pines, showering her vehicle with small twigs and pinecones.

She pulled her coat collar tight around her neck and bolted from the safety of her car. As she fumbled with the key, she paused. The last time she'd done this, intruders had been inside. Her pulse quickened, but only the wind whistled in the trees.

The curtains in the front window fluttered. Coop's paws clicked against the pane, and his bark reverberated in the house. If an intruder were inside, Coop wouldn't be at the window. She let loose a stilted breath.

Gritting her teeth, she pushed open the door. Coop's nails clicked on the entryway's hard grain, and her pet nuzzled her hand. A soft chuff eased from his throat. She ran her hand through his fur, plopped her purse on the entryway table, and shoved her keys in her coat pocket.

With a quick flick of the switch, she turned on the overhead light.

Her stomach lurched. *Someone had been here.*

She took a tentative step back.

Her living room furniture was in its usual place. Against the wall, the couch seemed normal, except for the stuffing protruding from the claw-like tears in the material. The broken glass from her mantle vase no longer littered the carpet. She swallowed and looked at the bookcase.

When she'd left, the cabinet was empty, the books strewn across the floor. Hardbacks and paperbacks alike were stacked in rows, the spines in perfect alignment. She brought her hand to her mouth, stifling the sob, hope welling inside.

"Tanen?"

Only Coop's soft whine filled her empty home.

Before she could stop herself, she ran to the bookshelf and traced her fingers along the edge, admiring his work. A tear crested over her lashes and splashed onto her cheek. She glanced at the coffee table. A solitary book lay on the surface.

As she approached, an object on top of the book twinkled in the light. She blinked. *Tanen's pin.* The beautifully engraved pendant had been placed on her book so the symbol aligned with the title—*The Hobbit.*

Her throat constricted and tears threatened once again. She seized his pin and held it against her chest. He'd left his precious adornment for her, reminding her of his gentle touch, his soft kisses, and the caring way he'd listened as she'd read to him. An ache built in her chest, and she'd never felt so cherished, so loved. A tear tracked over her cheek. *I miss him...*

With shaky fingers, she picked up her favorite book, turned it over, and examined the spine. Instead of the awful split down the middle, the back was firm. She flipped open the cover and scanned through the pages. All were attached, glued together with the utmost care.

She brought the book to her lips and kissed the cover. Even through the smell of fresh glue, the slight scent of pepper permeated her senses. She collapsed to her knees, cradling the book and his pin together.

Tanen...

Warmth bubbled up in her chest. She cared for him, more than she'd been willing to admit, but with this seemingly simple gesture, the truth burned in her soul. She loved him.

He's not human...and now, neither are you. Ram's haunted words replayed in her mind. Perhaps he'd told the truth. Her throat constricted, and she struggled to catch her breath.

If not human, what was Tanen? More importantly, what was she? The veil of doubt lingered and an old, scared part of her wanted to run, flee to Seattle as she'd planned. *What do I do?*

Tanen had returned, demonstrated his love for her by cleaning her place, fixing her book, and leaving his beloved pin. She took a deep breath and straightened her spine, repairing herself the way Tanen had repaired her book.

I choose to trust him...

The words solidified, emboldening her courage, and a new resolve built inside. She needed to find Tanen, find out who and what he was, and what she'd become. Wiping the tears from her eyes, she laid the book and pin back on the table, the way she'd found them. *Where are you, Tanen?*

Absently, she started to pick at her fingernail but stopped herself. He'd never said where he'd come from. *Think, Sheri, think.* She paced between the coffee table and the bookshelf, a headache building at her temple. Out of the corner of her eye, she spotted something out of place.

The light brown material of Tanen's jacket peeked from behind the couch, the edges just visible. She ran to the sofa and slid to the soft carpet, wrapping the coat in her arms. As she inhaled, his unique scent of pepper filtered into her lungs. Her chest constricted. *I have to find him, see him again, but how?*

Coop rubbed against her shoulder and his wagging tail batted her thigh. She gave him a quick pat. "Oh, Coop, we—" Her words bottled up in her throat.

Coop was an ex-police dog, trained to track by scent. Her stomach fluttered as hope flared to life. She rubbed behind her pet's ears. "You want to find Tanen?"

As if he understood, he barked. She placed Tanen's jacket under his nose. "Get a good whiff, Coop."

He snuffed the jacket, his nose twitching back and forth. With a quick bark, he whined and wagged his tail.

"Good boy, Coop!"

She tossed the coat on the couch, and ran into the kitchen to grab a flashlight. As she headed for the front door, she caught a glimpse of herself in the entryway mirror. Strands of hair had freed themselves of her bun, sticking out at odd angles. She shook her head at the deranged woman in the mirror, but her eyes were light with hope. *Maybe I am crazy.* But she'd made up her mind—she had to find Tanen.

What about the strangers who'd wrecked her home? Would she find them, too? Despite the niggle of fear that chilled her skin, she wouldn't back down, not this time.

She hefted the flashlight and the weight comforted her, spurning her on. "C'mon, Coop."

As she opened the door, the book and pin on the table caught her attention. Her chest constricted. She couldn't leave them behind. After picking up the special objects, she placed them inside her coat pocket.

A strange sense of foreboding ran over her shoulders. She wasn't going to Seattle, not anymore. For better or worse, her life was on a different path. In the back of her mind, she wondered if she'd ever see this place again.

With one last glance around the room, she hooked Coop's leash on his collar and stroked his fur. "Let's go find Tanen, Coop. Find him, boy."

As she walked through the door, she didn't look back.

CHAPTER 37

The lightening Lemurian sky was a welcome sign, a first for Alora. She paced from the small cook stove to the windowsill and back, following the same steps at each turn. A tratee fly flew in through the window and buzzed around her head. The light in its wing set off a small glow, but even her favorite night creature couldn't bring her solace, not after what had happened to Bellamy. *Hurry, Veromé.*

The fly exited out the opening as quickly as it came. If only she could get rid of the memories so easily. The rhondo beast's roar still echoed in her mind. Her pulse quickened.

Little pixels formed in the room, taking shape. Alora's chest expanded and a sense of relief washed over her. The small dots connected until Veromé's form solidified. Alora's muscles tensed. She was eager to race into his arms.

Veromé focused on her, and his features hardened, his brow pulling low over his eyes.

Her heart stuttered. She inhaled. *What's wrong?* Then, the memory returned—the fight, the accusation, the bitterness.

Blood pounded at her temple. "You're still angry. If I was having an affair with Zedron, would I still wear this?" She raised her arm. The bracelet he'd given her for their anniversary sparkled in the light.

He glanced at her wrist. His features softened. "I don't want to fight with you. Not about him."

"Then, don't."

A chagrined smile crossed his face, and he opened his arms. "Come, my love."

She raced to him like she'd initially wanted. He wrapped his arms around her, entwining her in his embrace. As she ran her fingers through his hair, she enjoyed how the soft strands cascaded around his shoulders. Her chest expanded, tears forming in her eyes. "I've missed you, so much. Kiss me."

He drew back to study her and cradled her head in his palm. "I've never been able to resist you. How could I now?"

He brought his lips to hers, giving her a slow, tender kiss. She melted under his care, absorbing all that defined him, his taste, his scent, the commanding way he took control. All she wanted was to enjoy every touch, every moment, before she disappeared. He deepened the kiss, pulling her closer. A low moan vibrated in his chest, sending a shiver down her spine.

Her stomach fluttered, and she peered into his eyes. "Veromé..."

"Shh..." He placed his finger over her lips. "I want to look at you, burn the image of your beautiful face in my mind. So, when I work, I have my memory to keep me going."

His enforcer work... The knot in her stomach returned full force. She glanced at the floor. *Bellamy.*

"Hey, hey, what is it?" He placed his finger under her chin, bringing her gaze up to his.

She pulled away. Her chest ached at the loss of contact, but she couldn't bring herself to speak of the latest tragedy, not yet.

"Something's happened. Tell me." His commanding voice left little room for argument.

She faced him. Her eyes stung from unshed tears. "Bellamy...she's gone."

"What? How?"

"One of the wooden walkways...sh...she fell..."

"No. A rhondo beast?"

Unable to speak, she nodded.

He trailed a finger over her brow and placed a stray strand of hair behind her ear. "I'm so sorry, my love." He embraced her once again, holding her tight.

The ache in her chest eased a bit. "I miss her already."

"She was a good friend. We'll both miss her. When did this happen?"

"It occurred just after the moon crested over the sky."

"Other enforcers will already have hunted the beast."

She placed her head against his chest. "I hate that you have to delve into these incidents. I worry—"

"Shh..." He held her tighter, and the warmth of his skin reminded her of how much she missed his touch.

She clamped her mouth shut to stave off the tears.

He leaned back to look at her, then peered out the window. His brow furrowed. "I don't mean to change the subject, but we don't have much time. My father gave me the details about your sanction."

Alora's throat tightened, and she pushed against him. "I don't want to talk about Radnor or his decree."

Veromé held on. "Alora, I'm sorry I made an assumption...about you and Zedron. I let my insecurities get the better of me."

The creases around his eyes, furrowed brow, and thin, pursed lips indicted the depth of his regret. Her nerves tingled, and she couldn't help but forgive him. "Veromé, you know I can't stay mad at you."

The first rays of the morning sun crested over the horizon. She gave Veromé one last kiss before her skin tingled. Dots formed in front of her eyes, her vision pixelating as her body transported molecule by molecule to her private cell.

Veromé's eyes widened, and his voice faded with each of her heartbeats, but not before she'd captured a few of his words. "Did...tell Noeh...Ursus? Friends...turned...enemies..."

A sudden coldness enveloped her. *No, oh, no.* In her distraction over Bellamy and the rhondo beast, she'd forgotten to warn Noeh. *The Ursus are coming...*

～

Tanen crashed through the heavy underbrush. Small ferns, clover, and moss squished beneath his shoes, extra wet thanks to the recent rain shower. He raced on, letting the beast close to the surface. This gave him the energy and power to burn off some of his frustration. The devastation Mauree could do with the blue sunstone was a nightmare of gigantic proportions. His need to warn the Keep's residents of the impending danger urged him onward. *Dearest Alora, I pray I arrive in time.*

Unbidden, a memory of Sheri with her warm smile and her beautiful hazel eyes entered his mind. The way she'd made love to him, her touch part salve, part elixir, had teased him, taunted him. A heaviness crept over his shoulders. He'd brought chaos and mayhem into her life, leaving destruction, uncertainty, and fear in his wake. To make amends, he'd cleaned up her place, repaired her book and left his most precious adornment—his lapel pin. Even so, it paled in comparison to his deeds.

His stomach heaved and this time, bile came all the way up. He choked, spitting out the vile fluid, the hot taste burning the back of his throat. Maybe this was his soul's way of cleansing himself from the inside. He prayed it would be this easy.

Movement flashed out of the corner of Tanen's eye. Before he could turn to look, something sharp nicked the skin at the base of his skull. He stiffened. A trickle of blood ran down his neck.

"Don't move, Tanen. You're wanted on suspicion of treason." Saar's deep voice rumbled through his chest.

A surge of adrenaline poured into Tanen's veins. "I came to warn you—"

Saar gripped Tanen's arm and whirled him around. He placed the tip of his sword under Tanen's chin, and narrowed his gaze. "Are you threatening me?"

Tanen curled his lip. "Mauree is on her way to Roan's Rock. She's gone rogue, joining forces with Jakar. For all we know, he's enlisted some new recruits."

A loud hiss escaped Saar's lips. "So she is coming...as we anticipated. Somehow, I'm not surprised she's with the enemy. How do I know you aren't working with her?"

"I give you my word."

Saar huffed and withdrew his sword. "Show me your mark."

Tanen unbuttoned his shirt and pulled the material free, exposing his chest. His marking for honesty darkened.

Saar inhaled. "Tell me more."

Tanen's muscles relaxed. "Mauree has the blue sunstone. I believe she intends to use it against the residents of the Keep at the Ostrum ceremony."

Saar's gaze narrowed on Tanen once again. "What's your involvement?"

Tanen clenched his jaw, and his beast growled. "It's complicated, but I'm not the enemy. We don't have time to discuss this."

"You stole the stone, didn't you?"

Tanen pursed his lips. "You have no idea how much I regret what I've done."

Saar's eyes darted back and forth as he evaluated Tanen. His mouth drew into a thin line. "We need to send the civilians inside. Many of the warriors are along the territory perimeter. I'll alert them. You continue on, call for a portal, and tell the civilians the ceremony is cancelled."

"Agreed." Tanen thanked the gods the commander had seen the light.

Saar gripped Tanen's arm. "One last question. Did you release Mauree from her cell?"

"No, I did not." Tanen's marking for honesty pulsed once again, darkening.

Saar glanced at it. "That bodes well for you, but not for the traitor...the one who betrayed us all. I'll catch up with you later."

Saar disappeared into the dark forest. Tanen ran on, eager to
arrive at his destination, but he couldn't stop dread's cold fingers from
running down his spine.

CHAPTER 38

A drop of water landed on the back of Sheri's hand, reminding her of tears. The brief rain shower had ended, but a few stray droplets still dripped from the trees. Wet ferns slapped against her legs as she headed down the trail, chilling her calves. Chasing after Tanen had seemed like the right thing to do, but now, doubt quivered in her stomach. Was he really out here? Her chest tightened, squeezing the ache in her heart. *I have to find him.*

Coop strained against the leash, pulling her along. His soft chuffs, punctuated by an occasional bark, kept her moving. He seemed to have Tanen's trail, traversing along the little-used path like he knew exactly where to go. After what seemed like hours, but was perhaps a few minutes, Coop slowed. His ears pulled back. A soft whine eased from his throat.

Sheri's pulse spiked. She stopped.

With a quick glance, she scanned the area. Dark shadows penetrating between the branches were broken only by the beam from her flashlight. Her hand started to shake, and the flashlight's glow turned the trees into monsters.

Strong and powerful, an astringent smell wafted by on the wind.

A deep rumbling formed in Coop's chest and he barked, again and again. His rigid stance and forceful display raised the hair on the back of her neck.

Strange, guttural grunts filled the air. The muscles in her shoulders tensed.

The branches of a nearby pine rustled. A bald man wearing a pair of jeans, a dark T-shirt, and a blue bandana around his throat crept onto the path. Even in the dimness, his dark orbs reflected the moonlight.

A scream threatened to break free, yet, at the same time, an unfamiliar urge to fight him, beat him at his own game flared to life. Where the impulse came from she wasn't sure, but she held on to it, using the energy to fuel her courage.

Coop strained against the leash, his front paws leaving the ground with each tug. His barks echoed between the trees.

From among the bushes another man stepped forward, one she recognized—the guy who'd ransacked her home—Jakar. He hissed and his long, barbed tongue snapped dangerously close to her face.

The scream she'd held in erupted from her throat. Coop's barking increased into a frenzy. She couldn't hold him any longer. Her pet yanked free and raced toward the bald man with the bandana. Her companion attacked, sinking his teeth into the man's leg. The man's fingernails turned into claws, scraping through Coop's fur.

"No!" Her chest constricted. Before she could think, she ran toward her beloved pet.

Jakar jumped in her path. "Who do we have here?"

She stopped. Blood pounded through her veins, feeding her anger and keeping her fear at bay. Over Jakar's shoulder, Coop bit into the creature's flank. The evil beast screamed.

Sheri focused on her opponent. Jakar's nostrils flared, as if he were reading her scent. "You, again. Though, this time, you're no longer human, you're...Dren." Jakar's mouth pulled into a grin.

A short pained whine tore through the trees. Coop sailed through the air, landing in the soft moss at the base of a nearby fir, motionless.

"Coop!" Sheri's blood boiled. Energy, hot and fast, built in her chest, growing in intensity with each heartbeat. Sparks pulsed from her fingers.

Jakar focused on her hands, his smile fading from his lips.

With all the rage she could muster, she ran at him. She clutched his biceps, her fingers tingling with energy. Little lightning bolts of electricity visibly trailed down his arms. A burst of light lit up the darkness. His scream pierced the night.

I'm...no longer human. What little doubt she had left was laid to rest. She couldn't ignore what she'd done.

With a quick turn, she faced his companion.

The evil beast sprinted toward her. His tongue whipped in and out of his mouth. She dodged, and the barbed tip snapped next to her shoulder. Spittle, sticky and warm, landed on her cheek. A sour tang ran up her throat.

He pulled her into his grasp, and his claws bit through her coat, piercing her shoulder. A ball of pain ripped through her and her heart thrummed, as if it were about to explode. Long trails of energy snaked from her fingertips, enveloping her and the unearthly being. He screamed. The deafening sound skated over her nerves.

His grip loosened, releasing her. With his mouth extending into a silent scream, he slumped to the ground into a pile of black sludge.

She placed her hands over her mouth, holding in her scream. How could any of this be real? But she couldn't ignore what she'd seen with her own eyes...what she'd done with her own hands.

Coop...

She glanced toward the tree.

He was gone.

She inhaled, fighting the fear coiling inside.

Creature after creature descended from the trees. Their dark eyes bore into her.

"Halt. Don't attack." Jakar emerged onto the path, Coop's limp form in his arms.

Her heart stuttered. "What did you do to him?"

Jakar curled his lip. Unmistakable red welts marred his biceps where she'd touched him. "Your pet is still alive and will remain so, as long as you cooperate."

A tendril of fear snaked its way into her heart. She couldn't speak, couldn't move.

"You love your little friend, don't you?" His tongue lashed out, snapping in the air.

She struggled to believe this was happening, yet, somehow, she knew this was as real as it came. "Wh...what do you want?"

"Well, your assistance, of course." His mouth curved into an evil grin. "You have a mighty fine gift. One that would come in handy in our little war."

"N...no." Her fingers trembled, so she curled her fist. She wouldn't show him her fear.

"I guess you don't care for him as much as I thought." Jakar opened his mouth, displaying his serrated teeth. Saliva dripped off the end of one long tooth, glistening as it fell.

"Wait!" She hated herself for giving in so quickly, but she couldn't let anything happen to Coop.

"Ah, that's better." He smiled, handed Coop to one of his cohorts, and nodded down the path. "You first. I'm with the scouting party, but the rest of my kind isn't far away." His dark eyes gleamed in the light.

Seems she didn't have a choice. She raised her chin and headed along the path. *Tanen, where are you?*

Not a minute later, two large males and a female strode onto the path. They were different from the others with bulky frames and dark hair. Mauree ran her hand over one of the male's biceps. The muscles in his shoulders tensed, and he crossed his arms. Mauree chuckled, and her attention focused on Sheri.

Sheri's jaw tightened as hatred, deep and powerful, welled from an unknown source, pushing away her fear.

Jakar shoved her forward. "Look what I found. She's a Dren now. Seems Tanen must've changed her."

Mauree snorted. "The only way that could've happened is if he got his saliva into an open wound. He wouldn't dare."

Sheri's mind reeled. *Three times the charm.* She'd bitten her cheek leaving the tissue raw and sore. Tanen had kissed her. A knot formed in her stomach.

"Why did you bring her here?" Mauree walked around Sheri, her gaze raking over her from head to foot.

Jakar tsked. "She has value. Killed one of my scouts…electrocuted him with her touch."

"What do you propose to do with her? If she's like any of the others, she'll need to feed, need to drink blood or go crazy. Melissa struggled with that when she came to the Keep and stole Noeh from…" Mauree's features hardened, and a tic formed in her jaw.

A Dren. Is that a vampire? A scream threatened, but Sheri swallowed the shriek before it could escape her lips. Pulling on her newfound strength, she raised her chin. At least there was someone else like her, this Melissa. Maybe she'd get the chance to meet her…if she survived.

Jakar shrugged. "I hadn't planned to keep her that long. Only want to see if there's a way to steal her power."

"You're no Ram." Mauree's clipped words echoed off the trees.

Sheri inhaled. The words tumbled from her lips before she could stop them. "Ram? You know my ex-husband?" How many Rams were out there in this world? It had to be him. That he'd somehow been a part of this sent a chill down her spine.

Jakar's gaze focused on her. "What's your name?"

She clamped her jaw shut and pursed her lips.

He raised an eyebrow. "It wouldn't be Sheri, would it?"

She tried to maintain her composure, but couldn't hide the slight flinch.

Jakar's smile revealed his serrated teeth. "Isn't that interesting…he wanted so much to reconnect with you."

Mauree waved her fingers. "Enough. This is a waste of time."

Heat flushed through Sheri, and the urge to fight, to hurt these creatures welled inside. Sparks flared from her fingertips.

Jakar raised his finger, and a long pointy nail extended from the tip. He wagged the gruesome digit in her face. "None of that, now. Remember, we've got your dog." He glanced at Mauree. "See, that's a taste of her power."

Mauree tapped her finger next to her lip, and studied Sheri. "Since we're almost there, you might as well bring her along. Once we win this battle, you can do with her as you please. If she gets in the way, kill her."

Mauree proceeded along the path. The woods teemed with the enemy, all following their leader. A snapped twig here and there, low whispers, and a few brief shadows foretold of the army marching through the forest. To where?

Jakar pushed her forward, and her fingers sparked again. She wanted to wrap her hands around his throat and give him a good dose of her anger. Her throat constricted. What were the chances she'd survive? Slim at best, but she wouldn't go down without a fight. If the opportunity arose, she'd grab Coop and run.

CHAPTER 39

anen approached the clearing, his ragged breaths heaving in and out of his lungs. Standing next to a large pine, he grabbed the bough's rough bark and peered between the branches. Sunstones encased in wrought-iron lanterns hung from poles spaced throughout the meadow. Light from the gems glowed through the trees, creating strange dance partners among the shadows.

Roan's Rock sat at the edge of the meadow, its surface pockmarked from weathering and age. Males and females, from merchants to council members, circled the giant boulder. Familiar faces appeared amid the throng—Noeh, Melissa, Anlon, and many others. An elder female, Chianne, with her hair wrapped in a bright yellow scarf, strode toward the rock carrying a small bowl of filberts. She scooped up a handful of nuts and tossed them onto a flat area of the stone, a tribute to Alora. Tanen's chest constricted. *The ceremony has already started.*

A slight breeze blew across Tanen's cheeks. The stench of Gossum, and an unusual, earthy scent filled his lungs. Taking a deep breath through his nose, he analyzed the smell. The new odor reminded him of bears, but had the underlying aroma of one of his kind. In one of the ancient texts, he'd read about some of the other Lemurian species.

Tanen's gut tightened. *Ursus... Were they friend or foe?* Another opponent in the war wasn't what his side needed. If anything, the Keep could use reinforcements. He gritted his teeth.

Focusing his mind, Tanen reached for the connection to the Keep. *Rin, open a portal.* He didn't wait for an answer and ran into the clearing. "Attention! Listen up!"

Nervous murmurs bubbled from the crowd, and several participants turned to look his way. The energy from the group heated and shouts of "Tanen" and "traitor" rose in the air.

Tanen raised his chin. "The ceremony is over. I've called for a portal. Return to the Keep."

Noeh stepped away from the mob. His face was drawn, his brow furrowed. His gaze focused on Tanen. "Explain yourself."

Tanen's pulse raced. He gave a quick bow. "Your Majesty, it's not safe here. Mauree is on her way and she has the blue sunstone. I ran into Saar. He knows of the danger. Everyone must return to the Keep."

Noeh studied Tanen for a long moment. After what seemed like an eternity, he turned to the crowd. "Do as Tanen requests." His voice boomed across the clearing.

Noeh hadn't called him "Council Leader." It was a good indication of Tanen's demise, but he couldn't worry about that. Getting the Keep's residents to safety was all that mattered.

Mist formed in the grass, coalescing, solidifying until the rough stone walls of the Portal Navigation Center appeared. Rin, the Keep's Portal Navigator, stood over the *porte stanen*, his fingers swirling over the central keystone. He met Tanen's gaze. "I din't believe it when I got yer call. What are ya doing here?"

"Long story, Rin."

A shrill whistle pierced the air. The warrior signal for danger.

Tanen motioned a group of civilians toward the gateway. "Hurry, one at a time. As fast as you can!"

Screeee. The battle cry from one of the warrior's swords swirled through the trees. The clashing of metal, feral grunts, and shouts followed close behind.

Screams rose from the mob. In a panic, several males and females ran for the portal.

Chianne fell, her hands and knees skidding on the wet grass. The male at her side gripped her under the arms to pull her up, but others pushed him down in their efforts to flee. In a matter of moments, the couple would be trampled by the crowd. Fear sent adrenaline into Tanen's bloodstream, fueling his muscles.

He raced into the melee and gripped Chianne around the waist. With a quick tug, he pulled her to safety, a few feet from the racing horde. Her soft sobs built into a loud cry. "Liam!"

Just visible between the fleeing resident, the male scrambled on his hands and knees. Someone's boot smashed his fingers into the soft loam, and someone else's knee banged against his ear. He stopped his forward momentum, as if stunned from the impact. Tanen's pulse raced. He thrust his way into the crowd and gripped the male's arm, pulling him to a standing position. With determined effort, Tanen pushed their way free, away from the melee.

Chianne wrapped her arms around Liam and glanced at Tanen. Her tear-streaked eyes held his gaze. "Thank you."

"Hurry, into the Keep, now." He ushered them along, toward the portal.

The astringent smell of Gossum intensified.

A male merchant screamed, his eyes wide with terror. The group surged forward and pressed those in front against each other. Panicked cries rang into the night and reverberated off the trees. The horde encircled Tanen, dragging him toward the portal.

"No!" Tanen fought the crowd. His need to capture Mauree and return her to the Keep to face her sentence, burned deep inside. He broke through a small gap and escaped the fleeing mob.

As he scanned the edge of the forest, his target stepped from the shadow of a large fir. Their gazes met. An insolent smile broke across her face, and she withdrew the sacred sunstone from her coat pocket. A blue glow lit up the surrounding area. "Hello, Tanen. Thank you, again, for this lovely gift. Now, you can reap what you sowed."

Tanen's pulse beat loud in his ears. He'd never imagined his compulsion to steal the blue sunstone from Noeh's desk could wreak such havoc.

CHAPTER 40

Shrill cries and shouts from the fleeing crowd competed with the drum of pounding feet, squeezing the air from Tanen's lungs. He focused on Mauree and the blue sunstone in her palm. Two large, imposing males kept close, their mouths drawn into thin lines, brows furrowed. Much bigger and heavier than the Gossum, they were the Ursus he'd scented earlier.

Craya! He hoped the Ursus were allies. Between the Gossum and the Ursus, it seemed Mauree had amassed her own army.

Mauree approached Roan's Rock and, with her free hand, picked up a rose someone had laid down as a tribute to Alora. A self-assured grin spread across her face. "Ah, roses, such a sweet, alluring scent. Don't you think so, Tanen?"

"The smell makes me sick—just like you." How she'd ended up with such a scent was an irony that didn't escape him.

She smiled, that wicked, sensual grin which used to raise his pulse with want. "And here I thought you had a crush on me. Well, too bad, dear Tanen. I have a better option." In a sensual tease, she traced her fingers over the arm of one of the males at her side. The skin around his eyes flinched at her touch.

192

Her focus returned to Tanen. "Seems like females always dump you, don't they?"

His marking for tenacity pulsed against his chest, and he pulled on the force, letting it build. His hand fisted at his side.

Gossum after Gossum and more of the large, hefty males, as well as a few females emerged from the trees, surrounding the far side of Roan's Rock. Mauree searched the mob. Her gaze pinpointed its target and a sinister grin formed on her lips. "Look...Noeh! Bring him to me."

A low, long whistle pierced the air.

Saar and a group of warriors, both Stiyaha and Panthera, raced from the pines. They flanked the fleeing civilians, placing a barrier between Mauree and the residents of the Keep.

"Attack! Attack!" Saar's words reverberated against the trees.

The two groups merged into one giant mass of clashing bodies, weapons glinting and claws gleaming.

A Gossum jumped onto a Panthera's back, gouging its claws over the panther's hide. Blood pooled in the welts. The nearest Stiyaha warrior stabbed the beast with his sword, and the creature disintegrated into a pile of sludge.

Several of Mauree's large males and females transformed into bears, their clothes disappearing underneath their fur. Long, sharp claws extended from their paws.

As fury built in his chest, Tanen let loose a growl. He pulled his dagger from his pocket.

A Gossum landed on his back, knocking him to the ground. Tanen rolled, using the Gossum's own momentum. Over and over, they tumbled through the grass and small pebbles that littered the clearing until they crashed into a large boulder.

The creature's grip loosened.

Tanen scrambled to a standing position, his dagger in his grip. His enemy struggled but couldn't get up. Stark-white and jagged, broken bone protruded through the Gossum's pant leg. The creature's scream filled the air.

Over the Gossum's bitter tang, the scent of fresh linen and lime infiltrated Tanen's senses.

The muscles in his back and arms tensed. *Sheri...*

He glanced in the direction of her scent. She stood near the base of Roan's Rock. Jakar held her hands behind her back. Coop lay at her feet—limp, lifeless.

Mauree raised the blue sunstone and the crystal radiated an iridescent light over the clearing. A shrill cackle eased from her mouth, drowning out the terrified screams from the remaining crowd.

Even as the battle raged around them, Tanen met Sheri's gaze. Although fear glinted in her eyes, she held up her chin, strength radiating from her pursed lips.

The urgency to get to his female became an overwhelming, driving need. His beast roared, eager to fight, kill, protect. The urge to change rippled over his skin. Synapses in his brain sparked, and the strands to his beast teased his psyche. Although he wanted to release his inner beast, brawn wasn't the answer. He needed to outsmart Mauree.

Instinctively, his beast growled, as if in agreement—this time.

Having rolled some distance away from the main battle, other than Sheri, no one seemed to notice him. With nothing but his dagger and his wits, Tanen stole into the forest.

Saar evaluated the scene, and his mouth went dry. Several yards away, at the far end of the clearing, an orange glow radiated around the opening to the portal. Inside, Rin swirled his hands over the central keystone and the sunstones that powered the gateway. At the back of the surging crowd, a male merchant pushed against a female, urging her forward. Since only one or two could fit through the opening at a time, the threat of attack had caused a panic among the mob. Screams and cries melded with the grunts and clashes of battle.

Nearby several warriors fought a horde of Gossum. For the moment, the soldiers held the brood at bay, but that wouldn't last long. Saar tightened his grip on his sword, his need to protect the Keep and all her inhabitants spurning him into action.

An unfamiliar scent wafted by on the breeze and a movement at the edge of the forest caught his attention. Out of the trees emerged a group of males and females. Tall and muscular, their dark hair blended well with their clothing. Were the new arrivals friend or foe?

One female stood out from the rest, her ebony hair tied in a long braid, bits of gold shimmering between the strands. As she evaluated the scene, her hazel-green eyes sparked with marked intelligence. She glanced at Saar and his breath bottled up inside. It was as if she could see into his soul.

One large male pulled a mace from a loop on his belt. Hanging from the end, the menacing spiked ball glinted dangerously. With a loud bellow, he raised the weapon into the air. The group charged, and the leader attacked one of Saar's males, his mace clashing against the warrior's sword.

Adrenaline surged through Saar's veins. He raised his sword and his weapon issued a long warlike screech. Before he could reach the enemy, the cry of a small babe pierced the air.

Saar's blood ran cold. *Prince Anlon.*

Saar turned toward the sound.

Queen Melissa, with the young prince in her arms, ushered the diminishing crowd of civilians toward the portal. Saar's gut clenched. If anything happened to either of them, he couldn't live with himself.

The muscles in his shoulders tensed. *Where's Noeh?*

"Don't panic. Keep calm!" Noeh's disheveled hair and the harried lines in his face affirmed Saar's fears. He helped an elderly female through the portal, then gripped Melissa's arm.

Saar sprinted toward his king. "Let me assist."

Too focused on helping Melissa and their son, Noeh didn't respond. The queen and the prince disappeared through the portal, now safe within the walls of the Keep.

Saar's throat tightened. *He doesn't hear me.*

Saar gripped Noeh's wrist, forcing the king to look at him. "Your Majesty, return to the Keep."

Noeh sneered and pulled his dagger from his waistband. "I will fight against our enemy."

Saar pursed his lips. "As your Commander of Arms, my responsibility is to protect *everyone* in the Keep, including you."

If Saar didn't know Noeh so well, he would've missed the small flinch under his eye. A pang of regret twisted inside Saar. He placed his palm on the king's chest. "Noeh, we need your guidance more than we need your battle skills."

Noeh's gaze bore into Saar, his eyes flitting back and forth. He exhaled and wiped his hand through his hair. The look of acceptance on Noeh's face pierced Saar's heart deeper than any sword.

Noeh squeezed Saar's shoulder. "Lead them well, my friend. Report to me when you return." He sheathed his dagger, glanced at the battle raging in the clearing, then jumped through the portal. No other civilians remained.

Saar exhaled. With the king in the safety of the Keep, he faced his enemy and ran into the fray.

CHAPTER 41

The blue sunstone warmed Mauree's palm, tingling her fingers with its energy. Situated at the north end of the clearing, Roan's Rock was the perfect observation point. The steady rise in elevation gave her a bird's eye view of the activity below. Her soldiers battled in the meadow, mace against sword, fist against flesh, tooth against claw. Gossum grunts echoed through the trees, the ominous sound was music to her ears.

Her soldiers advanced against the Stiyaha warriors and their partners, the Panthera. One of the large cats slashed its claws down a Gossum's back, shredding his skin. He retaliated, hitting the panther in the shoulder with his barbed tongue. The feline snarled, teeth bared, but the venom worked fast, and the cat developed a pronounced limp. Another Gossum joined in the attack, and the cat didn't stand a chance. Mauree smiled. Revenge tasted better with a little retribution.

Even though her soldiers advanced on the meadow, her enemies held off the attack, keeping her fighters from reaching the civilians—and Noeh. Mauree clenched her teeth. Noeh deserved to die for imposing the death sentence on her. Not that the punishment wasn't warranted, but all she'd ever wanted was to become queen. Her chest constricted, her heart hardening into something unrecognizable.

The portal entrance glowed a vibrant orange and the last straggling civilians, including Melissa and her son jumped through the entrance. Noeh stood next to Saar, his hand on his shoulder. He looked at her, his features hardening, then he turned and...

The muscles in Mauree's shoulders tensed.

"Don't let Noeh get away!" The bitter words carried across the clearing, but he was already gone. "No!"

Heat flushed through her chest, up her neck, and into her cheeks. She clutched the blue sunstone tighter, and as her anger overflowed, she slammed her fist against Roan's Rock.

Pain ricocheted up her arm. She couldn't move, the blue sunstone riveted in place by some unknown force. A low pulse beat through Roan's Rock, slow at first, then expanding with each second. The vibrations built until she quivered so hard her vision blurred. A bright light burst through tiny cracks in the boulder's surface, sending a blue glow over the entire meadow.

The tremors ceased.

Mauree's ragged breaths came in great heaves.

In her hand, the blue sunstone pulsed, beating in rhythm with the glow emanating from Roan's Rock.

Screams and cries of terror emerged from the battle. Encased in a blue glow, Stiyaha and Panthera warriors writhed in apparent agony. Mauree focused on Saar. His mouth contorted into an odd grimace, and his sword slipped to the ground. Close by a Panthera lay on its side with its teeth bared. A high-pitched scream issued from its mouth.

All around, Mauree's recruits appeared unaffected and recovered from their momentary shock. A Gossum stung a Stiyaha on the leg, and an Ursus slashed its claw over a Panthera's chest.

"Yes," she screamed, "defeat them! Kill them!" If she couldn't get her revenge on Noeh directly, she'd do the next best thing—take out his warriors—the Keep's protectors. The cries of the injured never sounded so good.

A chuckle bubbled up from somewhere deep inside. She let it build until it warped into a shrill scream. Somewhere in the back of her mind, a little girl, a remnant of her past, hid deep in her soul, afraid of what she'd become.

When the laugh subsided, she peered toward Noeh's escape route. Only the edge of the forest was visible at the end of the clearing. The portal was gone.

Saar reached for his sword, and even through the battle cries, his words reached her ears.

"Sword, come...to...me." His precious sword, his valiant companion, his most important weapon, scooted slowly across the grass. He gripped the weapon in his hand, but his movements were slow, lethargic.

A sense of euphoria spread through Mauree's chest. Hampered by the blue glow and under fire from her soldiers, it was only a matter of time before she secured her first victory.

CHAPTER 42

*C*rouched behind a large pine, Tanen peered around the rough bark. He tightened his grip on his dagger, and his fingers ached from the pressure. Sheri was in Jakar's grasp, her hands held tight behind her back. Heat flushed through Tanen's body, fueling his anger. He inched closer, until he was within striking distance.

"Don't let Noeh get away. No!" Mauree raised the blue sunstone and brought the sacred crystal down upon Roan's Rock. A steady pulse rocked the ground, increasing in intensity and speed. The vibration travelled up Tanen's legs, and he gripped a nearby pine for support.

A blinding blue light burst from Roan's Rock. Tanen shielded his eyes.

Agonized screams rent the air.

Tanen's pulse raced. *The blue sunstone...he was too late.*

He looked over his arm. Mauree held the sacred crystal against Roan's Rock. From cracks in the giant boulder, the blue glow suffused through the meadow, connecting the Stiyaha and Panthera warriors. All writhed in agony, their movements pained, sluggish. The Ursus and Gossum appeared impervious to the sunstone's rays. How could this be?

"Defeat them! Kill them!" Mauree's staccato voice echoed over the warrior's screams.

Her soldiers attacked with renewed vigor. The agonized howls intensified.

Tanen's gut clenched. His female was in the hands of his enemy, and his friends were under attack by Mauree's soldiers. *Why am I not affected?* Something in the back of his mind tickled his brain. What was the connection?

Images of ancient texts flew past his mind's eye. He closed his eyes and gave in to the vision—filtering, searching, looking for the relationship. The inscription on Roan's Rock played across his memory.

Lemuria. My homeland.
   Energy...
   Strongest...equi...
   Beware blue...warps...power.
   Those...spill blood...falter.
   ...pure of heart...stop...wrath.

He focused on the words, willing himself to make sense of it all. His marking for prudence, and the wisdom it represented, burned against his chest. Like a puzzle finally put together, the words melded, coalescing in his brain, and he filled in the gaps.

The energy from the blue sunstone is strongest at the equinoxes. *The Ostrum ceremony.*

Beware, the blue sunstone can warp power. *Mauree's evil nature.*

Those that spill blood shall falter. *The warriors... I haven't killed, that's why I'm not affected.*

Only one pure of heart can stop evil's wrath. *Sheri...*

A lump formed in his throat. Sheri was the key, their only hope to stop Mauree. Jakar still held Sheri in his grasp. Her attention was on the battle, anger radiating in her tight lips and tense shoulders. Tanen's chest swelled as respect for her burned inside.

Mauree held the sunstone against Roan's Rock, fueling the energy pulsing from the boulder. A couple of Ursus warriors graced her side.

None of them saw Tanen. He still had an advantage. Using the stealth tactics he'd learned in his warrior training sessions long ago, he closed the distance.

Mauree smiled and pointed to her two soldiers. "You two, go have some fun."

One of the male Ursus frowned, and he looked at his companion, before returning his gaze to Mauree. "If you insist."

"Oh, I do. Carry on, now." Mauree's cackle skated over Tanen's nerves, and he tightened his grip on his dagger.

All that remained...Jakar. *He won't defeat me this time.* The muscles in his legs tightened, and he launched himself at his enemy.

He bowled into Jakar, knocking both him and Sheri to the ground. Gravel scraped over Tanen's arms, digging into his flesh. The smell of his own blood filtered into his nose. He didn't care. There was only one thing on his mind. *Sheri...*

Tanen met Sheri's gaze. Relief radiated from her eyes, and the muscles in her arms visibly shook. His chest expanded as love for his female tore through him, shredding him on the inside.

A long, slow hiss eased from Jakar's mouth. His claws bit into Tanen's shoulder, pain filtering along the nerves. Tanen clenched his jaw, and all the years of criticism and ridicule over never becoming a warrior bubbled to the surface.

He slashed with his dagger, connecting with Jakar's arm. A loud shriek burst from the creature's lips, and he loosened his hold.

"Kill him." Mauree's shrill command pierced the air.

Only one pure of heart can stop evil's wrath. "Sheri, pull on your energy. Touch Roan's Rock...the boulder...stop the light."

Tanen gripped Jakar's shoulders, keeping him at bay. The barbed tip of the Gossum's tongue snaked by Tanen's ear. Spittle landed on his cheek.

Sheri's brow furrowed. "What?"

Tanen punched Jakar in the mouth, and the crunching sound bolstered his resolve. He peered at Sheri, love for her swelling his heart. Her favorite quote from her book, the one about courage and wisdom, spilled from his lips. "There is more in you of good than you know, child of the kindly West."

She blinked. A flash of understanding crossed her features.

Jakar broke Tanen's hold and he opened his jaw wide, aiming for Tanen's throat. The scales at the base of his neck flared. Tanen thrust upward with his dagger, through Jakar's scales, severing his spinal cord. Jakar stiffened. A weak hiss, like a deflated bag, escaped his lips. His black eyes dulled, and he slumped to the ground, turning to black slime.

The muscles in Tanen's entire body stiffened. Pain radiated in every corner of his being as if his nerves were on fire. The world turned a bright shade of blue. He'd killed Jakar, and in defeating his enemy, he'd become…a warrior.

I'm caught in the light.

CHAPTER 43

Sheri's heart pounded. The blue light surrounded Tanen, his arms and legs rigid. She cried out, fear for him squeezing her chest. *Touch Roan's Rock...the boulder...stop the light.* With a quick twist, she faced Mauree.

Mauree's confident smile burned a hole through Sheri. Deep inside, a well of energy built, the force so strong, white spots formed in her eyes. She focused on the energy, harnessing it, channeling it down her arms. After pushing against the ground, she launched herself at the boulder.

Mauree kicked her in the ribs, halting her progression. Pain radiated through her chest. Her lungs wouldn't work, and she couldn't pull in a breath. Unable to maintain her balance, she stumbled. Her knees hit the ground so hard her teeth chattered.

"You think you can stop me? Think again, little girl. You're not getting near Roan's Rock."

"Hurry, Sheri." Tanen's ragged breaths sent a chill along the back of Sheri's neck.

Coop whined.

Out of the corner of her vision, Sheri caught a glimpse of her pet. He raised his head, and his front legs twitched. A pang hit her in the chest. Of all the evil things to do, purposefully hurting an animal had to be one of the worst.

A fleeting impulse to grab Coop and run flitted over her nerves, but the thought was distant and didn't hold the same power over her it once did. *I'm not like my father.* She loved Tanen enough to fight for him, believe in him, as well as, believe in herself. If she could help Tanen and his people, then Coop would be fine, too.

There is more in you of good than you know, child of the kindly West. Tanen's words filtered into her heart. She rose to her feet. Sparks pulsed from her fingertips.

Mauree's eyes widened.

Sheri scrunched her brow.

Refocusing her energy, Sheri ran toward Roan's Rock. She plowed into Mauree, knocking them both against the boulder. With one hand holding the blue sunstone to the rock, Mauree struggled to keep Sheri away. Energy, warm and pure, traveled down Sheri's arms. As her hands touched the boulder's rough surface, the blue light wavered.

A loud rumble emanated from Roan's Rock. The ground shook. Pebbles rained from the rock's peak. Several pelted Sheri's shoulders and arms.

She glanced at Tanen. Even through his torment, his love for her radiated from his eyes. Her chest expanded and a wave of energy built deep inside. She pulled on his love and forced the energy down her arms. A pure, white light burst from her fingertips.

The blast of energy dislodged Mauree from the boulder, flinging her through the air. Her scream echoed into the night as she disappeared into the forest.

Little lightning bolts traveled around the rock, faster and faster, until the energy covered the entire surface of Roan's Rock. A loud hum rumbled from the boulder, growing in intensity as each second passed. The intense vibration shook Sheri to her bones, sending pain along her nerves. When she didn't think she could take anymore, the blue light extinguished. Darkness filled the void, only punctuated by the moon's soft glow.

An eerie silence filled the night followed by a soft moan, a cough, muffled voices.

A cheer rose from the meadow, and the sound of swords clashing echoed through the trees. By shutting off the light emitting from Roan's Rock, she'd freed the warriors. The blue sunstone lay among the rubble at Sheri's feet. She picked it up and caught her breath. *I did it.*

With a quick glance, she met Tanen's gaze. His sly smile built into a grin. "Sheri..."

She raced into his arms, and his warm embrace was where she belonged. As he leaned back, he studied her. "Are you injured, my love?"

Something in her stomach fluttered at his term of endearment, and tears welled in her eyes. He loved her, and she loved him in return. With her throat tight she couldn't speak, so she shook her head.

The tension lines around his eyes eased. "Thank the gods. How did you end up here? With Jakar?"

"I had to find you. We ran across Jakar, and Coop was injured. He used that to capture me."

"Why did you come after me?"

With a hitch in her throat, she choked out the words. "You repaired my book, and left me your lapel pin. I have them here." She patted her breast pocket. "You said we needed to talk, and I didn't give you a chance to explain. I...I want to hear what you have to say."

He blinked and trailed a finger over her brow and down her cheek. The comforting gesture calmed her nerves. "Indeed, we have a lot to discuss."

Several loud shouts burst through the air.

Tanen stiffened and tightened his hold on her. Sheri turned to see what had caused the commotion.

At the far end of the meadow near the edge of the clearing, the trees seemed to shimmer in a sudden mist. As it cleared, a few males emerged as if from a gateway. War cries emerged from their lips, swords raised for combat.

Sheri tried to catch her breath. She'd never seen anything so... otherwordly. All she could do was stare. What she'd seen so far of Tanen's world had been scary, but the beauty in the sparkling mist foretold of something more, something good.

Tanen squeezed Sheri's hand. "Reinforcements."

Sheri returned his squeeze, her heart lightening.

Coop barked.

Coop! She ran to him and fell to the grass at his side. He rose on unsteady legs and licked her cheek. Gripping his fur, she pulled him close, giving her pet a warm hug. Her chest constricted. "Good boy, Coop. Tanen..."

He kneeled next to her and placed his hand on her shoulder. "I'm right here, my love."

She peered at him. "Tanen, Mauree...she's out there somewhere."

His attention tracked to the trees, and the tic in his jaw pulsed. By the look of sheer determination in his gaze, he wanted to go after her.

Sheri gripped his arm. "There's no one else near here. Let's get her before she can escape."

He raised an eyebrow. "You don't need to—"

She placed her finger against his lips, silencing him. "I want to."

That was all the encouragement he seemed to need. He gripped her hand and helped her to her feet.

Sheri patted her leg. "C'mon, Coop."

As they headed into the forest, they encountered Mauree half-hidden behind a cedar tree. A burly Ursus male held her arm, supporting her weight as he helped her to her feet. Bits of hair stood out from her head at odd angles. Her skirt was torn and dark smudges, like burn marks, marred her top. Sheri's energy had done a number on the evil woman.

As if sensing Tanen and Sheri's presence, Mauree glanced at them. Her attention narrowed on Sheri, the blue of her eyes swirling with amber. "You little twit."

Sheri tensed, and Tanen's grip tightened around her fingers. Coop barked, the sound echoing off the trees. She ran her hand down his back, quieting him.

Tanen took a step forward. "Mauree, it's time you returned to the Keep, faced your sentence."

Mauree tsked and looked at her partner. When she returned her gaze, an evil grin broke across her face. "No, I don't think I will. Have you met Theron?"

The male stepped forward and crossed his arms over his wide chest. A mace dangled from his belt, the pointy spikes glittering in the moonlight. He peered at Mauree and his hooded, dark eyes burned with anger, but he stayed by her side. Thick, menacing power exuded from him in waves.

Instead of fear, a need to fight and defend herself flowed through Sheri's blood. She placed her hand on Tanen's arm. He peered at her, and she nodded.

Tanen widened his stance and raised his dagger. "If that's what it takes, then so be it."

CHAPTER 44

The blackness that surrounded Alora during the long Lemurian day was an endless torture. Her grief over losing Bellamy had haunted her, distracting her to the point she'd forgotten to tell Noeh the Ursus had switched sides. That was a colossal mistake and one she couldn't afford to make in this war. Unable to do anything from her dark place, she'd stewed all day.

The familiar pull started in Alora's chest. Her cells disintegrated, forming into the base particles necessary to transport her through time and space. After what seemed like an eternity, the tables and chairs in her main living quarters came into focus, along with the outline of a tall, sexy male...Veromé.

Her chest constricted at the sight of her mate. His smile and open arms were an invitation she couldn't resist. She raced to him, and he wrapped her in his embrace. His salty fresh scent overwhelmed her, and a stifled sob escaped her lips.

He pulled back, his brow furrowing over his blue eyes. "Hey, what's wrong?"

She stiffened, and broke away. "I have to hurry...need to see what's happened in the war on Earth."

Before he could respond, she headed to her visus bacin. The still water reflected her image, and her breath caught in her throat. Dark circles rimmed her eyes, evidence of her worry and anxiety.

Veromé's warm hand rubbed her shoulder, comforting her. Her muscles relaxed, and the tension in her shoulders eased. She placed her hands over her scrying bowl. A swell of energy released into her bloodstream. Concentrating on her task, she circled her fingers over the surface. Water in the visus bacin bubbled along the edges, the first sign an image would appear. Her heartbeat accelerated, and her breaths came out in short wisps.

A cool breeze passed over her arms. Goosebumps formed. The clash of swords filtered into the room, along with the groans of the injured. A mixture of scents—pine, dampness, and blood—filled the air. Her back stiffened as the image appeared.

A clearing materialized, shrouded in shadows. Night. Stiyaha and Panthera warriors engaged a brood of Gossum and the Ursus. So odd to see her characters fighting side by side with the enemy. *They're not my characters anymore.*

The stark reminder tightened her throat. She wanted to lash out at Zedron, hurt him the way he'd hurt her. She fisted her hand and slammed it against the edge of the visus bacin. Pain radiated up her arm, but she didn't care.

Under closer observation, a blue glow surrounded her characters, inhibiting their ability to fight. The source appeared to come from Roan's Rock and the blue sunstone. She scrunched her brow.

A tall Ursus male swung his mace in the air. He brought it down on his opponent, a Stiyaha warrior. The weapon connected with the male's thigh. Her soldier stumbled, his useless leg no longer able to support his weight, and his sword tumbled from his grasp. As the Ursus male raised his mace for another blow, Alora wanted to close her eyes, pretend this wasn't happening, but she couldn't pull her attention from the scene. The Ursus twirled the mace toward the Stiyaha's head. Alora flinched, and the mace's killing blow etched itself in her memory, becoming fuel for her fire.

A Stiyaha female stood at the edge of the trees, two Ursus standing guard. Even in the chaos, Alora knew her. The short skirt, tight sweater, and shoulder-length blonde hair were Mauree's patent signature. Her smug smile boiled Alora's blood.

The only saving grace was Sheri was with Tanen. He'd come through after all, bringing Sheri into the war. At least Alora wouldn't have to pull him from the game.

Before she could stop herself, Alora swiped at the water and the image disappeared. The quiet in the room chilled her skin. Her chest constricted so hard, spots formed in her vision. A loud sob escaped her lips.

Veromé tugged her to him, his front warming her backside. She turned in his embrace and stared into his eyes. "I'm...I'm..." The words wouldn't come, her throat too tight.

With a gentle caress, he ran a finger down her cheek. "Alora...shh...shh..."

She drew on some inner strength, a resolve to see this through. Her agitation getting the best of her, she slapped an open palm against Veromé's chest. "I'm losing the war. Damn Zedron!"

Veromé held her head in both of his palms, forcing her to look at him. "Hey, hey. This is one battle. It's not the end of the war." His furrowed brow and set jaw revealed his belief.

Her heart pounded. Yes, it was only one battle, but she couldn't help but wonder if the tide had changed. *No, that can't happen.* She pursed her lips and fisted her hands. "I'm not giving up, not on your life."

"Now that's the Alora I know and love so much." A comforting smile broke across his face. "I have no doubt you'll win this war, my love."

Her heart swelled with love for her mate. She wrapped her fingers in his hair and kissed him. He embraced her tighter, taking control, unleashing a passion she longed for every night. The waning rays of the sun disappeared, taking Veromé with them.

She cried out, and the emptiness in the room couldn't match the emptiness in her heart.

~

The blue glow that had hindered their ability to fight was gone, but the cries of the wounded warriors still echoed around Saar. Every scream was a reminder one of his soldiers was in pain, or worse. Some of the aged, retired warriors had come through the portal to help. Good thing they had. Between them and the remaining warriors on the battlefield, they'd held most of the enemy at bay. Saar held back, staying near the fringe of the war zone, ensuring the others made it through the portal and returned to the Keep. He clenched his teeth and focused on his current opponent.

A tall, muscular male with dark hair and brown eyes raised his weapon. His bicep flexed as he twirled the mace, increasing its speed. The chain rattled as the spiked ball whizzed in its circular path. With his mouth formed into a grim line, he approached.

Saar gripped his sword in both palms, angling the blade toward his adversary. Now that the blue glow had dissipated, his strength had returned. The muscles in his legs bunched, ready for his attack.

A loud shriek burst from the male and he ran toward Saar. His mace crashed down, connecting with Saar's sword. The vibration ran through Saar's arms and into his chest.

He pushed against the force. The tip of his sword nicked the male on his shoulder. Blood pooled along the thin line.

The male issued a loud bellow and transformed into a large bear. Long claws extended from his paws, and he swiped at Saar's head.

Saar ducked. Wisps of his hair caught in the breeze.

In a fast turn, Saar brought his sword around. The blade sliced through the bear's gut. Intestines spilled onto the grass. The scent of blood and bile filled the air. A low, needful cry escaped the bear's lips. Before Saar could finish the job, the animal slumped to the ground in a pile of sand.

Saar tensed. *Sand?*

To disintegrate in such a manner was a sign of one of Alora's characters. He rubbed his hand over his face, and a heaviness settled into his stomach. Something wasn't right...the Ursus couldn't be an enemy.

A soft whiz caught his attention.

He ducked.

A mace, with pointed, sharp spikes narrowly missed his head. The acrid smell of metal infiltrated his senses.

He glanced at his new opponent, and his heart skipped a beat. A female Ursus faced him, her eyes narrowed with her determination. She raised her mace above her head. The muscles in her arms and shoulders flexed, affirming her status as a warrior. Wisps of hair escaped her long, dark braid, framing the soft skin on her cheeks. Resolve sparkled in her eyes, and a grim smile formed on her face. An unbidden desire to kiss those plump limps raced through his mind. She was the beautiful female who'd captured his attention minutes ago. Against his will, his beast stirred.

She swung her mace. He raised his sword in self-defense.

She attacked, again, and again. He blocked her blows with his sword. Her frustration increased, her movements more agitated. He couldn't bring himself to fight back, and his skin tingled.

With a quick glance, he took in the scene around them. Gossum and Ursus were everywhere. A tightness coiled in his gut. His warriors were outnumbered.

"Retreat!" Bitterness coated his throat.

His opponent blinked. Instead of attacking him, she lowered her mace. Creases formed in her forehead as she furrowed her brow.

He raked his gaze down her body, whether to intimidate her or burn her into his memory, he wasn't quite sure. In either case, she'd haunt him in his dreams.

She curled her lip, and he couldn't help his overwhelming desire to touch her. Before he could stop himself, he closed the distance between them and trailed a finger along the side of her face.

She knocked his hand out of the way, but not before he'd seen her reaction—the quick intake of breath, the dilated eyes.

What am I doing? He shook his head and backed away.

Her eyes narrowed, her chest rising and falling with heated breaths.

His beast growled, and he fisted his hand. He quickly turned and ran toward the portal. *Don't look back, don't look back.* But of course, he couldn't help himself. She stood in the same place, her hand caressing her cheek where he'd touched her. His chest expanded. He'd never been attracted to a female like this. The intensity of his reaction and the realization she was his enemy hardened his stomach.

CHAPTER 45

*M*auree was so close Tanen could see the blue of her eyes. War cries and the clashing of swords from the battle in the meadow behind them rang in Tanen's ears, reminding him of the destruction she'd wrought. The urge to grab her by throat and drag her back to the Keep rose to the surface. He tightened his grip on his dagger and took a step forward, placing himself between Sheri and the male Ursus—Theron.

Sheri placed her hand on Tanen's back and stood next to him. That she was willing to fight by his side lightened his chest. Coop barked, but maintained his position at Sheri's feet.

"You need to pay for your crimes, Mauree." Tanen evaluated Theron and the mace that dangled from his belt, noting the sharp spikes on the end of the ball. He thrust out his chest and stared the male down.

Mauree tittered. "My, my, Tanen. Quite the warrior you've become, haven't you?"

"I've got him." Theron unhooked his mace and raised his weapon. As he swung the handle, the ball circled his head.

"I wouldn't get too close if I were you." Sparks from Sheri's fingers lit up the trees and reflected in Mauree's eyes.

Tanen's lungs expanded as pride for his female washed over him.

Mauree raised her hand. "Halt, Theron." She glanced between Sheri and Tanen and her mouth pulled into a thin line. "Tanen killed Jakar, and I've felt her power firsthand. I'd hate to lose you, Theron. Seems we're at a stalemate."

Theron lowered the mace, and Tanen could've sworn a flash of relief crossed his features.

"Retreat!" Saar's loud voice crossed the meadow.

Tanen's blood turned cold. That wasn't a good sign. He peered behind him, into the clearing. At the far end of the meadow, the portal beckoned. Saar assisted his warriors, ushering the injured toward the opening. Mauree's troops battled the remaining warriors, but the soldiers couldn't maintain their position.

Frustration built like a geyser, and Tanen clenched his jaw with hatred. He didn't know how long the portal would last, and his priority was to protect his female. "Someday, Mauree, you'll pay for your crime."

She laughed, the sound echoing off the trees. "Tanen, be sure to tell Noeh I'm alive and well."

Tanen wrapped his fingers around Sheri's hand. "Let's go."

They skirted the meadow's perimeter as they raced through the grass, avoiding those still battling the enemy. Sheri slowed, her grip pulling from his.

He looked at her. With wide eyes, she stared through the portal into the Keep. Tanen stopped and faced his love. "Come with me, through the portal."

Her gaze met his, flitting back and forth as she studied him. He was asking her to give up everything, leave her world behind including everyone she'd ever known. The gravity of her impending decision weighed on him, settling into the pit of his stomach.

He trailed a finger over her brow, moving back a stray strand of hair. "I'm well aware of the decision I'm asking you to make. I waited for you until nightfall, but had to warn my people. I planned to return for you."

She swallowed, her hazel eyes, the ones he'd fallen for not so long ago bore into him, squeezing his heart. The gleam of trust and acceptance in them almost brought him to his knees. "Tell me the worst thing."

"My world is full of danger. As you've seen, we battle and fight our enemies..." He exhaled and shook his head. "I can't make you any promises life will be easy. In fact, it's not, but there's good in there, too. Trust me, Sheri."

"Hurry, Tanen. We must close the portal." Saar stood at the portal's entrance and waved them forward.

Tanen raised his hand. "Hold on, Saar—"

"Take a leap of faith." Sheri's soft words were barely audible.

Tanen's heart leapt into his throat. "What?"

When she spoke again, her voice was firm. "Take a leap of faith. That's what my mother used to say."

The tension in Tanen's shoulders eased.

"So, you'll go with me?"

"Yes. Me and Coop."

Tanen's chest expanded. He grasped Sheri's hand and brought her fingers to her lips, giving them a gentle kiss. "Yes, you *and* Coop."

Her smile radiated all the way to her eyes.

As he pulled her toward the opening, his heart filled with joy.

Sheri's heart pounded. Through the opening in the mist, a small male about three feet tall with vibrant red hair and a goatee circled his hands over a stone platform in what appeared to be a cave. Several concentric rings of small crystals graced the large stone's surface, culminating in a vibrant red central stone. The glow emanating from the gems lit up his face, and he reminded her of the fabled leprechauns.

She pressed her hand against her chest. Everything in Tanen's world seemed so magical.

With a tight grip on Coop's leash, she leapt through the mist.

Her shoes, still wet and slippery, slid on the slick surface, and her knee banged against the stone floor. Pain, sharp and fast, blossomed from the impact. A soft glow radiated from yellow stones embedded in the cave walls. Warmth eased into her skin, chasing away the dampness and cold.

Tanen's warm fingers wrapped around her waist, and he pulled her to a standing position. She turned to face him. He encased her in his protective arms. "Are you okay?"

"Y…yes." As she laid her head against his chest, the steady beat of his heart calmed her, and the tension in her shoulders released.

Coop chuffed and nuzzled her leg. She bent down to stroke his fur.

The male Tanen had called Saar landed next to them, his boots smacking against the stone surface. "Rin, close the portal!"

The little male circled his hands over the stones, and as the mist dissipated, the meadow from which they'd come disappeared.

"This ain't all of ya. Where's the rest?" Rin's words echoed around the chamber.

Saar shook his head, and the little male's features hardened. Sheri's chest constricted. *How many perished tonight?*

The packed room was full of injured warriors. Some leaned against the wall, others sat on the stone floor. Pained cries and moans rose above the shouts of those attending to the wounded.

Sheri glanced at a male sprawled on the ground. His ashen face contrasted with his dark clothes, reminding her of the stories her father used to tell her about the man in the moon. She let go of her hatred. Her father had run from his problems, and had taught her to do the same. She didn't know if he'd ever faced his fear, but she had, and she'd grown because of it. Her father couldn't haunt her memories any longer.

Saar peered at her, then focused on Tanen. "Didn't expect to see you again."

Tanen stiffened, and his grip around her waist tightened almost to the point of pain. The tension between the two males was palpable, and a shiver ran over her shoulders.

Saar's mouth quirked at the corner, the scar over his lip and cheek pulling tight. "You have much to explain, but you did well tonight, battling the enemy, warning us about Mauree and the blue sunstone. That won't go unnoticed by Noeh."

Tanen's shoulders visibly relaxed. "I shall uphold the laws, whatever punishment is meted to me."

Saar raised an eyebrow. "Of that, I have no doubt."

His gaze tracked to Sheri. "Now, who's your friend...and her companion?"

Tanen ran his fingers up her back and gave her shoulder a delicate tug, pulling her tight against him once again. His warmth filtered through her skin, and she relaxed. "Saar, this is Sheri, and her pet dog, Cooper—Coop for short."

Saar's nostrils flared and his eyes widened. "You turned her. How did that happen?"

Tanen glanced at her, a chagrined look on his face. "It's a long story..."

"I look forward to hearing it, but there's much to do." Saar gave a quick nod, then headed to help one of the injured warriors.

Sheri placed her hand on Tanen's shoulder. "I thinks it's time we talk, don't you?"

Tanen grasped her fingers, and steered her to the side. "I've waited too long to tell you this, but you're no longer human, and—"

"You changed me into a Dren. I already know. I'd bitten my cheek and when we kissed..."

His brow furrowed. "How did you find out?"

"Ram, my ex-husband, shared that bit of info."

"Ram? He's your ex-husband?" Tanen's lip curled, and his gaze raked over his sweatshirt and pants. "I thought he was dead."

She shrugged. "Don't worry, he's no longer a Gossum. Tanen, what you did for me—"

"Sheri." He rubbed his hands over her shoulders, comforting her, tugging her close. "Why didn't you leave...go to Seattle when you had the chance?"

She pulled back to look at him. "I couldn't leave you, not then, not now, not ever."

He inhaled, his lips parting slightly. "What are you saying?"

"Your world...it's all so strange, but I can't imagine living anywhere else, nowhere but by your side." Her chest expanded as the words hit home.

His handsome face lit up when he smiled. He drew her fingers to his lips and gave them a gentle kiss. "I promise my love, I'll take good care of you, that is, if you'll have me. Would you...be my qithan?"

"Your what?"

His brow furrowed, his gaze flitting back and forth. "My...betrothed."

"Oh...oh...yes." She melted into his embrace, his warmth seeping into her skin.

He kissed her with his warm and tender lips, and her heart melted. Although she wanted to stay in his arms, there was much to do.

She peered at him, then glanced around the room. "There's no time like the present to get acquainted with your people. There are plenty of warriors here that could use some help."

He chuckled. "Indeed, where shall we start?"

A male sat against the far wall, his head lolled to one side. Sheri tugged on Tanen's sleeve, and pointed. "Over there."

He trailed a finger over her forehead, placing a few stray hairs behind her ear. "As you wish, my love. Welcome to your new home."

Whatever the future brought, Sheri would live here with Tanen and these honorable warriors. Home...it wasn't a place. It was a state of mind...being with the ones you loved. She smiled, her chest bursting with happiness. "Yes, Tanen, home."

CHAPTER 46

anen stood outside the double doors of the Throne room. A wrinkled shirt and a pair of loose pants were all he could find after his shower. His disheveled appearance would've bothered him in the past, but not anymore. There were more important things to worry about like what punishment Noeh would administer. He unbuttoned his collar, and the cool air trailed over the sweltering skin on his neck.

He wrapped his arm around Sheri's waist. "You ready to meet the royal family?"

She bit her lip and nodded.

"Don't worry, they'll be nice to you." *Maybe not me...*

He rapped on the door, the sound echoing down the empty corridor. This close to sunrise, most of the Keep's inhabitants had settled in for the day. Tanen longed to join them, but he couldn't put off the inevitable.

On a soft whisper, the door swung open, and a light breeze filtered past Tanen's shoulders. Sheri's hair swirled around her face, highlighting her pert nose and high cheekbones. He leaned down and kissed her on the forehead.

Jax peered at Tanen, and raised an eyebrow. His attention travelled to Sheri before returning. "Oh, oh, my. Noeh is expecting you. Yes, indeed, he is. Come, come, enter."

Tanen squeezed Sheri's hand and led her through the double doors. The king stood from his desk, his knuckles planted on the rough grain, his fingers turning white from the pressure. Noeh's assessing gaze roamed Tanen's face before flitting to Sheri. Unreadable, the king extended his hand in invitation.

Tanen swallowed. His need to serve his king, search the scriptures to find the appropriate sentence for Mauree's treason had sent him down this dangerous road in the first place. He couldn't help but glance at the spot on the desktop where he'd fetched Gaetan's satchel so long ago, stealing the blue sunstone from Noeh's desk in the process. His chest tightened. *I deserve whatever punishment he gives me.*

Noeh sat in his throne, and the wood creaked from his weight. Melissa was already in her seat at his side, the young babe, Anlon, sitting on her lap. A small ball levitated above his palm. To see Anlon using his gift sent a chill up Tanen's spine. What would he be capable of as he grew?

Tanen approached his king and kneeled, his head bowed in supplication.

"Tanen, please rise."

Tanen stood and met Noeh's gaze. "Your Majesty, I accept whatever punishment—"

"Tanen—"

"you deem required for stealing the blue sun—"

"Tanen!" Noeh's voice boomed through the room.

Tanen's marking for honesty pulsed on his chest, darkening. He swallowed and glanced at his king.

Noeh let out a long exhale. He tapped his red sunstone ring against the ornate chair's wooden armrest. The slight tick only increased Tanen's anxiety, and a bead of sweat rolled down his back.

"Noeh, please, don't make this warrior wait any longer than necessary." Melissa's soft words filtered through Tanen's ears.

Warrior? I guess I am... His father would've been proud.

Noeh ran his hand through his hair. "Your admittance of guilt is but a drop in the bucket."

Tanen's ears burned as heat raced up his neck. Sheri gripped his hand and gave him a gentle squeeze.

Tanen raised himself to his full height and trailed his finger across his forehead then over his nose to signify the symbol for Lemuria and life ever after. "As required under the scriptures for my crime, I submit my resignation as council leader. Whatever sentence you impose, I accept as my due."

"You shall serve a fair punishment," Noeh nodded, "but I do not accept your resignation as council leader."

The skin on Tanen's arms prickled. "What?"

Noeh scooted to the edge of his seat, his gaze focused on Tanen. "Without your warning of the danger at Roan's Rock, many civilians would've died tonight. For that, I am forever thankful." His words were gruff, full of emotion.

Tanen's chest expanded even as he tried to comprehend Noeh's words. "You're not sentencing me? I should be sentenced to one hundred years in the stronghold."

"What you did was wrong, yes, but if you hadn't stolen the stone and chased after Mauree, we would've been blindsided by the Ursus and the Gossum. We anticipated Mauree would show, alone." He ran his hand through his hair. "We lost a few warriors in the battle, but it could've been worse...far worse."

Tanen bowed low before his king. "Your Majesty...I don't have words to express—"

"Rise, Tanen." Noeh held Tanen's gaze. "I've made my share of mistakes as well. The Hall of Scriptures should remain open, always. Knowledge is power, you proved that to us all. I need my council leader."

Tanen swallowed, the king's words touched him deeply, and his marking for prudence burned on his skin. He didn't need to look to know it darkened.

Noeh smiled. "Now, for your punishment. Seems to me many of our warriors don't have a good grasp on the scriptures. Perhaps they've forgotten." He tapped his ring against his chair and his eyes twinkled. "As king, I sentence you to serve as Preceptor—teacher of the ancient texts. Remind these warriors, and me as well, of what's in those old books."

"Y...yes, Your Majesty." Tanen forced the words over his thick tongue.

"Enough..." Melissa stood and approached Sheri. "I want to meet your female."

Sheri stiffened and gave a short curtsy. "I don't know what I'm supposed to—"

Melissa wrapped her free hand around Sheri's waist and pulled her in for a quick hug. On Melissa's hip, Anlon giggled and held out the sphere. The toy hit the stone floor and rolled under Noeh's chair. It pinged against the wall.

Noeh pursed his lips. "I'm going to have to get that later."

Sheri stifled a giggle.

Melissa's smile was as welcoming as they came. She gripped Sheri's hand. "Welcome, Sheri. I'm afraid all I know is your name. I'm Melissa. It's so nice to meet another recent Dren. We have so much to discuss."

Sheri glanced from Melissa to Noeh, then focused on Tanen. "I... don't know what to say, other than, thank you for accepting me here. Tanen is my lifeline. Without him, I wouldn't have faced my fears and fallen in love with such a wonderful male."

Tanen's heart swelled. She loved him, and he loved her in return.

"Ow." Sheri grimaced. She opened her hand, and the faint pink lines were a bit darker than before.

Tanen gripped her hand and ran his fingers gently over her palm. "Does your skin burn?"

Sheri nodded. "The warm sensation comes and goes, sometimes more painful than others."

Melissa handed Anlon to Noeh and the babe squealed in delight. He stood on Noeh's thighs, his hands slapping Noeh on the arms.

The queen held out her hand. "May I see?"

Sheri nodded and placed her hand in Melissa's palm.

The queen traced her finger over the faint lines. She inhaled and let go. Melissa studied Sheri, her eyes darting back and forth.

Tanen's gut twisted. "Is something wrong?"

Noeh stood and glanced over Melissa's shoulder.

With deliberate care, Melissa held up her own hand, palm outstretched. "I never really thought much of it before, but I have something similar. Look."

Sheri inhaled. "The lines are in the shape of an "M." What do you think it means?"

"My guess—Mu—short for Lemuria." Tanen swallowed. "Melissa, how long have you had yours?"

"I received it after my transition from human to Dren. No one else seemed to have one, so I didn't think anything of it."

"So, the other Dren don't have this mark?"

"No, but Sheri and I are the only recent humans to survive the transformation. I wonder what this means."

Anlon fussed in Noeh's arms and he handed the small child back to Melissa. "We should discuss this with Gaetan. Something made you special, different from other humans. Perhaps our *Haelen* can help solve the mystery. You've done well, Tanen."

Sheri gave Tanen a quick smile, her eyes beaming with pride. His chest expanded, and he never felt so needed, so wanted in his life. He was born to fight for his king, but not on the battlefield. Instead, he would teach others as his contribution to winning this war for Alora. With Sheri at his side, he had no doubt they would be a formidable team. Happiness warmed his soul. He couldn't imagine anything better.

"Oh, the stone..." Tanen dug into his pants pocket and pulled out the sacred sunstone. He handed it to Noeh. "Sheri retrieved this from Mauree."

Noeh accepted the blue crystal and held it up. Light refracted from its edges, cascading a brilliant blue across the stone walls. "Seems to me you're more hassle than you're worth. I'll give you to Gaetan for safekeeping."

The king pocketed the stone and placed his palm on Tanen's

225

shoulder. "Before you leave, I need further information. Saar told me you didn't free Mauree from her cell. Do you know who did?"

Tanen blinked. *Ginnia...*

Noeh studied him, his gaze piercing into Tanen.

Tanen blinked, but maintained eye-contact with his king. Ginnia, the Keep's seer was but a child trapped in an adult female body. He couldn't bring himself to out her, yet his king had the right to know. He released the breath he'd held. "Yes, Your Majesty, I do, but you won't like the answer."

The skin around Noeh's eyes tightened. "I didn't expect to. Tell me who freed Mauree, and they will face my wrath."

Tanen frowned. "Ginnia."

Noeh audibly inhaled. "No! Not possible." He ran his hand through his hair.

Melissa touched Noeh's arm. "Noeh, I'm sure she had a good reason."

Tanen couldn't imagine what that could be. He shook his head and prayed for the little seer.

CHAPTER 47

*T*he scent of linen and lime woke Tanen. He inhaled, savoring the sweet aroma. Snuggled in his bed, Sheri pressed her backside into him. His member filled with blood, and he rubbed himself against her bottom. She stirred, stretching her lithe body. The contact drove him mad.

"Good evening." His voice was rough after their long day together. Memories of taking her in all kinds of positions—in the chair, against the headboard, over the sink—flooded his mind. He couldn't get enough of her.

She rolled onto her back, and a sexy smile tugged at her lip. Warmth radiated from deep inside. She was here with him, and he couldn't be happier.

"Hey, big guy." She gripped his shaft. "You seem happy to see me."

He groaned, and gathered her close. His erection strained against the soft skin on her abdomen. "Let me show you how happy I am."

She giggled. "You don't say…"

He cupped her cheek and poured all of his love for her into his kiss.

Coop whined. The thump of his tail beat against the floor.

Tanen stiffened. "I thought you left Coop in the main living quarter."

She sat up in bed, taking her warmth with her. "Nope, he's right here."

Tanen flopped onto his pillow. His erection pressed painfully against the sheet.

Coop stood, his nails clicking against the stone floor. He let loose a short bark followed by a small whine.

Sheri patted Tanen on the arm. "Seems like he's hungry. I'll be right back."

She flung the sheet back and, naked, left the bed. He couldn't help but stare at her round behind and shapely legs as she walked away. How he longed to run his hands over her soft skin. His fingers tingled, but he no longer had the urge to crack his knuckles. His knowledge of the scriptures and what he and Sheri had done at Roan's Rock had cascaded through the community like wildfire. A feeling of weightlessness lightened his chest. He was thankful Sheri had taken a chance on him, thus saving them all. The new confidence in himself along with Sheri's love had cured him of his need to steal.

The door into their main living quarters closed behind her with a soft click. He scanned his bedroom. One of her blouses lay on the edge of the chair, her pants were a ball on the floor, and a pair of socks hung over his mirror. In the middle of the dresser was her precious copy of *The Hobbit*, his lapel pin tacked onto the bent corner. His breath bottled up inside. She'd made herself at home. In the past, he would've cleaned up the mess, unable to handle the disorder. Now, though, he liked how she left her mark all over his place. He smiled.

The door creaked, and Sheri crept back into their room. Sunstones lining the walls reflected off his qithan bracelet, pulling his attention to her wrist. His chest expanded, as a happiness he never thought he'd experience snuck into his heart. At his first opportunity, he'd given her the precious jewelry—his promise to bond. He had to admit it looked good on her.

She closed the door and peeked at him. Her eyes gleamed, and a small giggle bubbled from her lips, building until the sound echoed off the stone walls.

Her contagious laughter brought forth a chuckle. "What's so funny?"

"You."

"Me?"

"Yes." She tapped her shoulder. "You have something here…"

He glanced at himself. Hanging over the headboard were her panties, the lacy end touching his shoulder. A loud laugh burst from his lungs. He picked up the panties and flung them onto the floor. My, how much he'd changed. "Next thing you know, you'll have me throwing my own clothes around the room."

She smiled and walked toward him, swaying her hips in an elaborate dance. With a sheepish grin, she slipped under the covers and snuggled next to him, kissing him on the neck. He welcomed her into his embrace.

"Melissa coached me about Dren feedings. Did you know…the bites are very erogenous?"

A rush of blood headed south, and his shaft jerked in anticipation. "Hmmm…no, I didn't know. Perhaps we should find out?"

"Yes, I think so." She nuzzled his chin, and he pulled her closer. Her soft breaths tickled his ear, flaring the fire between them. In slow, sensual circles, her tongue moistened the skin on his neck. A slow shiver built until she trembled in his arms. Before he could ask if she was okay, her fangs pricked into his skin. A soft pulling sensation increased his desire, sending a wave of love for his female crashing over him. He cuddled her close as she drank, and he relished in the knowledge he could provide for her in this way.

When she was done, she licked his skin, sealing the wound with her saliva. She hummed, and the vibration travelled from her chest to his, sending a tingling sensation to his groin. With a quickness borne of his species, he flipped her over, caging her in his embrace. He settled over her and one of his hands slipped under the pillow.

His fingers touched soft material, but the texture was different from the sheets and pillows. He stilled.

Sheri ran her fingers over his shoulders, and her brow furrowed. "What's wrong?"

He gripped the material and yanked. His grey underwear was in his hand. With deliberate intent, he tossed the clothing over his shoulder, not caring where it landed.

Sheri giggled, the sound filling his soul, marking him in all the ways that mattered. He could listen to her soft laugh for eternity and never tire of it. She'd helped him grow, helped him see his own value to the Keep. Her love for him had healed him, and he'd never be the same. *Good...*

~

Mauree stood on the balcony overlooking the lawn and the small lake beyond. The moonlight lit up the grass and the deer and her fawn that chose to graze there. Maybe she wasn't aware of the creatures that inhabited the house, or maybe she didn't fear them. Ignorance could be deadly.

Mauree fisted her hand. Her plot to kill Noeh had failed, thanks to Tanen. She'd also lost Jakar, her first lieutenant, and would need to find a replacement. Fortunately, she didn't have to look far. "Theron, come join me on the veranda. The moon is beautiful tonight."

Theron stepped over the sliding glass door's track and gripped the railing. His long dark hair blew in the breeze, framing his chiseled jaw and sharp cheekbones. He was the epitome of an alpha male. That she forced him to submit to her was a new thrill, one that burned in her veins. He'd do anything to protect his niece, Kaelyn, and Mauree wasn't above taking advantage of the situation.

"We almost had them last night." His low voice rumbled, sending a shiver over Mauree's skin.

"But not Noeh...he's the most important piece in this game. Topple the king and the war is all but over."

He placed his forearms against the railing, one foot secured between a couple of slats. His biceps bulged, displaying the immense strength the Ursus possessed. "What are your plans?"

"I don't know...yet. But between us, I'm sure we'll come up with something."

She stepped toward him and ran her fingers over his bicep and down his forearm. He visibly tensed, his muscles turning rock hard under her touch. The soft hair tickled the tender pads on her fingers. Warmth spread through her body. He'd proven himself to be more than she'd expected in the bedroom, and her nipples peaked at the memory. Time for another round.

She pulled on his arm, his firm muscle tightening beneath her fingers. His dark eyes hardened and his lip curled, but he followed her into the bedroom.

SNEAK PEEK OF UNDENIABLE LOVER

WARRIORS OF LEMURIA SERIES BOOK #4

CHAPTER 1

Saar curled his fingers around the hilt of his sword and pressed his lips to the cool steel blade. The skin around his mouth puckered, a constant reminder of the age-old, disfiguring scar that tracked from his cheek to his chin. Hot and bitter, bile rose in his throat, and the mixture of sweat and frustration blended into a toxic brew.

Dampness coated his skin. He took a step forward, his boots sliding over the smooth, polished stone floor.

Sunstones lining the underground Keep's cave walls flared to life. The light reflected in his opponent's cold stare.

"Come now, I didn't expect you to beat around the bush. You can do much better." Saar's adversary smiled, and his blue eyes swirled with amber flecks. So familiar, so chilling.

The taunt sent a rush of adrenaline through Saar's veins. He tightened his grip around his favorite weapon and hefted the heavy blade. Focused on his rival, he waited for the slight flinch around the eyes, the tell-tale sign his opponent would attack.

...and there it was, the twitch under Noeh's left eye. With a quickness bred into his Lemurian blood, Noeh brought his short sword down.

The clash of steel ricocheted against the Keep's stone walls.

Blade pressed to blade, Saar's muscles strained under Noeh's pressure. Although they didn't usually spar with real swords, both Saar and the king were on edge. Sparring with authentic weapons provided the extra rush they desperately needed.

Noeh's mouth lifted at the corner. "Concede."

The demand lit a fire of conviction in Saar's chest. He shoved his sword harder against Noeh's, forcing the male to step back. "Never."

Noeh relaxed his grip and swiped his sword under Saar's blade.

Saar used the momentum to his advantage. He brought his blade around, and the tip scratched Noeh's ear. Blood pooled along the cut.

"*Craya!* That's twice now you've nicked me." Noeh drew his mouth into a thin line, his gaze focused on Saar's lips.

Saar lowered his sword in deference to his king. "Actually, that's three. Set and match."

Noeh sheathed his weapon and wiped his palm over his face. The red sunstone in his ring, the one that marked him as king, glittered in the light. "Not long ago that wouldn't have happened, at least not so easily. Damn my deafness!"

If Saar could've absorbed Noeh's weakness, taken away his pain, he would've done so without hesitation.

Everyone had a weakness that wouldn't heal. Noeh's were his ears. Saar—the scar that marred his face. He cleared his throat to dislodge the ache that had formed there. "Your Majesty. You are our king. I, for one, would follow you to the grave."

Noeh exhaled, and a sad smile tugged at his lips. "You are my most trusted, my most loyal warrior. You've proven that to me, time and again." His attention focused on Saar's scar before drawing to his eyes. "I couldn't have chosen a better Commander of Arms."

Noeh almost died because of you. Father's words echoed in Saar's mind, and the familiar guilt weighed heavily on his shoulders.

He glanced around the room, taking in the empty weights against the far wall and the sparring dummies lined up in a row. Pictures graced the walls, many of warriors in battle, some with swords raised above their heads, others in beast form, long hair coating their tall, muscular bodies, claws elongated, tusks protruding from their jaws.

Saar longed to shift into his beast once again, but he wouldn't take the chance, not unless he needed to protect someone he loved, like Noeh.

In recent memory, only two Stiyaha had returned to their human state—Tanen, the Keep's council leader, and Noeh, their king. How had they shifted back? No one knew for sure, but some thought it had something to do with their new mates.

Three dark bands circled Noeh's neck, the sign of an unusually strong bonding. Most bonded males received two bands and those who received one often wished they'd never mated.

Saar brushed his fingers over his throat. No mark would ever darken his skin. A longing deep inside twisted his gut into a tight ball, and he clenched his teeth.

Although the sac under his tongue had filled with his bonding ink a time or two, he'd never pierced the pouch. The liquid that would bind him to a mate and produce the bands remained intact.

Not that it mattered. There wasn't a female in the Keep who would have him. Over his five hundred and fifty years on this planet, a few had lain with him for the experience, but all recoiled at his disfigurement. Now, he kept his distance from all females.

He placed his sword in his scabbard and faced his king so that Noeh could read his lips. "I do what I was born to do, fight this war for you and Alora."

In this elaborate game they played on Earth, Gossum were the enemy, the ones to defeat in this bitter fight for the right to control the planet's water. The fate of humankind, oblivious and caught in the middle, rested on the war's outcome.

Unfortunately, the last battle hadn't ended well. A tic pulsed in Saar's jaw.

Noeh narrowed his gaze, flecks of amber sparking in his eyes once again. "Speaking of the war, seems Zedron has some new players in the game. A new enemy for us. Perfect, just what we needed." He pursed his lips, the pink of his skin lightening from the pressure. "Where do you suppose those shape-shifting bears...the Ursus came from and why hasn't Alora, our illustrious goddess, mentioned anything about them to us?"

An unbidden image flashed across Saar's mind. During the last battle, a young Ursus female, mace in hand, stood before him ready to attack. She had long hair as dark as night, braided in a tight plait down her back, golden-yellow trim interwoven between the silky strands. Resolve glowed in her eyes, and she'd attacked him with a ferocity he'd never seen in a female before.

Although she was his enemy, he couldn't bring himself to harm her. A strange desire to touch her skin had flitted through him, and before he could stop himself, he'd trailed a finger down her soft cheek. His fingers tingled at the memory.

"Saar?" Noeh's voice broke through Saar's thoughts, pulling him back to the present.

"Your Majesty?"

Noeh paced to a rack of barbells, leaned down, and placed his hands over the heavy weights. The muscles in his arms bunched beneath the similar military-issued black shirt all the warriors wore. He tapped his ring against the metal, once, twice, three times. The ping echoed through the empty room. "You didn't answer my question. Where did the Ursus come from and why hasn't Alora said anything?"

Saar pulled a toothpick from a small pocket under his belt and twirled it between his lips. The ragged tip caught on the soft tissue of his inner lip, scouring the flesh. Blood, tangy and bitter, filled his mouth. He waited to reply until Noeh turned around. "I have no answer for you on the bears or Alora. It doesn't matter. In the end, we will prevail."

The lines around Noeh's eyes softened. "Your faith never ceases to amaze me and is only rivaled by your loyalty. Yes, my friend, we will succeed. We have to..." he blinked and peered at his ring. "I don't know what I would do without Melissa and Anlon. If I ever lost my son..." His jaw tightened.

Saar tugged the dagger from his belt clip, and ran the sharp edge over the jagged toothpick. A few shavings curled into a tight twist and slid to the stone floor. "Melissa would tell you not to invite trouble."

A short, stifled laugh emerged from Noeh's lips. "She'd tell me to get on with winning this war." He smiled and streaks of amber flashed through his eyes. "Put together a scouting party. Locate Mauree's hideout. With all those troops, she can't be that hard to find. We need to locate her before she attacks again."

Saar sheathed his dagger, returned the toothpick to his pocket, and bowed. On his shoulder, his marking for loyalty burned while the ones for courage and honor were eerily silent. A sense of pride lightened Saar's chest for his three dark, jagged lines. Born with his own unique marks at birth like all Stiyaha males, he'd honored his values well over the years and the markings had never faded. "Yes, Your Majesty. We leave at nightfall."

Saar's mind drifted to the beautiful female. Nothing good could come from seeing her again. She was the enemy. By all rights, he should kill her. He ground his teeth.

I pray I don't find her. Yet, a part of him deep inside wanted nothing more.

For more information on *Undeniable Lover*, visit www.rosalieredd.com.

ALSO BY ROSALIE REDD

Books in the *Warriors of Lemuria* series:
Untouchable Lover - book #1
Untamable Lover - book #2
Unimaginable Lover - book #3
Undeniable Lover - book #4
Unforgivable Lover - coming 2018
Unforgettable Lover - novella
Alora's Love Potion - short story collection
Marked by Love - novella

Reviews

Enjoyed *Unimaginable Lover*? The best gift you can give an author is an honest review. Please consider leaving a review on your favorite retailer to help spread the word and support an author.

Newsletter

Want access to free reads, special offers, and giveaways? Sign up here for my newsletter on my website and you'll receive a **free ebook**. Don't worry, your information won't be shared with anyone but my muse. You can visit me at my website at www.rosalieredd.com or contact me at Rosalie@rosalieredd.com. I love to receive email from readers!

GLOSSARY

Antorro stalks: A green, leafy vegetable imported from the planet Antorro.

Aridis: Lemuria's largest moon

Arotaars: People from the planet Arotin. Held as slaves on Lemuria. They have blue hair that sparks with electricity when they are emotional.

Craya: An expletive.

Dren: Short for "chil*dren*." Originally human adults, but were transformed into Dren through a Lemurian's bite. During the "turning," all Dren receive a unique, special power. Dren must drink blood at least once a week from the opposite sex or they become weak and lose their powers.

Gossum: Human converts turned by another Gossum through their bite. They have black eyes, and are hairless, with rough, scalelike skin down their neck and back. Gossum have a spur at the end of their long tongue which they use to paralyze their prey.

Haelen: Healer

Jixies: Small, dwarf-like characters that voluntarily serve the Stiyaha. Jixies tend to be quick, resourceful, and are great planners.

Despite their short stature, they can go amongst the humans to obtain special items not made within the Keep.

Keep: The underground home of the Stiyaha and Jixies, located in the mountains of the Pacific Northwest. The Keep is sentient and reacts to her inhabitants with minor tremors and/or by warming or cooling the environment through the sunstones embedded in the walls.

Lemuria: A planet in the Orion constellation. Lemuria is slowly dying and its people must rely on natural resources from other planets to survive.

Lemurians: Refers to both the people on Lemuria, as well as, the characters on Earth. The people of Lemuria appear as gods to the characters in the war on Earth.

Matronin colony: A Lemurian trade partner from planet Matron in a nearby galaxy.

Newbs: Young children

Panthera: Sleek and muscular, these highly skilled fighters are known for their speed and agility. They transform into black panthers and are highly arrogant and confident. They respect strength and cunning and will only follow a leader who can command them.

Porte stanen: The massive stone structure in the Portal Navigation Center used to transport characters in and out of the Keep through the portal gateway.

Qithan: Betrothed

Rhondo beasts: Fearsome creatures that terrorize the surface of Lemuria. They have black, oily skin with disproportionately long arms and short legs. A small amount of hair runs down its spine. They have a long tongue and sharp teeth, including tusk-like fangs.

Stiyaha: Stoic and just, Stiyaha are noble warriors. Tall and strong, they transform into large beasts, between eight and nine feet tall, covered in fur with large, protruding tusks.

Sunstones: Magical stones that line the ceilings and walls of the Keep, providing heat and light to its inhabitants. Sunstones are used in trade and have some healing abilities.

Tratee flies: Small flying insects on Lemuria that have translucent wings.

Ursus: A tough, burly species that shape-shifts into large bears. Tenacious and vicious, they are fierce warriors.

Visus bacin: Scrying bowl

Yandora vines: A trailing plant the lives on the bark of the Etila trees. The leaves have a melodic tingle when touched.

ABOUT ROSALIE

After finishing a rewarding career in finance and accounting, it was time for award-winning author Rosalie Redd to put away the spreadsheets and take out the word processor. She pens paranormal, science fiction, and fantasy romance in her office cave located in Oregon, where rain is just another excuse to keep writing.

www.ingramcontent.com/pod-product-compliance
Lightning Source LLC
Chambersburg PA
CBHW061615170626
46811CB00001B/440